Invidious

THE MARKED

BIANCA SCARDONI

INVIDIOUS, THE MARKED #2

First Edition: June 2016

All characters and events depicted in this book are fictitious. Any similarity to real persons, living or dead, is purely coincidental.

ISBN: 978-0-9948651-6-8

For my little one, Jaxon
So that, you too, might dare to dream big some day

CONTENTS

The steep descent into Hell is always paved with good intentions.

PREFACE

Truth fluttered in and out of my life like a butterfly, taunting me with its beauty—with its endless possibilities of change and triumph. No matter how hard I tried to catch it, to trap it inside my heart and own it, it evaded me at every turn.

Like my destiny, my truth had been written in my blood long before I was born, guided and misguided by those who sought to destroy me. I thought knowing the truth would give me power over it—over my destiny—allow me to shape it and bend it to my will. I thought I would be safe there inside the light.

I was wrong.

There was no light to be found.

Only darkness rising.

1. THIS MEANS WAR

Thick, heady coils of fog moved with intention, slithering methodically around my legs as I stared up at the starless sky from my bedroom balcony. The events of last night were on constant replay in my mind, racing through it like some death wish I couldn't remember making. Some ritual sacrifice I never signed up for. One minute I was at Spring Fling, dancing with the boy from my dreams, and the next I was fighting for my life in a burnt down church. My own personal hell where everything was a lie and everyone was in on it.

Everyone but me.

The betrayal clawed languidly at my insides, burrowing itself inside my soul as it fought to find a home in the agony. I wanted so bad to let the darkness take me in. To let it consume my shattered being and devour whatever was left of me. To erase everything that happened and make it inconsequential.

It was easier that way. Easier to give up. Easier to walk away and never look back. But *easier* wasn't always that simple.

My best friend, Taylor, was still out there—powerless in the hands of an omnipotent Revenant who was hell-bent on winning the grand prize. Her life was sitting in the palm of my

3

my hands, and walking away from this meant walking away from her; leaving her to the wolf the way I was left to mine. I couldn't do that to her, no matter how bad I wanted this all to disappear.

An awful heaviness pressed in over me like a gavel, cementing my sentence in stone. I had less than two weeks to fix this mess—to get the Amulet back and make everything right again. Unfortunately, I had no idea how I was going to do that. The only thing I knew for sure was that it would all come down to one person—the one responsible for all of this.

Trace Macarthur.

The beautiful boy from my dreams turned out to be nothing more than a trickster. An illusion I was too blind to see through. He played me right from the start, used me for his own personal gain, and then threw me down to the Gates of Hell when he was done with me, never bothering to look back once. Not even to see if I had stuck the landing.

I'd spent the last twenty-four hours inventing a million different ways to make him pay for what he did. To make him suffer the way he made me suffer. Unfortunately, all of that amounted to nothing because the fact of the matter was I *needed* him. I needed to get close to him again and gain his trust. Only then would I be able to get the Amulet back—to swipe it out from under his nose the way he swiped it from me.

Of course, in order to do any of that, I would first have to see him. I would have to look him right in the eye and finally *see* him for the fraud that he always was. Because that's all that he was—a fraud, a calculating liar since kickoff. Everything that came out of his cunning mouth was designed to deceive, and I lined right up, eager to buy every word of it.

Visions of his mouth pressed up against mine cut through my mind, puncturing the shaky barricade around my subconscious as I relived the scenes I didn't want to see

4

anymore. My heart throbbed with pain, with a brand of heartache I never knew existed, and I hated him more for making me feel it.

He was going to get what was coming to him. I was going to make sure of that. But, right now, I had to stay focused on what was most important and that was getting Taylor back.

I looked down at my phone and contemplated my options. Nikki Parker's last-minute e-vite glared back up at me like an unspoken dare. I knew there was only one reason she would have a sudden change of heart and extend an invitation to me. She was with Trace and she wanted me to know it. She wanted to revel in her conquest, bury me deeper in the wreckage that was now my life. Well, that was just fine by me. Kismet even.

And lucky for her, I already had a shovel.

Nikki's house was exactly what I expected from yet another upper-crust resident of Hollow Hills. Bloated and over the top with all the fixings of a glamorous life and none of the sustenance to carry it. A short drive from the bordering street took us up to a one-floor glass house that overlooked the town like an empress sitting on her throne.

I thanked Henry for the ride and then hopped out of the car, straightening out my skinny jeans and black halter-top. Cold droplets of rain dotted my shoulders like falling tears as my heart began to race in my chest, reaffirming the fact that this was the very last place on earth I wanted to be tonight. I wanted to be back home—back in Florida, living out my old life, with my old friends, where everything was simple and easy.

That life is gone, Jemma. Get the hell over it, I told myself as I pulled in a lungful of air and made a push for the door before my nerve had a chance to bail out on me.

Inside, the house was crammed with wall-to-wall students from both Weston and Easton Prep alike. Despite the history, the room mixed together like oil and vinegar, two rival schools blending over the promise of alcohol and a good time. Somewhere through the noise, I heard a girl call out my name as I forced my way through the crowd, but I didn't bother stopping to see who it was. I was here for one reason and she didn't sound anything like him.

Rounding the corner, I walked into what appeared to be the living room, though it was hard to tell since I couldn't see any of the furniture with all the half-dressed, gyrating bodies in the way. The air was thick with pheromones and perfume, and it was making the inside of my nose sting. It was hardly their fault though; they were here for a good time. I, on the other hand, was not.

I pushed up onto my toes and craned my neck, scanning the room for any Adonis-like liars I recognized. Before my eyes made it halfway around the room, I felt someone brush up against me from behind.

"What's up, Blackburn," said Caleb, his hot breath in my ear. He took a step forward and lined his shoulders up with mine. His chestnut hair was pointing skyward and had that messy-with-a-purpose look to it.

"Hey, Caleb." There was no point in wasting time with idle chitchat, so I didn't. "Have you seen Trace?" I asked him over the bone-rattling music.

He took a sip of his drink and ticked his chin towards the back corner of the room. It only took me two flat seconds to spot *them*. Trace and Nikki.

Together again.

My stomach bottomed out as I watched them from the doorway. He was leaning back against the wall, wearing jeans and a fitted white t-shirt that hugged him in all the right places, while Nikki was tipping into him, wolfing up all his personal space with her runway-ready body. She was all dolled up with a skin-tight pink dress and a pair of matching heels that looked like they belonged on a stage. And not the theater kind.

"That didn't take long," I muttered bitterly.

"It never does," said Caleb. His irritation was evident in both his tone and sour facial expression.

At least I wasn't alone in this. Maybe his fixation with Nikki was a good thing. Maybe we could team up and take the two of them down together. You know, like Bonnie and Clyde, minus the murder and romance.

"Why don't you do something about it?" It came out unexpected; frantic.

"Why would I do something?"

"Because you like her." I watched his back stiffen at my unexpected accusation. "Why don't you make a move? Stake your claim, get in the race—do *something*!"

"Easy, Blackburn." He started laughing but there was definitely a nervous pitch to it. "It's not like that."

God, he was useless. "Forget it. Just forget it."

"Bad day?" he quipped.

"Bad year."

"You want something to drink?"

I shook my head, still staring forward at the real-life nightmare unfolding before me.

I felt Caleb's eyes on me, assessing me as I watched them.

"You really like him, don't you?" It came out like an afterthought; a passing observation that had just occurred to him. "I mean, I knew you were into him, but it's more than that." He looked down at me in a pensive way.

"I don't like him," I said, watching Trace as he leaned into Nikki and whispered something in her ear. My heart sank all the way down to my feet, taking my stomach right along with it. "Not anymore anyway."

"Don't take it personal," he said, taking another sip of his drink as he watched the happy couple from afar. "You're not the first girl he did this to."

"Did what to?"

"You know" —he lowered his voice and leaned in closer— "hit it and quit it."

My ears damn-near melted off. "You can't be serious right now." Is that what he thought happened between us? What *people* thought? I wasn't sure if I wanted to laugh or cry about it.

"Come on, Blackburn. I'm not as dumb as I look." He took another sip of his drink and focused back on Nikki and Trace. "One minute I'm getting you a drink at Spring Fling and the next you're on the dance-floor with Trace. Doesn't take a genius to figure out why you both disappeared."

"You're way off, Caleb. Like on another planet. I didn't leave the dance to *hit it* or whatever you called it."

He shrugged his shoulders like it didn't matter either way.

"What about you?" I shot back accusingly. "I saw you that day in the locker room with Nikki. You obviously have a thing for her. Are you just going to let her play you like that?" I goaded.

"I don't have a problem with it if she doesn't."

"So you don't care that she's just using you? Why don't you go over there and tell Trace?"

He laughed as though I'd just dropped the punch line to some silly, little kid's joke.

"What? Are you afraid of him or something?" I couldn't believe how low I was stooping.

"I'm not afraid of that half-blood pretty boy," said Caleb. Despite his protest, I could tell his feathers were getting ruffled. "Besides, he thinks Nikki can do no harm. He wouldn't believe me anyway."

"No harm, huh? What a total crock." My anger notched up to volcanic temperatures.

They were so perfect for each other, it was sickening.

"Whatever," he said and tipped his head back as he polished off the remnants of whatever it was he was drinking. "It's not like she's the only game in town." He took a step towards me but I was too consumed with my own thoughts to pay it any attention.

"Look at them just standing there." I could feel the rage boiling inside of me, rolling through my blood like an inferno.

Caleb said something back to me but it didn't register.

"Someone needs to knock them off their pedestals," I said and then stormed off into the room.

Apparently that someone was me.

2. TO NIKKI, WITH LOVE

I kept my eyes fixed on Trace as I maneuvered my way through the room. As much as I hated to admit it, it hurt to look at him—to see him going on with his life as if nothing happened. As if *I* never happened. Somewhere in the back of my mind, I knew I needed to stay focused on my plan, on getting the Amulet back, but it was quickly being swallowed up by the burning desire to make him hurt the way he was hurting me.

He looked up just as I stepped around a couple. His eyes immediately found me as though magnetized to my being, and I faltered because they were even more beautiful than I wanted to remember them being. Even in the dimly lit room, they glowed like two sapphires that spiked my temperature to unimaginable heights. Heights that I no longer wanted any part of.

"Jemma." His voice was deep yet strangely soothing. For a split second, I thought I detected a tinge of relief in there but I quickly batted the fantasy away.

"It's so big of you to come," said Nikki, stepping in front of him and then leaning back against him as though she were his own personal dump truck. "No hard feelings, kay?"

Every fiber of my being wanted to slap the lipstick right off of her condescending mouth. With fingernails digging into my palm, I fought down the urge and held on to my composure. I needed to hit her where it hurt; not claw her eyes out. I squared my shoulders and plastered on the biggest, *fakest* smile I could muster. "Oh, yeah. Totally. I mean, if Trace could forgive you for messing around with one of his best friends, who am I to hold a grudge?"

Nikki's eyes doubled in size.

"Sloppy seconds aren't for everyone," I went on, turning my attention to Trace, "But some people aren't that picky. Right, Trace?"

He stared back at me expressionless, his eyes giving nothing away.

"Well, *technically*, Caleb had the sloppy seconds," I continued, anger stinging the corner of my eyes. "So I guess this makes it sloppy-thirds, right? But who's counting?"

"You bitch." Nikki tried to step towards me but Trace quickly pulled her back—his hands planted firmly on her hips.

The sight of it made my stomach turn.

"Happy fucking birthday," I said and walked off without bothering to stick around for the shit-storm that was undoubtedly about to start pouring.

"What did you say to them?" asked Caleb, grabbing my arm as I shot by him on my way to the nearest exit.

"What does it matter?" I shook my head, forcing away the budding tears I couldn't seem to shake. Tears that I refused to let fall in front of any of them. "He isn't going to believe it anyway, right?"

He paused, thinking about it. "Have a drink with me."

"No thanks," I said, staring at the front door. "I need to get out of here."

"One drink. Come on, Blackburn. You owe me for ditching me last night." He tilted his head to the side, letting the dim overhead light catch the copper highlights in his hair.

"Fine. One drink." I nodded, feeling a tinge of guilt for agreeing to go to the dance with him in the first place. I should have been doing my research on Trace. I should have been seeing through his phony facade.

"You got it." He snagged my hand and led us through the glass-endowed hallway and into an industrial-sized kitchen almost as big as the one at All Saints.

Apart from the stainless-steel appliances, everything else in the room was paper-white, right down to the glossy countertops and matching marble floor. I felt as though I'd just walked into some sterile plastic surgery office in the middle of Beverly Hills.

"You're going to love this," said Caleb, pulling me forward so that I was shoulder to shoulder with him.

A mammoth-sized plastic container sat on the kitchen island, nearly covering it from corner to corner. It was filled to the top with some brown-colored liquid and thick slices of lemon that floated around the surface like tiny life preservers.

Clearly, Caleb didn't know me nearly enough to be a competent judge of what I would or wouldn't love.

"What is that?" I asked, eyeing it with suspicion.

"Iced tea." He snatched two cups from the counter and dunked them into the container. "You'll like it. It's from Long Island," he said, laughing as he handed me a cup.

"Thanks." I swooshed the liquid around mindlessly, surveying it as it swirled around the edge of the cup.

I peeked up at my surroundings, gauging my enemy's territory. I couldn't help but wonder how many times Trace had been in this kitchen; hanging out with Nikki after school, eating dinner with her and her family...

"Cheers," said Caleb, raising his cup to mine.

"Yeah, sure. Whatever." I tilted my cup back and chugged it down as fast as my stomach allowed.

"Easy," laughed Caleb, pulling my cup away from my mouth. "You're going to want to slow down. Trust me."

I've taken more than a few sips of my dad's wine in the past and was *perfectly* fine. "I know what I'm doing," I informed, wiping my mouth with the back of my arm. "If I need your input, I'll let you know."

"You got it," he said, raising his hands as though backing down from some deranged mugger.

I polished off the rest of my drink and then filled up another one. Whatever was in this stuff, it was making me feel better, and I wanted more of it.

Caleb was going on about something beside me, but I couldn't hear a word of what he was saying. I was too focused on my escape—on getting it down fast enough, on *forgetting*. I wanted to forget the devastation that had implanted itself inside my life, the heartache that followed me around like a curse. I wanted to obliterate every last painful memory that imprisoned my mind, no matter how short-lived the escape would be.

Tomorrow was another day. Tomorrow, I would dive back into my reality and let the crushing waves of expectation wash over me again as it drowned me under its unrelenting weight.

I filled up another cup.

"Seriously, Blackburn. Slow down."

"You should probably listen to him," said a familiar baritone voice from behind. "Unless you want to get sick tonight."

I felt the humming sensation even before I turned around to see him. Trace, that is. He was standing there with his hands in his pockets and an innocent look of concern on his face. Obviously fake concern. I looked him dead in his eyes and took another long, deliberate sip.

"Can we talk?"

"Nope."

"Jemma." He reached out and tried to slip his arm around

my waist.

The gesture threw me off. But only for a second, and then I realized what he was trying to do. He was trying to touch me—to read my thoughts. I slapped his hand away and took a step back. My cup—and defenses—went back up, and I took another sip.

"Knock it off," he said, grabbing the cup out of my hands. "You've had enough."

"As if you even remotely have a say in the matter." I swung around to get another cup from the counter and stumbled forward, losing my footing like a blundering ballerina.

Caleb's arms quickly caught me before I could face-plant into the oversized punch bowl. Iced tea bowl. Whatever. I looked up at him and tried to focus. He appeared to be swaying a little. Or maybe it was the room that was moving?

"You have really pretty eyes," I said to Caleb, staring up at his Sahara Desert-colored eyes. "They'd look smokin' with some black mascara."

"Thanks, I think," he laughed. "Yours are pretty nice too."

"Alright, that's enough," said Trace, clutching my hips as he pulled me off of Caleb. "You're going home."

"And miss Nikki's bitch-bash? Nah-uh," I quipped, pivoting around to face him. "I—" My words drifted off into nothingness as I glanced up at his gorgeous face—at those eyes—those beautiful, shimmering, storm-churning eyes.

His dimples appeared as his plush lips hiked up at the corners. Apparently, he liked what he'd heard.

"Only if you meant it."

"Let me go," I demanded, though it lacked punch. Being this close to Trace was no good for me, and I knew that, but the room was definitely spinning now and I wasn't even sure I could stand upright anymore.

"I'm not letting go." He lowered his head to mine, bringing

our faces within a dangerous whisper. "Come home with me."

My heart rate picked up its thrum, a desperate song that begged for my submission, for my utter destruction. I couldn't allow it to take me under.

"No."

"Jemma—"

"I said no."

"Then let me take you home."

"I have no home." Bitter, angry tears pooled in the corner of my eyes without my permission. "I have nothing."

"You have me."

"And that's the biggest nothing of all." I shook my head, but it was small and tethered, like a dog on a leash. "You're nothing but a liar and a fraud."

"It's not what you think, Jemma. I wouldn't lie to you. Not about us. Not about this," he said, veering his eyes down to our touching bodies.

"I don't believe you." I pushed him hard, causing him to stumble back a step.

"Come on, Jemma, don't do this," he said, closing the gap again. He drew me in, holding me possessively as though he owned me in some small way. "This isn't the place."

"It's never the place, Trace. And yet here we are." I peeled his hands off from around my waist, slow and measured.

Every inch of my body ached from the withdrawal. I was like an addict, addicted to his brand of toxicity. There was no rhyme or reason to it, no understanding of heart. The smaller, more lucid part of me knew the truth. I had to hold onto that part and stay strong. I couldn't let the addict within me lead me back into the pits of Hell.

Not until I was sure I could withstand the inferno.

I turned to Caleb. "Dance with me?"

"Jemma—"

"You got it," said Caleb, snatching up my hand.

Somewhere in the peripheral of my awareness, I knew Trace was watching me as I disappeared into the crowd with Caleb. I knew I'd hit a nerve, and I knew it was what he deserved.

I pulled Caleb in closer and glanced over my shoulder at Trace. He met my gaze with what looked like pain-filled eyes and then lowered his head. A strange heaviness filled my heart, and I had to look away.

By the time my eyes found their way back to the spot Trace had been standing in, he was gone. I'd done exactly what I set out to do, and yet the satisfaction of hurting him the way he hurt me never came.

Inside, I still felt broken.

Fragmented...

Incomplete.

3. THE PURGE

The rest of the night was a messy blur, like a palette of colors that weren't meant to blend. I remember dancing with Caleb and then with some guy from my chemistry class, and I remember bumping into Hannah and her blindsiding me with questions about Taylor. I remember lying to her through my teeth about it and doing a piss-poor job of it at that. Mostly, though, I remember the guilty ache in my stomach, followed by the mad dash to get another drink down fast enough to drown out the uncomfortable feelings—sink them all deep enough so that I couldn't feel *anything* anymore.

And then I remember a toilet.

"Here's some napkins," said Carly, kneeling down beside me. Her silky, chestnut-colored hair was parted down the middle and fell just below her shoulders in straight sheets of satin. She looked so put-together and beautiful with her lightly bronzed skin and kind caramel eyes.

It was an embarrassing stark contrast to my puke-covered face.

I took the napkins from her and wiped around my mouth before slumping down onto the bathroom floor. Definitely not one of my finer moments in life.

"Knock, Knock." Caleb tapped on the door as he peered his head inside. "You ready to get back to the party?"

"Seriously, Cale? Get out of here!" yelled Carly. "Can't you see she's sick?"

I never really thought they looked alike before, despite the fact that they were twins, though under the bright bathroom lights, I suddenly saw a striking resemblance...though it could have just as easily been that demonic iced tea talking.

"Move!"

Caleb stumbled forward into the bathroom as someone behind him pushed their way through the doorway.

Gabriel Huntington, my transitory Handler slash full-time savior stared down at me unimpressed.

"It's Gabriel, you guys. My knight in shiny leather."

He didn't look amused. "Can you walk?"

"No, but I think I can crawl."

"Jemma, don't!" cried Carly.

Nikki joined the intervention just as I dropped on all fours and started my trek over to Gabriel.

"Oh, this is rich. Are you seeing this?" I heard her say. "This is what he's leaving me for?"

"Jemma." Gabriel knelt down to my lower-than-dirt level and picked up my chin, his moss-green eyes bouncing around my face as he inspected my current state of affairs. "I'm taking you home," he said, slipping his arm around my waist and then lifting me up to my feet.

My head pounded in protest as the room began circling around me like a merry-go-round I couldn't get off of. I tried to focus my eyes on Gabriel. "Can you take me home, please? I don't feel so good."

"I already—never mind. Come on," he said and led me out of the bathroom, his arm fitted securely around my waist.

I stumbled through the packed house wearing my own version of a searing scarlet letter. Judgment-filled eyes followed me at every turn, whispering mistruths and spreading their lies like a flesh-eating bacteria. I felt like some pariah being ushered out of a party I was never meant to attend in the first place.

I bet they couldn't wait to get rid of me. I bet they were all cheering and singing victoriously as they rid themselves of the outsider who couldn't hold her liquor. I could probably hear them if I listened close enough...

"Speech it up," I yelled, though my drivel was promptly swallowed up by the dance track blaring through the speakers. "I can't hear a goddamn thing!"

The room suddenly flipped upside down, and I found myself face to face with Gabriel's butt.

Honestly, the view wasn't half bad.

"What were you thinking?" scolded Gabriel as he carried me out to his truck. He had me strung over his shoulder like a listless sack of potatoes. "This isn't you. This isn't the girl I've been training with."

"Maybe that was the point," I mused, my arms dangling down towards the fog-kissed ground. "Maybe I didn't want to be that girl anymore."

"Unfortunately for you, you don't have that luxury."

He opened the passenger door to his black SUV and plopped me down into the front seat. After buckling me in, he hurried around the front of the truck and climbed into the driver's seat.

"This isn't a game," he said, continuing his tirade as we pulled away from the scene of my apparent crime. "You're not entitled to blow off steam. You're not entitled to a night of teenage idiocies. You're a *Slayer*. Every minute of every day for the rest of your existence. Don't you understand that?"

I squeezed my eyes shut in an effort to slow down the incessant spinning in my head. "Please, Gabriel. I seriously can't handle a lecture right now. Have at it tomorrow, but please, just give me tonight." I rolled down the window and stuck my head out. The cold wind slapped at my cheeks like a reality check.

"If Tessa finds out about this—"

"She won't find out as long as you keep your freaking mouth shut!" I flopped back into my seat and rubbed my temples, trying to stave off the beginnings of an epic migraine. "Dammit."

Gabriel leaned over my leg and popped open the glove compartment. "Here," he said evenly, handing me a bottle of over-the-counter painkillers. "Take two of these and drink plenty of water before you go to sleep."

I instantly felt horrible about being short with him. "Thank you," I muttered, fumbling with the bottle in my hands. "Look, I'm sorry about what I said before. I know you're just trying to help, okay? I get it. I made a mistake. I messed up tonight. I'm not perfect," I defended, though I'm pretty sure that fact had already been clearly established tonight. "It won't happen again."

That was the absolute cold, hard truth. I'd learned my lesson. I had no intention of ever taking another drink from an oversized container *ever* again. The momentary escape wasn't even almost worth the aftermath.

He nodded once, seemingly satisfied with my guilty plea.

"How did you know where I was anyway?" I asked him after a few beats of peaceful silence. I was fairly certain, even in this inebriated state, that I hadn't shared my plans with him.

He didn't meet my eyes when he answered. "Trace called me."

"Figures," I said, shifting my gaze to the window.

The liar was also a snitch.

Sunday came at me like a freight train. My eyes snapped

open to a pounding headache as a mess of lights and shadows danced behind my lids like some kind of hellish kaleidoscope I couldn't turn off. Flashbacks from yesterday came cloaked in regret, making me cringe at the prospect of having to face anyone from last night—*ever* again.

Rolling onto my side, I glanced over at the clock on my nightstand. It was almost noon and I had less than an hour to get myself ready and head over to All Saints for my shift. Undoubtedly, my cosmic punishment for last night's slip up.

To my relief, my uncle was already gone by the time I came downstairs. I wasn't in the mood to answer any questions about my whereabouts last night, or be forced to *lie* to yet another person. I was doing so much of it lately, it was getting harder and harder to keep all my stories straight.

The doorbell rang just as I pulled a cereal bowl from the cabinet. I assumed it was somebody selling something I wasn't going to buy anyway, so I ignored it, hoping they'd get the message and go away. By the third ring, though, I could see that wasn't going to happen. Pulling in a calming breath, I set my bowl down on the kitchen island and went to answer the door.

Trace was standing on the other side of the threshold. His long, dark hair was wet from the pouring rain and clung to his jawline and neck in a way that robbed me of all my attention. He lifted his eyes to mine, and my breathing ceased.

I *so* didn't need this right now.

I slammed the door shut in his face. Two seconds later, another knock. I squared my shoulders and opened the door again, working hard not to get distracted by the brilliant blue eyes that seemed to glow against the dreary gray backdrop.

"Can I come in please?"

"No."

He pumped his jaw as his eyes had their way with my face. "We need to talk."

"Yeah? About what?" I asked, my tone rich with merciless sarcasm.

"Come on, Jemma. Please."

As mad as I was—as much as I hated him—I knew I had to hear him out. The clock was ticking and I needed to find a way to mend this thing with him if I had any hopes of getting the Amulet back for Taylor.

I only hoped I had enough willpower to do it.

I stepped back and held the door open for him. Neither one of us said anything as he stepped inside, careful not to brush up against me as he passed.

"How are you feeling?" he asked as he followed me into the kitchen. "After last night, I mean."

"As if you even care," I said, grabbing the cereal box from the counter and dumping some into my bowl. "And thanks for snitching on me by the way."

As if my night wasn't enough of an epic walk-of-shame, I had to have Gabriel see me in all my post-underage drinking glory.

Trace watched me from across the island. "You refused to let me take you home. What was I supposed to do?"

"Mind your own business, maybe?"

"You are my business." It came out hushed, like a secret he didn't want anyone knowing.

I speared him with contempt from across the island. "I stopped being your business when you left me for dead."

His head snapped back. "What are you talking about?"

"I'm not in the mood for your games, Trace." I couldn't believe his audacity. "Just tell me where it is."

"Where *what* is?" His eyebrows pulled together as if to demonstrate his utter confusion.

Not only was he *fine*, but he was a fine actor too.

"Stop playing games with me," I warned, my fists balled up at my sides. "Where's the goddamn Amulet?"

"What the hell are you talking about, Jemma? How would I know where the Amulet is?" he asked, his iridescent eyes piercing holes right through me. "I thought this was about Nikki."

"Nikki?"

"Because I went to her party," he said with a hint of guilt spattered over his otherwise perfect face.

"I don't give a crap what you do with Nikki," I hissed back, lying through my clenched teeth. "I'm talking about what you did to me at the church after the dance. You set me up. You stole the Amulet from me and left me for dead!"

"What church? I didn't leave you anywhere." His volume kicked up several decibels. "*You* left *me* at the dance."

I shook my head at him. He was lying. He was trying to confuse me—throw me off. "You took it. You were there. I *saw* you do it. Stop lying to me!"

"I'm not lying, Jemma. I swear it." Palms down, he pushed forward across the counter and locked eyes with me as if to drive home his point. "I didn't take anything from you. I don't know what you *think* you saw, but it wasn't me."

"Then who was it?" I shouted indignantly. "I spoke to you, Trace. I saw you. It was you!"

"You spoke to me?" he repeated incredulously as though I were making the whole thing up. He started to shake his head, but the movement weakened and then his eyes shifted away as though he'd become distracted by his own thoughts. "You saw me?" It came out in a whisper this time, almost as though he were asking himself the question, and not me.

What the heck was he trying to pull? "Let me guess, it wasn't you, right? It was your long-lost twin."

"No." He looked back up at me with deep, impenetrable eyes. "But I think I know what happened. I know who you saw."

23

"Congratulations. I already know who I saw," I said, crossing my arms over my chest. "I saw *you*!"

"Yeah. You saw me." He straightened his back. "Just not the 'me' from this Timeline."

"Exactly. Wait, *what*?" I felt like someone just sucker-punched the wind right out of me. "What the hell are you talking about?"

"I didn't take the Amulet. I wasn't there. I *know* I wasn't there, yet you saw me."

"Clear as day."

"There's only one thing that could explain that." His voice was low—shrouded in mystery. "Time travel."

"Are you trying to tell me that some other version of you traveled back in time to steal the Amulet from me?"

"It's the only thing that makes sense."

I tried to process what he was telling me, but my thoughts were spiraling so far out of control, it was making me dizzy. "Why? Why would you—or *future you* do that?"

"I have no idea why my *Alt* traveled back, Jemma." His dimples made a minor appearance as he clenched his jaw muscles in frustration. "All I know is *I* wasn't there."

I wasn't sure what to believe. In fact, I couldn't seem to tell up from down anymore. "How do I know you're not just saying this to cover up the fact that you actually have the Amulet and you don't want me going after you for it?"

His face twisted as though my accusation inflicted actual pain on him. "I wouldn't do that to you."

His voice was so sincere, it was hard not to believe him. Mostly because I wanted to. I wanted to believe him more than I wanted to breathe air, and if this were seven days ago, I would have taken his word as gospel.

But everything was different now.

"That's just it, Trace. You already did it to me." My voice

cracked as the reality of the situation sobered me. No matter which way I spun it, it was still a jagged pill that hurt to swallow. "Whether you did it the other night, or you do it in a few months from now, it doesn't change anything for *me*. The other night still happened. *You* still did it. The *when* is just a matter of time."

His jaw muscles pumped as he followed my logic.

"I can't trust you," I realized. The crushing weight of the bitter end descended on me like an ice storm. "I can never trust you again."

"Don't say that—"

"I think you should go."

"I didn't do this, Jemma. I *wouldn't* do this—not now or ever." His glimmering eyes fell heavy on me; on my soul. "You have to believe me."

"How do I do that, Trace? Tell me how to know for sure, and I'll do it. I'll believe every word you say."

The admission came out without my permission and it terrified me to hear it. On some level, I knew it was true. I desperately wanted to hear him say the words that would explain it all away—that would chase away the doubt and make everything between us right again.

"Jemma." He lowered his eyes, unable to deliver.

"Go home, Trace." I pushed the bowl of cereal away from me, my appetite having gone the way of our almost-relationship—right down the gutter. "Just leave me alone."

He shook his head. "I can't do that."

"Yes, you can. It's easy. All you have to do is walk away from me. Just like you did at the church." I squared my shoulders as the gut-wrenching memories of that night assaulted my mind. "I can't trust you, and until I do—until I have proof that you didn't do this—I don't want you anywhere near me."

"And if that never happens?" Worry creased his features as he cocked his head to the side. "What if you never find proof that I'm telling you the truth? Then what?"

"Then this is how it stays between us."

"Is that really what you want?"

"Yes," I answered, though the lump in my throat was singing an entirely different tune.

"I know you don't mean that," he said quietly, moving around the island towards me.

"Yes, I do," I assured him, but my eyes faltered and I was sure he noticed it. "You're dead to me."

"And you're *everything* to me." His eyes never left mine as he rounded the corner.

My heart hammered in my chest as he closed the distance between us. Trembling, I took a step back, but he followed me, keeping the gap between us at a minimum.

"Stop it." I held my hand out, preventing him from advancing. "Stay away from me."

He was a storm—a raging hurricane capable of obliterating me, and I wasn't sure I was strong enough to withstand its power. Every inch of my body wanted me to surrender to it—to him—to let him take me apart at the seams.

He covered my hand with his, holding it against his chest like a quiet love song. I let the warmth from his touch linger on my skin before pulling my hand back.

"I'm not what you think I am." His hand moved to my face, his thumb grazing along my cheek.

My eyes slipped shut as the pulsating sensation overtook me.

"What I told you that night at the dance," he said, lifting my chin so that I was looking up at him. "*That* was the truth. Don't ever forget it, because I won't ever forget you."

He lowered his head and dropped a soft kiss on my forehead. Before I had a chance to react, he pulled back and walked away, leaving me spinning, reeling, completely alone and utterly confused in the middle of my uncle's kitchen.

4. A GIFT FROM JUDAS

The rain poured down from the heavens like falling hatchets, heavy and unforgiving of our sins. Inside All Saints, memories of Taylor haunted me at every turn. There was no escape from it—no reprieve from the pain. She was at every table I served, behind every door I opened, in the shadows of every corner I passed. I wondered if she was okay; if she was even coherent enough to understand what was going on. My heart was heavy with grief.

She didn't deserve to be thrown into this mess. She deserved to be at home, safe with her family, gossiping on the phone with Hannah or Carly, and getting her last-minute homework done.

I put in the last order with Sawyer, the head cook, and started clearing the tables. The day had dragged on to unfathomable lengths, and I was beyond ready to get away from this place and everyone in it. I had so much on my mind; so much weight to carry on my tired, sagging shoulders, and I hadn't even scratched the surface of my problems.

The door swung open, interrupting my thoughts. "Kitchen's closed," I called over my shoulder.

"That's quite alright. You don't serve my kind of food here, anyway," answered a sultry voice I knew and hated well.

I turned with trepidation as Dominic made his way over to me, smiling deviously as though he could hear the fear pounding in my chest. He was dressed in his usual all-black attire and overcoat, and his blond curly hair was damp from the rain.

"Good evening, angel."

"Go to hell, Dominic."

"Ah, such a lovely mouth. A moment of your time if I may? We have some pressing matters to discuss."

"Discuss *this*," I said, giving him the middle finger. I tried to walk away, but he cut in front of me, quick as a fox.

"As much as I would enjoy exploring the definition of such a gesture with you, I must insist you hear me out." He leaned in closer and lowered his voice to a hiss-like whisper. "It appears we have a shared goal. Perhaps it would be wise of us to lower our arms and join forces."

"Join forces?" I repeated, repulsed by the very notion of it. "The only thing I want to join with you is my wooden stake in your empty heart."

He flinched back, feigning hurt. "That was rather harsh, angel. Even for you."

"Get out of my way, Dominic." I pushed him aside. "I don't need anything from you, and definitely not your help."

"Very well." He followed me through the room as I shuffled between empty tables and chairs. "I *was* going to tell you about Engel's plans for a certain piece of antique jewelry we both know; however, if you're not interested in what I have to say—"

"So help me God, if this is another one of your games," I said, stopping dead in my tracks, "I will end your pathetic existence." I turned to face him, arms crossed over my chest.

"No more games, angel. I promise." His lips curved up into a devious smile I knew not to trust.

I didn't believe him, nor did I trust him, but I was alone in this thing and desperately needed something—anything—that could give me the edge over my growing list of enemies.

"My shift's almost over," I said, deciding to hear him out—for whatever it was worth. "Meet me outside in ten."

His grin reappeared. "I'll be counting the seconds."

I stepped out of All Saints and into a torrential downpour. The rain came down fast and hard, making it difficult to see even a few feet in front of where I stood. Opening my umbrella, I searched the parking lot for Dominic and was just about to call it quits when I saw headlights rolling up at a steady pace, high beams flashing like a beacon of false hope. Dominic's black Audi pulled up beside me and the passenger side door popped open, swinging wildly as though plagued by a mind of its own.

I took a step back and peered in at Dominic. "I'm not getting in there," I called out. "We can talk out here."

"In the rain?"

I glanced around looking for some kind of shelter or safe grounds to talk, but came up empty.

"Come on now, angel," said Dominic, leaning across the armrest like a wolf on the hunt. "If I wanted to hurt you, I would've done it at the church where there weren't any witnesses. Doesn't that afford me any points with you?"

"Nope." But, he *did* have a point. And it was raining an entire ocean's worth of water.

"You're breaking my heart, angel."

"That would require you actually having one." Rolling my eyes at him, I closed the flimsy umbrella and hopped into the passenger seat of his car, probably against my better judgement. "This doesn't mean we're friends," I clarified, rubbing my arms for warmth. "And keep your hands and teeth off of me," I warned for good measure.

"I wouldn't dream of touching you, angel," he said as he sped out of the parking lot almost as fast as the lie sped out of his mouth. "Unless you absolutely wanted me to."

"Right. Well, that will never happen. Like *ever*."

He didn't bother looking over at me when he said, "Never say never."

"Um, okay there, Justin."

"*Justin?*" He arched his brow at me, looking thoroughly confused.

"He's a—never mind. Start talking."

The wipers slashed back and forth at full speed though they barely made a dent in the blur of falling water.

"Straight to the main event?" His onyx eyes poured over me like hot caramel. "I like it."

"Get to the point," I snapped while grabbing the armrest for security. "And keep your freaking eyes on the road!"

Dominic's laughter filled up the space around me, irritating with its silky smooth vibration. I kept my eyes pinned on the road ahead, refusing to give him even an inch to work with.

He settled down fairly quick. "Alright, angel. On to the matter at hand." He took a hard right towards the hills and then settled into a steady pace as we coasted up the winding roads, the rain hammering hard against the windshield.

"It appears we have a shared goal now that we've found ourselves on the same side of the war."

"What are you talking about?"

"Well, we both want the Amulet. We both want Romeo dead—"

"I don't want Trace dead," I quickly cut in. Death was far too easy of a punishment for what he did to me. I planned on making him suffer for a long time to come.

"I guess I'm alone on that."

"Dominic." I wasn't even *almost* in the mood for this.

"I jest," he said, though there was no humor in it whatsoever.

"We both want to get the Amulet back from Romeo," he amended. "Is that better?"

"Get on with it."

"The way I see it, we're both after the same outcome; therefore, combining our efforts would only increase our chances of accomplishing our task."

"Why do you want the Amulet back?" I asked, spearing him with suspicion. "I know you don't give a crap about Taylor's life, so what's in it for you?"

"The satisfaction of helping—"

"Don't even try," I said, halting him before he could shovel any more crap at me. "What's in it for you, Dominic?"

"Self-preservation."

I shook my head. "I don't understand."

"Have you ever bothered to ask yourself why Engel wants the Amulet in the first place?" he asked, turning serious. "What could a centuries-old vampire possibly need with some old necromancy necklace," he asked mockingly as though I should have already figured this out.

"I assumed he wanted it for its protective powers," I said, though that hardly made sense now that I thought about it. He'd already survived just fine on his own and even defeated several generations of Slayers. Why the newfound need for protection?

"If only it were that mundane."

"Then what is it?" I could feel a thickness burrowing in at the back of my throat. "Why does he want it?"

"There is only one thing a man truly wants in life," he said, ready to impart his two-bit wisdom on me. "And that's power. *Absolute* power."

"That's what *you* want," I corrected.

"That's what all men want."

"Fine. Whatever." I nodded, deciding to play along for

argument's sake. "And how exactly does the necklace achieve that for him?"

"Because by possessing the Amulet, he would then possess the ability to control the dead."

I looked at him like he was nuts. "Are you saying he wants to raise the dead?" They couldn't even do it right two thousand years ago with the best Casters on hand. The only thing Engel would raise would be a couple of zombies—if he was lucky.

"No. Not the dead, angel," he said, glancing over at me ominously. "The *undead.*"

"Revenants."

"Precisely." He pulled up to the Blackburn Estate and put the car in park before twisting around to face me. "He wants to create an army of undead and come out of the shadows. An army of Revenants that will rise and fall to his every whim. Walking immortals that would be programmed to do one thing for him—overtake the world. Town by town, city by city—"

"Oh my God." The thickness in the back of my throat tightened into a noose-like choke.

"And believe me when I say, I will not be controlled by anyone. Least of all Engel."

"You never had any intention of giving him the Amulet, did you?" I suddenly realized. "You were going to keep it for yourself all along."

He nodded, his expression haughty and unfazed. "The only person I trust to be in possession of an artifact that would essentially strip me of my free will is myself."

"So what now?" I asked, my head spinning a web of tangled possibilities. "You'll help me get the Amulet back from Trace and then what? You'll just try to take it from me again," I accused.

"I assumed we'd be on the same side now that you've been made aware of Engel's plans," said Dominic, visibly perplexed by my loaded question.

"If I don't give him the Amulet, Taylor dies. If I do, Engel wins and we all die."

"This can easily be resolved with a simple sacrifice for the greater good of all."

"I'm not sacrificing Taylor if that's what you're implying," I snapped, glaring at him. "That's not even an option."

"Very well then," he said, thwarted by my refusal to abandon my friend. "There's only one option left then."

"What's that?" I asked, swallowing hard.

"We kill Engel."

5. THE USUAL SUSPECTS

Monday morning came at me jagged and unrelenting. Taylor's parents showed up at school with two police officers after she failed to make it home for curfew Sunday night. They'd spent most of the morning interviewing faculty and students about her last known whereabouts, and since I was the one she was supposed to have been with this weekend, I was also the first one from the group to face the firing squad.

I stuck to my story as best as I could—what with two seasoned cops hammering questions at me, and her parents watching on with tear-filled eyes. The truth was, it broke my heart to lie to her parents, but what choice did I have? I couldn't tell them the truth, and as far as I was concerned, this was all going to be over with soon enough anyway.

Taylor *would* be reunited with her family and friends...even if it was the last thing I ever did.

"So, she never made it to your house Friday night?" asked Detective Morrison, the taller officer with the slicked-back, dark hair.

I shook my head. "She told me she was going to stay over at Hannah's instead," I lied.

"Hannah...?"

"Richardson."

"Did she give you a reason?"

"Well, I was planning on leaving early and I guess she wanted to stay until the end of the dance."

"Did you witness her meeting up with the other girl— Hannah Richardson, was it?" asked Detective Jones, the other officer with the sandy blond hair.

I shook my head again and bounced a glance at her parents. I instantly regretted it. "N-no. She was walking back inside when I last saw her. I just assumed—" My voice cracked. "I'm sorry," I whispered, turning back to her parents. "I didn't know this would happen. If I would've known, I—"

"We know, sweetheart," said Mrs. Valentine amidst a steady stream of tears. She had the same blue-gray eyes and golden hair as Taylor, though hers was pulled into a coil at the back of her head. "You couldn't have known. None of us did."

"We'll get her back," said Mr. Valentine, pushing his glasses up the bridge of his nose. Judging by the confident tone of his voice, there wasn't a single doubt in his mind.

"So, you aren't sure if she ever made contact with Hannah, correct?" continued Detective Morrison, holding a small writing pad in his hands, presumably going over his notes.

"Correct."

"And you haven't heard from her since Friday? No texts? No phone calls? Nothing?"

"I tried calling her, but her phone was off." That part was the truth. I must have called her a dozen times, hoping by some miracle that she still had access to her phone.

It was a long shot, but I figured it was worth a try.

"Alright then," said Detective Morrison, nodding over to his partner. "I think that about covers it. We appreciate your cooperation, Miss Blackburn. If you remember anything else, please give us a call," he said, handing me his business card.

I nodded and then slipped the card into my pocket.

"Send in Miss Richardson on your way out," instructed Detective Jones as he flipped through his notes again.

I made my way out of the office and into a waiting room stained with the familiar faces of my friends and foes. Nikki's eyes followed me across the room like two aquamarine stones hell-bent on burning holes into the back of my head while Morgan leaned in and snickered something beside her.

"You're up, Hannah," I said, walking past them as I headed straight for the first exit I could find.

The crisp afternoon wind rushed up against me as I bolted through the front doors. I couldn't bear being in that building for another minute. It was stifling, suffocating. The air was too thin, and the walls too close.

Taylor's memory was everywhere, following me around like a ghost hissing in my ears and gnawing at my insides. I wasn't sure how much longer I could stand the torture. I needed to put an end to this—to all of it—and get her back home where she belonged.

But how? How was I going to dig us out of this?

As much as it hurt to admit it, I needed help. I was in way over my head, and I had almost zero experience dealing with Revenants. Certainly none that were as powerful as Engel was. I needed someone with some insight into his ways, someone with the guts to go against him. Basically, someone who was even more warped than he was.

And only one person fit that bill.

Without even making the decision, I started heading across town towards Huntington Manor. I told myself it was because I needed Dominic's help forming an actual plan—a plan that would require his particular brand of diabolic manipulation—

but a part of me also knew it was because I didn't want to be alone.

And I hated that part of me even more than I hated Dominic.

6. A TRIP TO THE DARK SIDE

It was almost noon by the time I made it across town. The sun was buried deep behind a thicket of gray, swollen clouds, apparently still refusing to grace my dimming world with its presence. I tried to recall the last time I'd felt the sun on my skin, reveled from the warmth in my bones, but it all seemed too far away to remember—just another unreachable memory of some distant world I used to know.

I looked up at the imperious mansion that sat on an acre of fog-covered land and felt my pulse quicken as memories of my prior visit resurfaced.

It's different now, I told myself. *I know what he is, and I can protect myself.* I doused myself in the false bravado and strutted up the front steps.

Knocking twice, I took a step back and bit the inside of my cheek as I waited. I was just about to turn and walk away when the door finally snapped open.

Dominic stood there wearing nothing but a fitted pair of black slacks and a haughty smile. It was as though he knew I was coming over and decided to put on the one thing that would leave me speechless. I didn't want to look and yet the curiosity called at me like a black cat on a Halloween prowl.

"What a pleasant surprise, angel."

My eyes traveled north, examining the lean, angular muscles that decorated the upper half of his body.

He leaned into the door frame and smirked. "Came to enjoy the sights, did you?"

I shot him a warning look. "I came to see you—to talk to you about a plan."

"Is that the story we're going with?"

"Forget it." I turned on my heel and started down the steps, grumbling, "I don't know why I even bothered coming here."

"Just a minute," he called, but I didn't slow down. When words failed to call me back, he tried speaking to my mind instead. *Come back, angel.* His voice crawled through my brain like a tickle I couldn't scratch.

I stopped dead in my tracks. "Get out of my head, Dominic!"

"Please come inside. I'll behave, I promise."

I swiveled around to face him. The smug expression he usually wore had diminished. His eyes, normally dark and menacing, looked almost vulnerable—lonely even. I wasn't sure why, but for the first time in my life, I felt pity for him.

I walked back up the stairs, my eyes spearing him with an unspoken warning. It was as though he heard me because he immediately lifted his hands in the air and stepped back from the doorway, giving me proper room to enter.

"Where can we talk?" I asked.

He closed the door behind me and ticked his chin towards the den-slash-study at the end of the hall. "After you," he said, motioning ahead.

I moved with the kind of speed and confidence that said I knew exactly what I was doing, but my heart rate was singing a different tune and I was sure he could hear it. I sat down on the red leather sofa in front of the fireplace and took in the room around me as Dominic poured himself a drink.

Floor to ceiling bookcases covered the back walls like wallpaper, darkening the room into a cave-like chamber. I noticed there weren't any picture frames or family portraits hanging on the walls; no throw pillows or magazines lying around—basically, nothing that would indicate people lived here...that a *family* lived here.

"Care for a drink?" he asked, holding up his glass as he stood behind the wooden console table.

I shook my head, nauseated at the sight of it.

"Can I offer you something else?" He walked over to the sofa and took his seat beside me. "A juice box perhaps?"

My eyes narrowed. "You're hilarious."

"And you're beautiful." His lips twisted into a grin as he reached out and caressed my cheek with the back of his knuckles. Despite his cool temperature, it was a gentle gesture that made my skin warm in a strange way...

A way I didn't particularly care for.

The truth was, I didn't want to respond to Dominic's touch in that way; not in *any* way. I told myself it was just the lingering effects of his bite—of the falsified connection he made between us when he bit me—but I couldn't help but wonder if maybe there was something more to it.

Maybe I was lonely too.

"Don't, Dominic." I pushed his hand away.

"Are you sure, love?" He tilted his head inquisitively as his eyes poured over me like rain. "I can make the hurt go away," he said softly, his voice a quiet promise of rapture.

My cheeks flushed. I wasn't sure what that entailed but I was certain I didn't want to find out. Whatever it was he was offering, it was poisonous and I wanted no part of it.

"Just stay on your side, and I'll stay on mine."

"As you please, angel." He pushed back into the sofa and then focused in on me like a puzzle he was trying to solve. "Does our proximity make you nervous?"

"No." I rose my chin to back up the lie. Of course he made me nervous—and scared, and angry, and so many other uncomfortable things I didn't yet understand, but I wasn't about to admit that to him. "I just don't want you cramming up all my personal space, that's all."

"If you say so." He smirked, his dark eyes fixed on me as though they could see right through the lie.

Refusing to meet his gaze, I turned my attention out the window at a small gazebo that overlooked the rose garden. There was something so warm and peaceful about it, almost as though it didn't belong here amidst the stony darkness.

"My mother's garden," said Dominic, swiveling his drink.

"It's beautiful," I noted. "She must spend hours in there."

"Once upon a time, I suppose. Now, it's just the gardeners." He stood up and moved to the fireplace. Bending down, he picked up a log and tossed it into the hearth. "I don't know why I still commission it. I should have it cut down."

"*What*? Why would you even say that? It's perfectly beautiful right where it is." I stared back out the window at the arched trellises and imagined myself sitting there, reading a great book without a single care in the world.

"It's useless."

"I'm pretty sure your mother would disagree."

"And I'm fairly certain she wouldn't have much to say on the matter." He pulled out a shiny, silver lighter from his pocket and kindled the wood. "Unless she's begun conversing from her grave without my knowledge."

My face blanched. "Oh. I—uh, I'm sorry. I didn't know."

"*Saint* Gabriel didn't tell you?" He straightened out and watched the fire for a moment before turning. The flames danced around the edges of his taut shoulders as he buried his hands in his pockets. "I was certain he would've jumped at the chance to out me as her executioner." A darkness washed across his face, looming over his expression like an inky shadow of death.

"Her *executioner?*"

"In the flesh."

My heart sped off in a frenzy, banging against my ribcage like a lunatic in a padded white room. "You k-killed your mother?" I sputtered, my eyes darting to the nearest exit, calculating my distance to safety.

His eyes followed mine to the door. "I did."

I swallowed hard, my throat as dry as cotton balls. What the hell was I thinking coming here?

"The very first thing I did upon entering this world," he continued. A smile crept across his lips, but it lacked veracity. "I suppose you could say I've been a killer since the day I was *born.*"

My heart sunk in my chest as the sad reality of the situation burrowed in. "She died giving birth to you."

"Poetic, isn't it?" He picked up his glass from the mantel and took a long, purposeful sip.

"That was hardly your fault, Dominic." I couldn't believe I was defending him, but it had to be said. "You were just a baby."

"And yet, still culpable. My father made sure to remind me of the fact every day of my life." He walked back over to the sofa and took his seat again. "Such is the price you pay for the crime, I suppose."

"Your father is a jerk," I said before thinking twice of it. "He was wrong then, and he's wrong now."

He looked over at me thoughtfully, his pitch eyes tempering as he studied me. "Don't do that, angel."

"Don't do what?"

"Don't feel bad for me." He leaned in closer. "Don't feel *anything* for me. I know what I am and I have no reservations about it. You'd be a fool to think anything else."

I wasn't sure what to say to that.

I'd always been the kind of person who believed in second chances, that everyone had redeemable qualities and deserved a fair shot. But Dominic was an anomaly. He didn't fit in with my preconceived notions of the world. He was a monster and he made that clear to me—time and time again. And yet here I was...feeling bad for him.

It's got to be the trauma from this past week finally catching up with me, I decided. I shuddered the misplaced feelings away. "Don't worry, my feelings for you haven't changed. Hatred is still pretty much at the top of the list."

"If you say so, angel."

"But I stand by what I said," I added quietly so that no one but the two of us could hear. "He's wrong."

He nodded, accepting it in whatever capacity he could.

The fire crackled a quiet song as the hungry flames tore at the log like a cannibal on flesh. There was something eerily comforting about the silence, about being here with Dominic— with the devil I knew.

"So, about the Amulet," I finally said, chasing away the spell and anything it could have stood for.

"Yes, on to business." He perked up at the prospect of a new scheme. "Any chance you changed your mind regarding the blond-haired sacrifice?"

"No, Dominic," I said, stale and unimpressed. "I didn't change my mind about letting my best friend die."

He rolled his eyes as though my humanity was a nuisance to him. "Then we're going with the original plan."

"Which was what?" I asked, still unclear after our

inconclusive conversation last night.

"We kill Engel, and we get the Amulet back from Romeo." He paused momentarily. "Though not necessarily in that order," he added, extending his arm along the back of the sofa.

"We kill Engel," I repeated, shocked that he was actually sticking to his harebrained idea from last night. "You say that like it's actually a possibility, like he hasn't murdered generations of Slayers already."

"It most certainly is a possibility." His lip pulled up on one side. "With the Amulet in hand, of course."

"Right. Of course." I nodded, deciding to go with it for argument's sake. "And remind me again how we're getting the Amulet back exactly? Trace isn't just going to give it back to us. I don't even know what he wants with it in the first place, let alone where he's hiding it. Not to mention, it might not even be on our Timeline anymore. We need to—"

"Slow down, love," he cut in, halting my mouth diarrhea. "One thing at a time."

Easy for him to say.

"Care to explain why you suspect it's no longer on our Timeline?" he asked, visibly bothered by the news.

"Trace said so. He swears he wasn't there that night. That it wasn't him." Just saying the words aloud made me long for them to be true.

"Is that right?" He faced forward, distracted with his own sinister musings. "Interesting."

"Well, what do you think?" I watched him closely, gauging him for his reaction—desperately seeking out his unspoken confirmation that it might be true.

He took a slow sip of his drink. "I think he's either a complete idiot, or an absolute genius."

"Do you think he's telling the truth? You saw him that night too, and probably a bunch of times before that, right?"

He picked up a loose strand of my hair and twisted it around his finger. "Indeed, I did."

"Did you see anything different about him?" I asked, pushing his hand away without missing a beat. "Did he look like he was, I don't know, from the future?"

"It's hard to say. If he was from the future, it wasn't the distant future."

"Great. That's no help at all."

"Well, you know him better than I do, angel. What are your instincts telling you?"

"They're telling me nothing." I shook my head, frustrated by my lack of information and control. "All I know is, he's been keeping things from me—things about his ex-girlfriend...and some other stuff," I added, not wanting to disclose anything about Morgan's vision. Something Trace conveniently left out. "If I can't trust him to be honest with me about those things, how am I supposed to trust him now?"

"Easy. You don't," he said simply. "You assume the worst and prepare yourself for all the possible outcomes."

There were only two possible scenarios here. Either he was lying to me and he had the Amulet, or he was telling the truth and it's in the future with an alternate version of himself.

"If he has the Amulet, he's going to go back to the past and give it to Linley." Of that, I was sure. Why else would he want it? "Either way, it's off our Timeline and out of our reach."

"That certainly does complicate things."

"So what do we do now?"

Running his lean fingers along his jawline, he mulled it over. "Figuring out the Amulet's whereabouts and Trace's intentions for it is the first part of the plan. You have to determine whether or not he has it, and you have to be sure." He tipped his head in as though leaning in to tell me a secret. "That part, however, will be solely up to you."

"How am I supposed to do that?"

"Use your feminine wiles, of course."

"Get serious."

"I am serious." He flashed his teeth in a cunning way. "You need to gain his trust and make him believe you no longer care about his affront to you—that your feelings for him far outweigh his betrayal. Get as close to him as you humanely can."

"I don't know if I can do that." Faking it was one thing; being that close to Trace without hopelessly sinking right back into him was a whole different story.

"The other option is to go straight for Engel, though we'd be at a great disadvantage without the Amulet."

I bit the inside of my cheeks. Neither one of my options sounded appealing, though the latter seemed far more risky. Engel was old—and not the decrepit bad-hip kind of old; the experienced and powerful kind of old—and going up against him without any backup was just plain stupid.

I was a lot of things but stupid wasn't one of them. I needed the Amulet. End of story.

"Alright." I looked him dead in the eye and nodded. "I'll do it."

7. SANGUINARIUM

Training with Gabriel was just the kind of outwardly aggressive expression I needed. In keeping with my usual ways, I decided not to tell Gabriel about what was going on. For one, I knew he would tell my sister, Tessa, and I wasn't ready to deal with the consequences of that. Not to mention I had the nagging suspicion she wouldn't give much consideration to Taylor's life in her pursuit of reclaiming the Amulet. She would look at the bigger picture—the greater good of all—and I couldn't risk her bypassing Taylor like that.

Of course, I also didn't mention anything about Dominic or how I'd spent the entire afternoon with him, hashing out the details of our plan. As far as Gabriel was concerned—or anyone else for that matter—Dominic was still my sworn enemy.

Either way, this was just a temporary cease-fire until I got what I needed. As soon as I was done with this whole mess, I would be done with Dominic too.

"Concentrate, Jemma." Gabriel stepped back, dropping his arms in frustration. "This is important. You need to understand the mechanics involved in vanquishing."

I grunted my displeasure. How the heck was I supposed to

concentrate with everything that was going on?

"You should listen, kid. This isn't a game of point-and-stick," interceded Julian, the annoying Sentinel charged with overseeing my training with Gabriel.

"Point-and-stick?" My tone was riddled with ridicule. "How about I point my foot and stick it up your—"

"Precision is key," cut in Gabriel, ignoring both our remarks in equal parts. "And your timing is vital. *Every* time or it could be your last time." His moss-colored eyes turned hard. "Do you understand what I'm telling you?"

"Yes, I understand," I said, crossing my arms. "I'm not stupid."

"You need to be able to do this with your eyes closed and your hand tied behind your back," he said sternly. "Instinct, preparation, muscle memory—this is what we're building on and it's what's going to keep you alive. You have to be prepared for anything, *everything*, because a million things *can* and *will* go wrong out there."

I swallowed a hard lump of pride as his words sobered me. "I get it, I'm sorry. I'll concentrate."

His face relaxed with something that looked a lot like sympathy. "This is for your own good, Jemma. You have to learn to anticipate your opponent's next move and always stay one step ahead of them." He straightened his back like a soldier standing his ground. "The objective is always the same," he said and pounded his fist into the center of his chest. "Right here."

"Right." I nodded and then finished the thought. "And then what?"

"I beg your pardon?"

"What happens after you stake a Revenant?" I asked, curious since my last attempt clearly didn't go as planned. Besides, if we were going up against Engel and his men, I needed to know exactly how to get the job done right this time. "Do they like, disappear in a cloud of dust like they do in the movies?"

"Of course not."

Julian snorted.

"So, they just keel over and die?" I asked, choosing to be the bigger person and just ignore the irritating giant.

"Not exactly," said Gabriel, pushing his hand through his hair. "We'll get to that eventually. All of that is secondary to you mastering your strike—"

"No. I want to know now," I pushed, taking a step towards him. "I'm tired of all the holes and half-stories. If you want me to grow up and take this serious then stop treating me like a child." I squared my shoulders and asked again, "What happens after you stake them?"

"They become incapacitated," he finally answered. "But only for as long as the stake remains *in* their heart. Removing it reanimates the body."

My eyes rounded out at this unexpected detail.

"Incapacitation, of course, is not the end goal. While vital to the process, and useful in instances of interrogation, it is simply the first step," he continued matter-of-factly. "The objective is to vanquish them which requires dousing the incapacitated body in Cinderdust."

"Cinderdust?" *Now we're getting somewhere.* "What is that and where do I get it?"

"It's a synthetic element created by the *High* Casters which essentially ignites upon contact with a Revenant."

"Like a fire?"

"It's slightly more colorful and substantially faster, but yes, more or less like a fire."

"Okay." I nodded, absorbing the new information. "So, basically, the stake to the heart puts them to sleep, and the Cinderdust is what makes it permanent?" I verified.

"Precisely."

"Can't we just throw some Cinderdust and be done with it?" I asked, frustrated by all the extra steps. "Why even bother with the stake?" It seemed like a big risk to take; especially for those of us who weren't on top of our game when it came to the whole *aiming* thing.

"The Order dictates protocol. I assume it's because the Revenant's heart must first stop beating in order for the Cinderdust to do what it was designed to do, though it's simply just a theory of mine. I'm not privy to all the details regarding the actual transference."

"Wait." I crinkled my nose at his strange statement. "Did you just say 'transference'?"

"Well, a Revenant is never *truly* dead. Vanquishing them simply removes them from our world—a relocation if you will. That is the true purpose of Cinderdust."

"You just lost me," I said, shaking my head and feeling more confused than ever.

"Revenants are *immortal*," answered Julian, lifting his head up from his magazine. "That means they live forever, as in, they don't die."

"I know what it means."

"So what's the confusion then?" he asked, sounding irritated even though this conversation didn't involve him in the slightest. "They're immortal, not immortal *until*."

"Revenants are indestructible," explained Gabriel. "They've always been indestructible. Because of this, the Order was forced to find a way around it and did so with the creation of Cinderdust," he nodded into it, waiting for me to catch up. "Much like a Reaper's ability to realm jump, Cinderdust transports Revenants to another realm."

"So we're not actually killing vampires, we're like, u-hauling them out of here?" I didn't like the sound of that. "What if they get a return ticket?"

"*Sanguinarium* is a one-way ticket." A strange look crossed his face. "There is no way out. No life form to feed on, no place to rest, no peace for your soul. It is eternal perdition for Revenants."

I shuddered at the thought of it. Not that I had any issue with sending Revenants there—they were murderous predators void of any humanity. But what about Revs like Gabriel? I couldn't stomach the thought of Gabriel being sent to perdition.

"So I guess I need to be careful where I point this thing, huh?" I tried to make light of the situation, but Gabriel's smile only reached halfway to his eyes.

"Just stay focused on what you were created to do. Your job is to rid the world of my kind. Never hesitate."

I flinched at his self-inclusion. "But you're not one of them, Gabriel. You're Anakim above all else," I said, tilting my head to the side as I tried to get him to see it my way. "And you're good, and kind, and decent. That's a lot more than I can say about most people."

"Shucks. Someone get me a tissue," sniffled Julian.

"Why don't you get one yourself?" I snapped, whipping around to face him. "And pick yourself up a muzzle while you're at it."

"Jemma." Gabriel tried to call my attention back.

"Why is he even here?" I asked Gabriel, livid now. "All he does is sit in that chair like a stupid beanstalk and make stupid comments all day."

"He's here for your protection."

"From what?" I asked with mock-laughter. "From *you*? You would never hurt me, and besides, he'd probably let me get killed anyway." I'd had enough. Finding the patience to deal with Julian on top of everything else I had going on was becoming a job in and of itself.

And I already had more than enough jobs.

Gabriel pursed his lips, though I could tell he was thinking the same thing I was. "I'll talk to the Magister tomorrow. This obviously isn't a good fit."

"Obviously," said Julian.

"You think?" I spat, staring him down as though I might jump in for a round of that point-and-stick game.

If the Magister had any sense at all, he would find another Sentinel to oversee our training because the current one was two short words away from being forced to eat his own tongue.

8. MEAN GIRL

Fog wafted over Hollow Hills like a translucent cloud of smoke, masking our world from the outside like some cosmic barrier that sought to keep us imprisoned. I walked into Weston early the next morning, eager to get a head start on my new plan, *operation get close to Trace*. The clock was ticking, and I desperately needed to figure out a way to put my hurt and anger towards Trace aside if I had any chance of getting the Amulet back. He was my one and only link to it, and pretty much the only lead I had.

I still wasn't sure whether it was *future* Trace or *present-day* Trace who took the Amulet from me, but one thing was for sure; one of them had it and that made Trace the only one who could get it back for me.

Unfortunately, my target was already there when I arrived, which consequently, threw me right off my game.

He was standing against his locker when I rounded the corner, his cell phone planted firmly in his hands. From the corner of my eye, I saw his head pop up as I approached, and even though my instinct was to look away from him—to avoid those storm eyes at all cost—I knew that wasn't going to help me get the Amulet back. I had to get close to him again—as close as I could stand to get—and I had to do it without tipping him off.

I met his curious stare and gave a meager smile, letting my eyes linger on his a while longer than they needed to. As dazzling as he was, I didn't falter. I knew my place, and I knew my plan, and I was sticking to it no matter how good his just-showered-hair looked.

The seed had been planted.

Reaching my locker, I tossed my schoolbag inside and pulled out my homeroom books just as my phone vibrated in my jacket pocket. I glanced down at the screen and saw my sister's number.

Ignore.

An early morning interrogation with Tessa was the last thing I needed. What if she started questioning me about the Amulet? What if she suddenly wanted it back, or worse, knew I wasn't in possession of it anymore? I wasn't even *almost* ready to deal with Tessa right now. And definitely not at this ungodly hour.

My phone buzzed again.

Voicemail.

I threw the phone in my locker and shut the door.

"Hey, Blackburn."

I jumped at the sudden sound of Caleb's voice in my ear.

He placed a steadying hand on my shoulder and laughed. "Sorry about that. Didn't mean to scare you."

"It's okay," I said, squirming back a step. "I'm just a little on edge lately."

"Anything I can do to help?" He flashed his pearly whites and leaned his shoulder into the locker beside mine.

Unless he knew a way to get the Amulet back, save Taylor, and kill a centuries-old vampire, there wasn't much he could do for me. "No, but thanks for asking."

I secured the lock and bounced a glance over his shoulder. Trace was still leaning against his locker, though his arms were crossed over his chest now, and he wasn't alone. Ben was standing beside him, talking his ear off, but it didn't look like Trace was paying any real attention to him since his eyes were still pinned on me.

And they didn't look happy in the least.

"You coming to the game tonight?" asked Caleb.

"I don't think so," I said, shaking my head as I turned my attention back to him. He really had that frat-boy look down pat with his crisp letterman jacket and perfectly tousled hair. "I have some stuff to take care of." My eyes veered back to Trace, who was still watching me like a foreign movie he didn't understand.

My heart rate picked up again.

I hated that that he still had an effect on me. It would be so much easier to hate him—to move on and forget him if I knew for sure that he betrayed me. At least then I'd have some resolution, some closure...and a clear conscience when I pulverized his heart the way he pulverized mine.

"Maybe I can take you out sometime." Caleb's eyes fell heavy on me. "Like on a date or something."

"A date?" It took a while for the word to even register.

God, when did that happen? When did something as normal as a *date* become such a foreign concept?

"I don't know. I have a lot going on right now." I nearly cringed at how lame I sounded. "I still have tons of homework to catch up on. I really need to stay focused," I added, hoping to lessen the sting.

"Right." He raised his chin in a nod, slow and weighty with disappointment. "Got it."

"Maybe when things calm down?" I offered, though we both knew that wasn't likely to happen. The way things were going,

I'd probably never get a chance to go on another date again. Those kinds of things tended to take a very distant backseat when you find out vampires exist and that your sole purpose in life is to destroy them.

"Yeah, maybe."

My gaze shifted over Caleb's shoulder again. Ben and Trace were both staring now, and I could see Ben's lips moving. It definitely looked like I was the topic of their discussion.

I couldn't help but wonder if Ben knew the full story; if he was up to date on what was going on. I had a hard time believing he would still be talking to Trace if he knew he was partly responsible for Taylor's disappearance. Either he hadn't fessed up yet, or he really wasn't there that night.

The not-knowing was killing me.

I needed to dig deeper into Trace's story, to disentomb his secrets and find out what the heck was really going on. There was only one place I could think of to start.

"Have you seen Morgan?" I asked, turning back to Caleb. If anyone could provide insight into the truth, it was Morgan. She was a Seer after all. Maybe she'd like, *seen* something.

He shook his head. "Check the washrooms. That's where the girls usually hang out."

"Right." *I should totally know this.* "Thanks."

Morgan was standing in front of the bathroom mirror applying a thick coat of mascara when I walked into the girls' washroom. Luckily, Nikki appeared to be nowhere in sight which elated me to no ends. I much preferred to have this tête-à-tête without the ice queen present; especially since I had the nagging suspicion that she controlled most of what her friends *did* and *said*, and I really didn't want to risk her interference.

I darted across the washroom, checking under each stall to make sure no one else was in there with us.

"You do know how weird that looks, right?" she said, looking at me through the mirror, her lash brush mid-air. "And it's probably illegal too."

"I'm just making sure we're, um, safe. You can never be too careful, right?" I said, heading back the other way to lock the door. "That mascara looks great on you by the way," I added—my pathetic attempt to soften her up a little.

"I know." She blinked hard. "What do you want?"

"I need to talk to you."

"About what?"

"About Trace."

"Why don't you talk to Trace about Trace?" she said, pulling a tube of red lipstick out of her makeup case.

"Because I need the truth and Trace seems to have a hard time with that."

She didn't respond.

"That vision you told me about at the dance," I started.

"What about it?"

"Is it true?" I moved beside her and watched her through the mirror. I needed to know if there was any truth to what she'd said or if it was all part of some sick game.

"Of course it's true." She tossed her red curls over her shoulder. "Why would I make that up?"

I decided not to answer that question honestly. I wasn't sure how much she knew about what happened that night after the dance. "I'm just trying to sort everything out," I said, aiming for vague. "So you saw Trace die in a vision, and it was because of me? To save me?"

"Pretty much." She smacked her lips together and ran her finger along the edges, removing the excess lipstick.

"To save me from what? When? And why would he do that? Why would he risk himself to save me? Does he—"

"Oh my God, stop," she cut in, making a face. "I'm not a

fortune-teller, okay? You're asking me questions I don't have answers to." She tossed her lipstick back in the makeup case.

"But you're a Seer!"

"Yes, a Seer—not an *Oracle*. I have visions, like tiny little glimpses of the future. That's it. I try to call them like I see them, but I don't always have the full picture."

I took a deep breath and tried to compose myself. "Okay, so what *did* you see?"

"I saw you. I saw Trace. I saw blood. A lot of it. I saw you pull each other in, and then a final, you know..."

"A final *what*? A final word? A final breath? A final kiss?" Goddamn her, I needed answers!

"All of the above. More or less." Her evasive emerald eyes flickered to me through the mirror. "Look, you told him you loved him and then he was dead. That's what I saw. Okay?"

I couldn't seem to pull in enough air to fill my lungs. "When did you see this?"

"Right before you moved here."

"Did Trace know?"

She nodded.

"So you guys knew I was coming here before it was even decided?"

"Pretty much."

I wasn't yet sure how to feel about that. "Have you had any other visions?"

"Tons."

"About me?"

"Some."

"Can you be more specific?"

"No." She swept some powdered blush across her cheekbones. "Like I said, I'm not a fortune-teller." She paused for a moment and then turned to me. "And I'm not a therapist either, so if you have relationship issues with Trace, you need to take that up with him."

I lowered my head. "That's not exactly an option right now. Things are really...messed up."

"I'd say so." Her gaze softened with what looked like pity as they looked me up and down. After a brief pause, she said, "Look, for what it's worth, I know he cares about you, okay? A lot."

I felt a tug at my heartstrings—a dazzling spark of hope that lit up my insides like a Christmas tree. "You had a vision about it?"

"No. I had a conversation about it." She dropped her blush brush into the makeup case and tossed it into her bag. "He's my friend. I don't need a vision to know what he feels."

She grabbed her purse from the counter, draped it over her shoulder and walked out of the washroom, leaving me spiraling with even more questions than I started out with.

9. THE COMPANY YOU KEEP

The lunch bell blared through the speakers, prompting me out of my seat so fast even Taylor would have been impressed. Tossing my books in my locker, I discarded the lunch I had no appetite for and headed straight for the library, fully intent on hiding out among the cobwebs and books for the remainder of the hour. I may have made some progress with Trace this morning, but sitting across from him at the lunch table for the next hour wasn't a part of my plan.

Pushing through the doors, I smiled at the librarian eating her lunch at the counter, and then took off for the deepest corner of the library. Pacing slowly down the aisle, my hand swept across the book spines as I browsed the titles. I wanted to find a book to escape into, something to lose myself in for the next sixty minutes, but I wasn't sure there was one thick enough to erase my reality.

Reading hadn't always been my thing. Back in Florida, I always preferred being out with friends to being alone with myself. Shopping, cheerleading practice, pep-rallies; that was my thing. As superficial as it may have seemed, it filled up the silence around me—the void from my non-existent mother, and my too-far away sister—and I loved every minute of it.

All of that changed after I watched a vampire murder my father in cold blood, and consequently, landed myself in the hospital. Lucid conversations and social mixers weren't exactly an option anymore, but reading always was. It quickly became my way out; my escape from captivity. I didn't have to live inside my pain anymore. I could live inside my books, each one taking me further and further away from the barred windows that held me prisoner.

I heard muffled voices at the front of the library. I peeked over a row of books and saw Trace talking to the librarian. He nodded, flashed a dimpled smile, and then arrowed his eyes in my direction. I took a hasty step back as if I'd been caught watching something I shouldn't have seen. Composing myself, I peered back over the books at him.

He was walking now—moving straight for my aisle.

I snatched a random book from the shelf and flipped it open. I read two lines (something about an Alpha werewolf) and tried to put it back, but it was too late. The book fumbled out of my hands as Trace rounded the corner.

Our eyes met, and I swallowed hard.

He glanced down at the book on the floor and then calmly walked over to me. Bending down, he picked it up, flipped it to the front cover and then looked back up at me under dark, fanning lashes.

"Interesting choice." The tantalizing depths of his voice sent a shiver down my spine.

"I like to keep it interesting," I said, staring down at him casually as though looking into his eyes after what he'd done to me wasn't torturous in every sense of the word.

He handed the book back to me and straightened out. "So you're talking to me again?" he asked. His voice was low, like the books were alive and he didn't want them to hear us.

Working hard to keep steady eye contact, I nodded.

"Really?" He took a hopeful step closer. "So you believe me then?" His dark brows pulled together making his eyes look like two drops out of the bluest ocean.

I tried not to get swept up in the waves.

"I don't know what to believe anymore." I *wanted* to believe Morgan. I *wanted* to believe him. I wanted to believe him more than I wanted to be alive because every breath I took without him was shallow and suffocating. "I wish I could trust you again," I admitted quietly, sliding the book back in its place. I needed someone on my side now more than ever.

His jaw muscle pumped. "I would never hurt you."

"You say that now, and maybe you even mean it, but something changes because you *did* hurt me. It already happened." Visions of him walking away from me that night sliced through my mind like taunting reminders of what we'd become. I could feel my eyes well up as the burn at the back of my throat intensified. I didn't want to cry—I didn't even want to care, but it seemed to be out of my control.

Seeing the agony on my face, he immediately erased the gap between us. I wanted to step back and keep the space alive, but my legs—my heart—couldn't bear the strain of separation.

"How do I fix this, Jemma?" He lifted my chin, forcing me to look up at him. "How do I fix something I didn't break?"

"I don't know," I said, but the truth was, I wasn't sure this could *ever* be fixed.

Pain flashed through his eyes.

"You weren't supposed to hear that," I whispered, realizing he'd been listening in.

He looked away as he tried to conceal the hurt that was already written all over his elegiac face. When his gaze met mine again, his eyes were harder, more determined. "Tell me what to do, Jemma. Tell me what I have to do to prove myself to you.

Whatever you want, I'll do it."

My hands trembled as I tried to contain all the emotions funneling through me. "Are you sure you mean that?"

"Try me," he dared, wetting his lips.

"I want the truth, Trace. About *everything*."

"I told you the truth," he said confidently.

"No." I shook my head and clarified. "I want to know the truth about your trips to see Linley. I want to know about the vision, and about you and Nikki. I want to know all of it."

"There is no me and Nikki," he affirmed, clenching his jaw. "And I don't want to talk about my sister."

"But you said—"

"Why does it matter to you?" he cut in quick as a knife. "What does my sister have to do with *us*?"

"Everything. Nothing. I don't know, but that's the point. Maybe it's related. At the cabin, you said you were trying to find the Amulet for her," I recalled.

"So what?"

"What were you going to do with it once you found it? If you tell me what you were planning, maybe it could help us figure out where it is now, or at least understand why your Alt would want to take it."

He shook his head. "I can't risk it."

"But you can risk *me*?" Feeling the hurt prickle through me, I pushed his arms down and took a step back.

"Don't you get it? Involving you *is* risking you. It's risking all of us." His jaw muscles popped. "I won't do that. The less you know, the better. This is the way it has to be."

"You don't get to make all the decisions, Trace. You don't get to play God with my life—with Taylor's life!" Anger slashed through me, firing off my mouth. "I'm getting that Amulet back one way or another. Either you help me get it or stay the hell out of my way."

"You won't find it." His voice was barely a whisper, but it resonated in my ears like a gong. "Even if you figured out where it is, you can't get there."

"Why not?" My eyes narrowed, suspicion reigning again.

"For starters, you can't time travel," he pointed out smugly. "And secondly, if my Alt went back in time to get it, that means it's now in the future. And since I can only travel backwards, you're shit out of luck."

Panic set in, making my skin crawl with unease. "There has to be another way," I said, racking my brain. "Maybe it's in the past again. Tessa said Linley was trying to recreate the First Rising spell—"

"Leave it alone, Jemma." There was a definite edge to his tone, but I wasn't about to give up that easy.

"That's not going to happen, Trace." I had to make him see it my way. I had to appeal to his sensibility. "If Linley's the reason you wanted the Amulet before then she's probably still the reason you'd want it in the future." I glanced over the row of books to make sure we were still completely alone. "We need to go back and talk to her. She might know what's going on. She might be able to help us—"

"That's not happening," he cut in before I could finish pleading my case.

"Why not?" I asked, and then it dawned on me. "You're still helping her, aren't you?"

"She doesn't know anything," he said, ignoring my accusation. "If she had the Amulet, I would know it."

"You can't expect me to just drop it. This is the only lead I have." Frustrated, I shook my head at his lack of cooperation. "Taylor's still out there. Doesn't that matter to you?"

"Of course it matters," he said, his head dropping down a notch. "Just not as much as my sister does."

My conversation with him in my bedroom came back to me.

He had confessed that he would do anything to save his sister...even if that meant sacrificing innocent people.

Apparently that included Taylor and me.

I needed to switch gears and get him back on my side. "No one has to be left behind, Trace. If we work together, we can save them both," I said, desperate for his concession. I wasn't sure that was even a possibility, but I had to put it on the table. Taylor's life was depending on this and I wasn't about to hold anything back.

He didn't answer.

"So I guess you were just lying when you said you would do anything."

His eyes hardened. "This isn't a game, Jemma. If the Council finds out—if they even suspect anything—you'll be banished. And I'll be Bound, or worse." He took a step towards me. "Is that what you want?"

"No." I took a step back, but he quickly matched it.

"Then stay out of it."

"I can't do that." I swallowed hard as he closed the gap. "You already involved me. *You*. Future you. Same difference."

His dimples pressed in as he tensed his jaw.

"If you care about me at all, you'll tell me the truth about Linley," I said, retreating slowly down the aisle as my chest rose and fell at his mercy. "You'll tell me what you know, and you'll help me get the Amulet back."

"And what's in it for me?" he asked, forcing me further back as he studied my face. His eyes settled on my mouth. "What do I get in return?"

I swallowed the lump in my throat. "What do you want?"

"You."

My back hit the bookshelf.

"I want *you*, Jemma." He grabbed the shelf on either side of me and leaned in. "All of you. Just like before."

My face flushed red. I could hear my heart beating—pumping so hard I thought it might punch a hole through my chest.

"What about the vision?" I blurted out because it was the only thing I thought might actually slow him down.

"That's my problem." He moved in closer—so close I could feel the heat emanating from his body. It was as close to the sun as I'd gotten in weeks.

"Morgan told me everything."

"Good for her," he said, staring at my mouth as though he wanted to paint a portrait of it, to devour it.

"Why didn't *you* tell me?"

"Because I didn't think it mattered." He shifted again, erasing any semblance of space between us. "I wasn't planning on falling in love with you."

I pushed back against the bookshelf, but there was no room left to retreat. "And now?" I asked, working hard to keep an even tone as I fought away the urge to wrap myself in the intoxicating scent of his spicy cologne. "Where does that leave us?"

"Right where we are."

My lips parted, but no words came out. I knew I had more questions—more thoughts, but I couldn't seem to make enough sense of them to get anything out.

And definitely not with him standing this close to me.

"You're everything to me, Jemma," he said, still staring down at my mouth. "I need you to believe me." He moved in to kiss me, but I stopped him right before he connected.

"Prove it, Trace."

He licked his lips, his eyes never straying from my mouth. There was a war raging behind his eyes, a battle of opposing wills, and I had no idea which side was going to win.

I bit my bottom lip in anticipation.

Heat flashed through his eyes like molten rock. "Fine. You win. I'll tell you everything you want to know."

"When?"

"Tonight."

The last thing I cohesively remembered was Trace's mouth as he lowered it to mine and kissed me with the heat of a thousand broiling volcanoes.

10. GAME CHANGER

Trace and I met up later that evening as planned. Our steamy make-out session in the library (while a pleasant distraction) hadn't derailed me one bit. In fact, I was as determined as ever to get the Amulet back and bring Taylor home, and with Trace finally willing to answer my questions, I was beginning to feel like I had an actual chance of making it happen. He had the answers I needed, and I was ready to do everything in my power to get them.

I was done taking things at face value—I'd already learned my lesson the hard way—and I refused to accept anything less than full disclosure.

From *him*, that is.

On my end, I was still planning on keeping Dominic my dirty, little secret for as long as I needed him to be. He was my backup plan, my safety net, and I wasn't about to screw that up for myself. Besides, chances were, I'd probably need someone like Dominic on my side when it came time to square off against Engel. The last thing I wanted to do was burn that bridge.

The rain had finally tapered off into a light drizzle by the time Trace and I pulled up to his house. All the lights were off, and the driveway was empty, making the house appear daunting, almost haunted, as it blended into the starless night.

"Where's your dad?" I asked as I stepped out of the blue Mustang and cast a glance at him over the roof of his car.

"Business trip."

"Oh. Okay, cool." I wasn't sure it was such a great idea being here alone with Trace like this, but I couldn't seem to summon the words to object to it.

Once inside, we headed straight for the kitchen. As per the rest of the house, it was spacious, clean, and had all the trappings of a well-cushioned lifestyle. Stainless steel appliances and charcoal-colored granite countertops topped off the dark wood cabinets like an exclusive price tag.

"You hungry?" he asked, flicking on the lights. "Training always made me hungry."

"I'm starving," I admitted, pulling out a dark leather chair at the kitchen island.

He yanked open the double-door refrigerator and started digging around inside before resurfacing with an armful of food and condiments. He set his pickings down on the counter and got to work.

"How long did you train before you quit?" I asked, realizing I didn't know much about his time with the Order.

"Officially? From eleven to seventeen."

"And unofficially?"

"Since as far back as I can remember." He spread some mayonnaise on a slice of bread. "As soon as I really understood what I was, it was the only thing I wanted to do."

I thought back to myself at that same age. It was a stark contrast. At eleven, I was still playing with dolls. At fifteen, I was headed to nationals with my cheer squad, completely oblivious to what I was and the hidden world around me. My life revolved around pep-rallies and obsessing over the exact moment when my first kiss would happen. It all seemed so much smaller now, so trivial, and yet, if I was completely honest with myself, a part of me still longed for it.

"Do you ever regret leaving the Order?" I asked. "I mean, now that you know they weren't keeping the Amulet from Linley."

He shook his head. "They didn't have the Amulet, but they knew how to get it. And they knew about the Scribes." I could hear the anger building in his voice. "They have all this power— all these beings with the ability to make things happen, to stop things from happening—and they do nothing with it."

"But maybe there's a reason," I offered. "Maybe they know better than to intervene."

"Or maybe they're just weak." He slapped on a few slices of ham and cheese and then topped it off with another slice of bread. "Maybe our lives aren't valuable enough to them. Maybe they don't think saving one is worth the effort."

I could see the vexation in his eyes, icy and sharp like a slow-building storm. I knew better than to play there.

He sat down at the island and slid my plate over to me.

"Thanks."

"What about you?" he asked, biting down into his sandwich. "What do you make of them?"

"I don't know," I said, covering my mouth as I chewed. "I haven't been around them long enough to know whether I can trust them or not." All I had is what people told me, and that wasn't very much at all. "Gabriel says everything is fated— predestined on the Paradigm."

"Yeah."

"So what's the point in trying to change something that will always be no matter what you do?"

"What if that's not true?" he challenged. "What then? Gabriel himself is proof that the past *can* be changed."

"Yeah, but he cheated the Paradigm by dying and coming back as something that isn't even human." Or technically alive for that matter.

"Exactly." His dimples flashed briefly as he swallowed. "There's a hole there, an opening. If you can cheat your fate that way, who's to say there isn't another way—another hole."

"So how are you going to do it?" I watched him as he devoured the last of his sandwich. "How are you going to cheat fate and save Linley from her destiny?"

He looked down at me with apprehension. "I don't have all the details figured out yet."

"But you have an idea, right?" I watched his jaw muscle pop under my interrogation. "You wanted the Amulet for a reason. Were you going to bring it into the past and give it to her? To stop her from dying?"

Shaking his head, he pressed back in his chair. "Doing that would create a Ripple. It's too risky."

"So what then?" I pushed. I could tell from his ever-guarded expression that he had a plan. That he knew exactly what he was going to do if given the chance. I just had to dig deep enough to get to it, push harder through the wall. "Were you going to try to bring her back from the dead?" I cringed just saying the words out loud. But the Amulet, after all, did have necromancy capabilities.

He shook his head again, slow and calculated.

"Then what?" I leaned in closer, forcing him to keep eye contact with me. "How were you going to do it?"

I could see the unease in his face, the tension in his shoulders. This was his lifeline, his one chance to save his sister. Letting me in meant slicing it wide open to the possibility of interference—of failure.

With his head cocked to the side, he tapped his thumb on the table and watched me, studied me, read me like an open diary. The truth was right there on the tip of his tongue, peeking through like a sliver of sunlight spilling through a crack. I just had to chip at the edges a little more, push a tiny bit harder.

"We can do this together."

The crack split and acquiescence brimmed through.

"I'm going to bring her into the present," he said carefully, scrutinizing me as he spoke.

"You can do that?" I asked, shocked by this revelation. "You can just grab people from the past and pop them into the future?"

"Something like that." He watched my face for any signs of panic or distress. When he found none, he went on. "Once she's on our Timeline, she only has a limited amount of time."

"Why?"

"Because it's coming for her," he said ominously. "Death is coming whether she's on our Timeline or hers. The outcome will be the same." He leaned forward in his chair. "That's where the Amulet comes in. As long as she's wearing it, she'll be protected."

And there it was. The reason he needed the Amulet.

"But, that's only a temporary fix to buy us some time," he went on. "The minute the Amulet comes off, she'll be a goner and everything we did will be for nothing."

"So what then? How are you going to stop her from dying?"

His dimples winked at me like the promise of a sweet, painless death. "I'm going to finish what she started. I'm going to recreate the First Rising spell."

11. RAISING THE DEAD

Skeletal branches tapped against Trace's bedroom window as the howling wind pushed the trees back and forth, hissing voraciously as though it wanted in. I sat down on the edge of his bed, watching him as he moved around his room.

"The spell has to be modified first," he continued without missing a beat. He pulled out a change of clothes from his dresser drawer. "I'm not looking to turn her into a bloodsucker," he clarified, unbuttoning his shirt.

"Don't you need the Scribes for that?" I asked, staring at his peeking flesh without really meaning to. "Wasn't that the whole reason she went back to the past with Tessa in the first place?" When they changed the past and stopped Gabriel and Dominic from perishing in a fire.

"I already have them," he said, dropping his shirt to the ground. "The only thing I'm missing is the Amulet."

My eyes nosedived after his shirt as I tried to force myself not to look up while processing what he'd just said. "You have the Scribes? How? When?" I sputtered, eyes wide and pinned to the ground.

"Linley got them," he answered, and I was sure I detected a

hint of pride in his tone. "That night with Tessa."

"She lied to Tessa?" My eyes snapped up to his, and I instantly regretted it. Not because the view wasn't good—like *insanely* good—but because I could hardly tear my eyes away from it and stay focused on the grave matter at hand.

"She had to."

"Did she, um..." His naked upper body was all I could think about. Ridges and edges as sharp as the rugged coastline taunted me with their perfection, daring me to look out at them—to venture closer—but not to touch.

"Did she *what*?" His head was tilted, his arms flat by his side. He looked like an Adonis without even trying to.

"Did she, um, ever tell Tessa? Like, does Tessa know?" I kicked myself inwardly. *Get it together*, I scolded myself as I shifted my gaze towards the window to give him some privacy.

Beads of water splattered against the glass, blurring out the outside world as though it didn't even exist anymore. Sometimes when I was alone with Trace like this, it almost felt like it didn't.

"I don't think so," he said.

His belt buckle clinked.

"What are you doing?" I bounced a glance in his direction just as the edge of his pants slid over his hip bone. My head snapped back so fast I almost got whiplash. "You can't do that in here!"

He laughed, the sound of it throaty and completely sexy. "Why not? It's my room."

"Yeah, but I'm in here with you."

"So?"

For the love of all that was holy. How was he not getting how inappropriate this was?

His belt buckle made another clink as it hit the floor. "Haven't you ever seen a naked guy before?"

My heart came to a full stop and then kicked off into

overdrive. "Of course I have. I mean, well technically—look, that's not the point!"

God, was the heating on in here or something?

He laughed again. "Relax, Jemma." My name slid off his tongue like silk. "I'm wearing shorts."

I peeked at him from the corner of my eye. Skin. Skin. More Skin. *Shorts.* Okay, so he was wearing shorts—more like boxer briefs—but at least it was something.

And, oh my wow, was he ever *something!*

He pulled on his jogging pants and then rolled out his desk chair across from me. "Good?"

"And a shirt please." Not that I wasn't enjoying the view, but I had to stay focused, and I knew that would be impossible with Reaper *MacSteamy* sitting across from me.

"Alright," he said as he reached over and grabbed a cutoff-sleeve t-shirt from his clean laundry pile. "Satisfied?"

Hardly, but that was precisely the point. "Thanks."

He flexed back in the chair, his legs spread out wide. "So where were we?"

"You were telling me how you got the Scribes," I reminded him. "So, basically, you're all set."

"Not exactly." His jaw muscles ticked again. "The Scribes are just a starting point. We need a new spell—one that will make her Immortal without turning her into a Rev."

"And how exactly are you planning on pulling that off?" I asked with cynical undertones.

He hesitated before answering. "Nikki."

Just hearing her name gave me heartburn.

"That's why we've been hanging out more," he quickly added as if defending himself against my unspoken accusation. "She's been working on a new spell for me."

I bet that wasn't all she was working on.

"Is she even capable of doing something like that?" I asked, curious about the magnitude of her witchy powers.

"I hope so." He leaned forward in his chair, his elbows resting on his knees. "She's the one that came up with the spell to hide my trips to the past."

It made me sick to hear him speak about her. Like her name was vomit and didn't belong coming out of his mouth.

"So all of this is resting on Nikki's shoulders?" There was something severely and innately wrong with that.

"For now, yeah." If he was worried about it, it didn't show on his face. "Unless you have a better idea."

I shook my head, but I sure as hell planned on coming up with one. I wasn't about to put anyone's life in freakin' Nikki Parker's hands. And definitely not my own.

"So that's it." He shrugged his shoulders with nothing more to offer. "Now you know everything."

I wasn't sure how I felt about him having the Scribes in hand and Nikki by his side. The combination seemed lethal and dangerous. "Looks like you have it all figured out," I noted, leaning back. "All you're missing now is the Amulet."

He nodded. Studying my face, his eyes turned serious. "I hope you know I never had any intention of taking it from you. I don't know what happens to change that, but it must have been big because the last thing I would ever do is hurt you."

Without even realizing it was happening, something had changed in me over the course of the evening. The more I listened to him, the more I believed him. I believed he wouldn't hurt me that way. At least I did in my heart, and for now, that would have to be enough to keep me going.

Trace was on the cusp of something big, something huge, and there were only a few minor obstacles standing in the way of it. Namely, the missing Amulet. Either way, the fact still remained. One way or another, if he was going to resurrect his sister from the dead, he *needed* that Amulet.

The more I heard, the more I was certain that future Trace had found a way to fill in the missing piece once and for all. By taking the piece right out of my hands.

But then, why travel back in time to do it? Why not just take it from me in the future? Did I no longer have the Amulet?

Or was I no longer around to take it from?

12. HEARTSONG

As soon as I was up to speed on Trace's plans for Linley, I tried to make a quick exit with the lame excuse of a last-minute homework assignment. I was literally on my feet and about to head out the door when Trace said something funny about Mr. Bradley's almost-see-through dress shirts. I couldn't help but laugh. And then I joked about the way he combed his hair over the bald spot on his head, and we both laughed. And suddenly, I'd forgotten I was supposed to be leaving.

It was always that way with Trace. Time seemed to just melt away from me when I was with him. It didn't matter where I'd been, or where I had to go. When we were together, it was the only place I wanted to be.

"How have you never heard of this band before?" he asked some time later, aghast by my admission. His electric blue eyes locked on me like a beacon of hope.

"I haven't exactly had time to sit around and discover new music lately," I pointed out.

"True." He studied me for a moment and then smiled, dimples blazing. "I think you're going to like it. I mean, I *hope* you do." The way he said it made it sound like he had a real stake in it.

I watched curiously as he flipped through his playlist and then plugged the MP3 player into the dock before grabbing the remote control on his way back. He flopped back on his bed and propped a pillow up behind his head.

"Come here," he said, gesturing for me to get closer.

"That's okay, I'm good here," I said, waving him off as I hunkered down on the corner of his bed.

"Come on, I don't bite."

"I know," I said, but the truth was, I was afraid to get too close to him. I still didn't trust myself enough to risk the proximity.

He seemed confused. "Are you scared of me or something?"

"No." I swallowed the lump of nerves at the back of my throat. "Of course not," I said. But that wasn't entirely the truth, and we both knew it.

"We've been alone like this before."

"I know."

"It's not a big deal."

"I know," I said, more firm this time.

"So stop playing and come here. I'm not starting the song until you do," he baited, interlocking his fingers behind his head—which consequently, highlighted the bulky muscles in his arms rather nicely.

I wasn't sure if he was doing it on purpose, but I suddenly felt inspired to move. I scooched down closer and carefully laid myself down next to him.

His dimples exploded on both sides in victory. "See, that wasn't so bad, was it?"

"Define *bad*," I sassed, refusing to give him the full satisfaction.

Laughing, he picked up the remote from his lap and hit play. Thick, black lashes lowered over his eyes like a curtain; his jaw set in a line of anticipation.

I tried not to watch him—not to stare at him so damn hard, but it was like trying not to look at a shooting star.

"Close your eyes," he said.

"I'm not closing my eyes."

"Just humor me for me a minute." His pleading eyes were damn near impossible to turn down. "Please. Close them."

I closed my eyes.

The music started; a steady, soft drum beat, lulling and poignant like the strum of a loving heartbeat.

Already I liked it.

"This is my song to you, Jemma." His eyes were turned away from me when he said it, like he didn't have the nerve to say the words and face me at the same time.

And, now I loved it.

My breath hitched as the lyrics begun. Soft, careful promises of love danced in my ears, taking me away to a place I'd never been, but always dreamed of going. It was the happily-ever-after to a story I desperately longed to live. I couldn't move. I couldn't stop listening. I couldn't risk missing a single beat. All I wanted to do was stay right where I was—to live and breathe this moment with him forever.

"What do you think?" he asked as the song came to the end, his voice twisted with uncertainty and hope.

I tried to steady my breathing, to compose myself. "I love it. I've never loved a song more in my entire life."

His hand slipped into mine, and I shivered from the connection as he laced our fingers together. It felt right like this with him—flawless—just like the last time we'd been here.

Only it wasn't like the last time. Sadness seeped into my heart, weighing it down with pain and grief. So much had happened since then. So much hurt.

"I wish I could take it away for you," he said, turning over to face me. The wounded look in his eyes told me he knew he was the one that put it there.

"I do too," I said, wishing he could make *all* of it go away; all the hurt and pain, and the mind-twisting memories of that night at the church.

"You think you'll ever be able to forget it?"

"I don't know," I said simply, because it was the truth. "In my heart, I know it wasn't really you, but it's hard to erase the image of you walking away from me." That picture had seared itself into my mind like a third-degree burn. The scars were painful to touch and hideous to look at.

He moved in closer. "Will you let me try to erase it?" His voice was a husky whisper, hot in my ears.

I swallowed my butterflies, unable to formulate an actual response. Instead, I veered my eyes to the ceiling. The plain, white ceiling. It was safe to look at. Trace wasn't.

His hand came up to my cheek and steered my face back to his so that I had no choice but to look at him. His iridescent blue eyes ran all over my face, taking in my features as though he wanted to memorize them.

"I already have," he said, answering my thoughts as though we had always been this way, easy and natural. "I've memorized every inch of you and I still find something new every time I look at you. Like this freckle right here," he said, touching his finger to the top of my lip. "It's my new favorite."

My heart raced in my chest as he wet his lips and began inching closer to me. I knew exactly what that meant, and all I could do was watch with anticipation as he closed the gap.

In the next second, his mouth was pressed against mine, sending my entire body into a state of euphoric exhilaration. Sparks ignited all around me, crackling against my skin like a full-blown electrical storm.

It didn't seem fair that I felt this way when I was with him;

that my body reacted this way without my consent. After everything that happened, and everything that had yet to happen, my heart still felt the same way. It was confusing, and trying, and all-encompassing, and I knew it would devour me whole if I let it. If I didn't stop it from taking over again.

"I'm sorry." I pulled back from his warmth. "I can't do this right now."

"Jemma." He licked his lips, savoring my kiss with his tongue.

The sight of it made my head swarm. It took everything I had not to dive back into him; not to let the billowing heat lure me back into his inferno.

"I have to go." I hurdled myself off the bed before I had a chance to change my mind.

"*What*? Wait." He jumped up and rushed after me. "Hang on a second," he said, grabbing my hand and spinning me back to him as I tried to open the door. In one dizzying move, he kicked the door closed with his foot and leaned me back into it.

My heart somersaulted in my chest as he eliminated the space between us, leaving nothing there but the thin fabric of our clothing. And it wasn't nearly enough to quell the heat.

"Where are you going?" His breath tickled my lips as he spoke, tantalizing and inviting in every way.

"Home," I answered, watching as his mouth twitched a small frown. "I have to go home."

"It's still early."

"What time is it?" I asked, as if it remotely mattered.

"No idea."

"Then how do you know it's early?" I asked and then immediately gasped as he pressed himself against me. Thigh to thigh, chest to chest, pounding heart to pounding heart.

"I just know." His eyes sparkled an illicit invitation I wasn't sure I was strong enough to decline. "Stay with me."

My knees trembled, threatening to take me down. Trace instantly sensed my weakness and tightened his hold on me.

"I can't," I said, twisting out of his grip. "It's too soon, Trace. I...I'm sorry." I pushed him back a step to open up the space between us. I couldn't think straight with him standing that close to me—and that was precisely the problem.

His hands dropped.

"There's too much going on right now," I tried to explain. My head was all over the place, bouncing from Taylor and Engel to the Amulet and Morgan's vision, and then all the way back again. And I still had to figure out where the Amulet was. "I need time to make sense out of everything that happened and figure out what it all means. I have to be careful," I added quietly.

His eyes were filled with longing as they poured over me, studying me as though the secret key to unlocking me were hidden somewhere on my face.

"You still don't trust me." He pushed his hands through his midnight-black hair and dropped his head, terse and abrupt as though shot down by the very words he uttered.

"I'm trying to," I admitted.

"I hate this, Jemma," he said, every word soft and delicate as though birthed from the deepest part of his truth. "I never wanted for you to hurt like this."

"I know," I said, and a part of me truly did. But there was still another part that was screaming for me to tread carefully; to expect the worst and prepare for all possible outcomes, as Dominic had said. "Too much has happened, and too much is coming. I have to stay focused on what I need to do and I can't do that while trying to navigate my feelings for you."

"So, you still have them?"

"Have what?"

"Feelings for me." He clenched his jaw in anticipation of my answer.

"I'd be lying if I said I didn't."

He moved in closer to me—to touch me, or hold me, or connect with me in some way, but I stepped back out of his reach.

"But it doesn't change anything."

He lowered his head.

The seconds ticked by languidly like sand in a frozen hourglass. The silence, both deafening and heartbreaking, was emblematic of the standstill we were now in.

When he looked back up at me, all I saw was the searing pain in his eyes. "It kills me to see you look at me like this, Jemma, and maybe that's what I deserve for not being honest with you from the beginning, but it still knifes my insides." His lids slid closed, banishing his blue eyes from the world for the longest, darkest moment of my life.

"Trace." I called out his name like a prayer, urging him to open his eyes, to let the sun pour back into my world. I needed his light, his sustenance to carry me forward, yet getting too close to him was still dangerous; a fiery burn I wasn't yet sure I could endure.

They opened again, and I breathed in fast and deep because the air had once again returned to my stifled lungs.

"Maybe it would have been better to just lie to you and tell you I did it," he said, his eyes meeting mine in a revealing way. "That I did it for my sister, and then beg for your forgiveness."

"Why would you say that?"

"Because at least then I'd *know* I deserved this. It's not like it never crossed my mind," he confessed and then looked away as though too ashamed to face me. "The only thing standing in the way of bringing Linley back was that Amulet. And you had it. I'd be a liar if I said I never thought about taking it."

I crossed my arms, unsure of where he was going with this

and if I really wanted to hear it.

"But I didn't do it," he stated firmly, meeting my eyes poignantly. "I couldn't take the risk of losing you." Shaking his head, he pumped his jaw muscles in frustration. "I didn't do it, and I lost you anyway. All you see is betrayal when you look at me. It's in your mind every time I touch you."

I couldn't find the words to deny it. Probably because I knew it was the truth.

"I'm paying for something I never actually did."

I lowered my eyes in regret, realizing I'd driven him to this—to wishing he had lied to me instead. As hard as it was to hear the truth, I respected him more for putting it out there, for letting me hear it, no matter how ugly it was. If present Trace really didn't do this, as my heart was telling me, it wasn't fair that he was stuck footing the bill for it.

I needed to find a way to separate the two of them and to forgive him for the thing he had yet to even do.

"I'm trying to let it go, Trace. I want to get back to where we left off, but it's going to take some time. And with Morgan's vision..." I looked away from his troubled eyes, afraid to go on. "I need time to sort through it." I hadn't even begun to consider the implications of her vision and what that really meant for us.

He exhaled his frustration.

"I understand if you don't want to wait around. I wouldn't ask you to anyway—"

"I'll wait." He blinked slowly as he took me in. "I'd wait until the end of days for you, Jemma. I don't know if I should be admitting that to you or not, but it's the truth."

I smiled up at him, at his words.

"For whatever it's worth, I know you're the one, Jemma. I know we're meant to be together, and I'm not messing with destiny anymore." He pierced me with a look of complete want. "Not when it comes to you, anyway."

My heart stopped and started at the unexpected declaration. I wasn't sure what part of that to process first. "*Destiny*, huh?" I raised a skeptical brow at him, deciding to graze right over the whole "you're the one" thing. There wasn't enough CPU in a computer to process that one yet.

His lip hitched up at the corner as he buried his hands (and his secrets) in his pockets.

Obviously, I wasn't about to let him off *that* easy. "Why do you keep saying stuff like that?" I asked him, curious, since it wasn't the first time I heard him say we're going to be together; that I was going to love him someday.

"Morgan," he answered simply, shrugging off her name like it was no big deal.

"What did she say?"

"That you're going to fall in love with me." His mouth twisted into a beautiful, perfectly dimpled grin.

I thought back to what Morgan said in the washroom—that I told him I loved him right before she saw him die.

My stomach dropped. "Why didn't you ever say anything?"

"Why do you think?" He shook his head. "It's kind of an awkward conversation to have with a girl who doesn't even know you. Besides, I hadn't even really accepted it myself at that point," he explained with an air of detachment. "Accepting it meant I had to accept her other visions, and I wasn't ready for that."

My throat tightened as a heady feeling of dread washed over me. "Like her vision about your death." There it was again; the enormous elephant in the room.

He nodded, though barely.

"What are you going to do about it?"

He laughed, dark and gruff, as though the situation were entirely void of any hope. The sound of it ripped a hole right through the middle of my heart.

Trace was on a fast-track to the end of the line, and I couldn't even stomach the thought of it, let alone contemplate surviving it.

"There has to be something we could do to stop it," I said, my voice tinged in the kind of hysteria that started in the pit of your stomach and then shot up through your esophagus like vomit. "There has to be."

"Jemma." He moved a little closer to me, spoke a little softer. "There isn't."

"No. I don't accept that." There had to be a way to change it, to stop it from becoming real. Tessa and Trace both said that Death comes for us no matter what we do, so maybe it wasn't a matter of stopping it from happening, but a matter of cheating it. Maybe bringing Linley back from the dead would be the key to bringing Trace back too. "If we find a way to bring Linley back, we can do the same for you" —I swallowed hard— "you know, if it comes to that."

"Maybe." His head cocked to the side as he watched me.

"Maybe?" *What kind of answer is that!*

"I don't want to talk about that right now," he said and then took a slow step towards me. "I don't want to talk about anything. I just want to be with you." His hands found their way around my waist again and pulled me into him as though he were a lost soul and I was his one and only way to salvation.

My heart sped up as he lowered his head to my neck and breathed in the scent of my hair, of my skin.

"Stay with me, Jemma."

A swarm of butterflies took flight in my stomach. I didn't know how to say *no* to that, to him, and I wasn't sure I wanted to. Despite knowing this could very well be the beginning of my end—of his end—I couldn't find the strength to pull away.

Not even to save our lives.

"I promise I won't do anything more than this," he added in

an attempt to seal the deal that had been made long before I came here. "Just stay with me tonight."

Without waiting for my response, he flicked off the light switch behind my head and began towing me back towards his bed. I followed freely and completely, a willing servant of his heart and anything it desired. He sat down on the edge, every move unhurried and designed to keep me from fleeing, but the truth was, I wouldn't have anyway. Fleeing meant running away from the very air that filled my lungs with life.

With his hands planted firmly on my hips, he lay back on his bed and pulled me down with him. Down into oblivion; into bliss; into the warm space where I have always belonged.

It had been a long time since I had a place to call home. Most days, I couldn't even remember what that felt like anymore. My anchor had chipped, cracked, rotted away to the bottom of the ocean, leaving me lost and stranded in the open sea alone.

Until now.

Fate had brought us together, and as it stood, it would soon take us apart, but in that small moment, I was no longer lost. I was finally home again.

Trace was my home.

13. EYES WIDE SHUT

My eyes blinked open.

The dull-gray light of morning poured into the room, covering everything in a hazy, fog-like filter. With my entire body humming, I glanced down and found Trace's arms still wrapped securely around me. He'd held onto me throughout night and I'd never felt more at peace.

And then reality slapped me right in the face.

I'm finished!

"Oh, my God! Get up!" I shrieked, jumping out of Trace's arms like a ripped off bandage. "We fell asleep! Get up! Where's my phone?" I searched around frantically, yanking the covers up and tossing his pillows around the bed.

"What time is it?" he asked, his voice and eyes still groggy and doused in slumber.

"I don't know, but I'm so dead!" I spotted my phone on the floor in front of his bed and dropped to the ground on all fours to grab a hold of it.

Nine missed calls from my uncle.

"Oh, my god, he's going to kill me. He's literally going to kill me. I might as well say my goodbyes now because my life is about to be over." I was practically hysterical about it.

"Calm down," said Trace as he sat up and dropped his feet over the edge of the bed. Rubbing the leftover sleep from his eyes, he said, "Just relax. I'll give him a call."

"And say what?" I screeched, staring at him like he'd just escaped from the looney bin. "We fell asleep in your bed? Whoops, our bad? No freaking way! He's going to kill us *both*!"

"Don't worry. I'll take care of it." He picked up his phone and dialed my uncle's number before I could further object.

Watching from the foot of the bed, I nearly chewed a hole through my cheek as I waited for him to make contact.

"Hey Karl, it's Trace." Pause. "Yeah, she's with me." Another pause. "I know. We ran into some Revs last night and ended up hunkering down until it was safe to come home. We lost our phones getting away otherwise we would have called sooner." Another long Pause. "Yeah, you got it." He put the phone down on his nightstand and turned to face me. "There."

"*There*? There *what*? What did he say?" My eyes were doing all sorts of crazy things. There may have even been a twitch involved.

He shrugged like it was no big deal. "He said to call my dad and let him know we're safe. They figured we were together when we both came up missing last night."

"And that's it?" I asked incredulously. "He wasn't angry? He didn't yell at you or anything?"

"Nope." He got up from the bed and strode towards me. "Told me to make sure I got you to school on time." He bent down and dropped a soft kiss on my cheek and then took off for a shower.

What the—

Okay, so apparently my uncle had been possessed by some kind of *really* easy-going demon because there was no way he would've let me get away with not coming home or even calling to check in. He just wouldn't.

Would he?

Trace and I walked into our World History class together. Several sets of curious eyes looked up and took notice of this new development; a few of which seemed genuinely disappointed, like had it not been for me, they may have had a chance with him. Of course, none more so than Nikki. Her glaring turquoise eyes were shooting knives at my head from across the room, letting me know exactly what she thought about me.

I shuffled down the aisle and took my usual spot next to Ben. When I glanced back up, Trace was standing beside my desk, but he wasn't looking at me. He ticked his chin offside, gesturing to the guy sitting behind me, who promptly packed up his books and abandoned his seat.

"Nice," said Ben, reaching back for a fist bump just as Trace sat down in the newly available seat.

I swiveled around in my chair. "That's not your seat," I pointed out. Captain Obvious to the rescue.

"It is now." His dimples went off in tandem as he fought back a smile. "Is that alright with you?"

I wasn't sure sitting this close to Trace was the best idea. I had a hard enough time concentrating in class without his good vibrations shooting through my body, but I wasn't about to let him know that. "I guess so."

His eyebrows rose. "You guess so?"

"I happened to like that guy."

"Yeah?" He lifted his chin, seemingly to the challenge. "What was his name?"

Crap, what the heck was his name? Mm...Ma...Marty... "Marshall! His name is Marshall."

"*Maxwell,*" whispered Ben.

"Maxwell. That's what I said."

Trace stared back at me with a half-smile plastered across his beautiful, heart-shaped lips, not saying a single word. There was something shimmering in his eyes, something soft and loving.

It made my cheeks warm. "Stop looking at me like that," I said, trying to bury my smile long enough to bark out the order with any semblance of authority.

"Damned if I know how." He leaned back in his chair and kicked out his legs in front of him, still staring at me in the same, exact way.

The heat quickly spread from my cheeks to every other part of my body, threatening a complete system meltdown. Buckling under the heat of his stare, I abruptly turned back around and waited for Mr. Bradley to start his class.

A few seconds later, I felt a tap on my back followed by a piece of paper flying over my shoulder and landing squarely on my desk. I unfolded the note and read the message.

I'm going to Starry Beach before work. You in?

I half-turned my head and nodded. A few moments later, another note landed on my desk.

You looked really good in my bed BTW. Like really good.

A tropical storm erupted inside me at the sight of his words on paper. I didn't dare turn around to acknowledge him this time out of fear that he'd see the cherry shade of red splattered all over my face and know just how much he affected me. Instead, I directed my eyes forward and tried to concentrate on Mr. Bradley, who was busy checking names off his attendance sheet.

"I'm looking forward to a repeat," added Trace, loud enough for most of the class to hear.

"Mr. Macarthur?" called Mr. Bradley at the front of the room. "Care to share that with the rest of the class?"

"That's alright," said Trace, his voice as deep and edgy as an underground cave. "I'm keeping this one for myself."

I didn't have to turn around to know his eyes were pinned on me. I really wasn't sure exactly what had changed between us since last night, but he was definitely bolder now—more determined to stake his claim.

"Before I begin today's lesson," started Mr. Bradley, "I'd like to take a moment to speak with you on a more personal note. As most of you know, Taylor Valentine, a student and fellow classmate of yours, has been missing since last Friday."

My heart sank into the pit of my stomach.

"While her parents are remaining hopeful that she will return safely, they aren't leaving any stone unturned. Together with law enforcement, they have organized a town-wide search party to take place this afternoon at four o'clock. We encourage all of you to head down to Town Hall and sign up. A vigil will also be held later this evening..."

The sound of his voice seemed to be moving further and further away from me. My head was spinning, my stomach roiling. I wasn't sure what side was up anymore.

"Miss Blackburn?"

All eyes were on me. I was standing up and I wasn't even sure how that happened.

"Is everything alright?" he asked.

"I-I..." I shook my head but it only made the dizziness worse. "I have to go," I said, stumbling down the aisle and then barreling out the door.

"Jemma!" Trace called out after me as he chased me out into the hall. "Wait up!" he yelled, but I didn't stop.

I wasn't stopping for anything. My feet pounded against the floor like gunshots.

"Jemma!"

I needed to get away from it; from this building, from my

reality, from my guilt, my helplessness—

Trace's arm shot out from behind me and lifted me off the ground, easy as plucking a dying rose from the earth.

"Let me go!" I cried, tears streaming down my face as I kicked out at the air.

It was futile. His hold was ironclad.

"Stop running," he said, holding me against him. "Talk to me."

"She's gone and it's all my fault!" Tears flooded over like a busted dam.

He muttered a string of curse words into my hair as realization set in. "Come on, Jemma. Don't do this to yourself."

"Why not? I did this to her!"

"No, you didn't. It's not your fault, Jemma. It's not." He buried his face in my neck, his long hair brushing against my cheeks as he molded his body around mine. "We're going to fix this, okay? We'll get her back."

"How, Trace? How are we going to do that?" Breaking out of his grip, I turned to face him. I needed to see those eyes. I needed them to bring me back to my happy place. My safe place.

"We don't even know where the Amulet is and we're running out of time."

"There's still time."

"Even if we figure out where it is, we have no way of getting there. Just like you said, remember?"

"We'll figure it out." He tried to pull me in again, but I put out my hands and stopped him.

"I need to get out of here."

"Okay." He nodded, taking my hand into his. "I'll take you home."

"No." I pulled my hand free and looked away. "I need to be alone. I can't be around you right now."

"Jemma."

"I'm serious, Trace! While we were busy rolling around in your bed last night, Taylor was out there all alone—waiting for us to remember her."

"It wasn't like that." He shook his head, trying to dissuade me. "There's nothing we can do until we get the Amulet back," he reminded me, but it was useless. I was already beyond that point.

"We're not getting the Amulet back, Trace. It's gone and there isn't a goddamn thing I can do about it anymore. It's time to accept it and move on to plan B."

He looked over his shoulder and then back at me. "What are you talking about? What plan B?"

I still hadn't told him anything about Dominic or how we'd been working together on a plan to kill Engel. And now definitely wasn't the time to open up that can of worms.

"What plan B, Jemma?" he asked again.

"I'm still working on it." I squared my shoulders and hardened my backbone. "The only thing I know for sure is that I have to take Engel out, and I have less than two weeks to do it. I can't do that if I'm busy wasting time with you."

He flinched back at my words, his expression creased with hurt. "*Wasting* time?"

"You know what I mean," I said and instantly felt a pang of guilt for being so harsh with my words. He didn't deserve it, but I wasn't sure how else to get through to him. "Look, I'm sorry, okay? I didn't mean it that way. I just meant that I have to stay focused right now."

He nodded once, slow and tempered, like a sunset bowing down to the world. "It's all good," he said, but I could see that it wasn't. "Do what you got to do, Jemma. I won't get in your way," he added, and with that, the armor he once wore like a second skin reappeared.

Something told me I'd regret this later, but I didn't stick around long enough to contemplate it.

14. THE TIME TRAVELER

The Blackburn Estate was as quiet as the Hollow Hills cemetery when I tore through the front door. My uncle had already left for work, or errands, or whatever it was he did when I was away at school. Rushing upstairs, I barreled down the hallway and into my bedroom, slamming the door shut behind me.

The rain hammered down against my balcony window like a rabid creature clawing and scratching at the glass. I paced back and forth in front of my bed as tears ran down my face in bold streaks of hopelessness. My thoughts were racing, sweeping, spiraling through my mind like a tornado. Everything had fallen apart, busted wide open, and the pieces that remained were leading me to one horrible, godforsaken place.

I had to *kill* Engel, and I was going to have to do it without the Amulet.

But how? How the hell was I going to go up against a Revenant that had already killed four generations of Slayers? How was I going to defeat him with no experience, minimal training, and no one to back me up?

Gabriel was an immediate dead-end, if for no other reason than his loyalty to Tessa. Dominic was a wildcard, and even though we had a shared goal, I still didn't know if I could fully trust him. And then there was Trace...

Trace was strong, capable, and he cared about me. He would be there by my side if I asked him to, without question. But Morgan's vision alone was enough reason for me to not involve him in this. I couldn't risk letting him know when or where this was going to happen or he would be there with me, ready and willing to walk into his own demise.

I couldn't let that happen.

I had to do this alone. I had to kill Engel and bring Taylor home by myself, and even though it very well may be the last thing I ever did, I would go to my death trying.

A hard knock at the door jolted me out of my thoughts.

I circled back to the balcony door and pulled back the curtains. A soaking wet Trace stood on the other side, dark strands of hair sticking to his beautifully defined jaw.

"God, you look beautiful." Even though his voice sounded muffled through the glass, I could still hear the longing in his words. "Can I come in?"

I unlocked the door and pulled it open. "What are you doing here, Trace? I told you I wanted to be alone—" I stopped cold in my tracks as he pulled out the Amulet from his pocket and dangled it in front of my eyes.

"I think you should let me in."

"Where did you—" I shook my head. "When did you—"

"I don't have a lot of time." Ignoring my half-baked questions, he walked inside and quickly locked the door behind himself as though he were being followed. "Please sit down."

"How did you get it back?" I asked and watched as he closed all the curtains, isolating us from the outside world.

There was no way he managed to get the Amulet back in such a small time frame. I had just left him at school less than an hour ago. "You had it all along, didn't you?" I couldn't believe what I was seeing. "You were lying all along!"

"It's not what you think," he said, shaking his head.

"The hell it isn't. Give it back," I snapped as I reached out and tried to grab it from his hand, but he moved it out of my reach before I could make contact with it.

"Please, just sit down, Jemma." He slipped the Amulet back in his pocket and waited for me to do as he asked. "I'll explain everything," he said, checking his watch.

Gritting my teeth, I took two slow steps backwards and sat down on the edge of the bed, ready and willing to tear him a brand new one.

"Do you know who I am?" he asked, surveying me from across the room.

"Is this a joke?" I could feel the rage prickling through my blood as he waited for an answer. "Yes, I know who you are. You're the liar who's been playing me since day one."

"I'm the liar who's been *protecting* you since day one," he quickly shot back.

I snorted at his convoluted retelling of the past. "You're in serious need of a new dictionary."

He cracked a smile as though amused by my indignation. "I'm not from this Timeline, Jemma."

"Excuse me?" I leaned forward to get a better look at his lying face. "Are you seriously trying to tell me you're not the same exact Trace I just left at school not even an hour ago?"

The hell he wasn't. They looked identical and not a single day older.

"That's exactly what I'm telling you."

I snorted my disbelief. If he really was from the future, why would he take the Amulet from me and leave me for dead only to show up with it a few days later? None of this made any sense. He had to be lying. *Again.* But why? What the heck was he up to?

"I don't know what kind of sick game you're playing—"

"I'm not playing any games," he said emphatically.

"Yeah? Then prove it," I dared him, my gaze hard and unrelenting. "If you're from the future then prove it to me. Show me something with a date on it, and I'll believe you."

He tapped his pockets and then shook his head. "I don't have anything on me."

I crossed my arms. "Then go get something."

"Excuse me?"

"You're a Reaper, Trace."

"Yeah."

"So mosey on back and grab a newspaper."

"I can't. I've been Bound, Jemma." His eyebrows pulled together in frustration. "This is a one-shot deal."

"How convenient," I scoffed. "If you've been Bound, then how did you get here?"

"Another Reaper." He took a step forward as though trying to command all my attention, as though trying to distract me from his blatant lies. "I needed to come back one last time."

I wasn't buying his story for a minute. He was the same old trickster that had already shown me his true face at the church, and this time, I wasn't looking away from the truth.

"What you *need* to do is get out of my house before I do something we both regret." I shot up from my bed and stepped towards him, ready to make good on my promise.

"Hang on a minute," he said suddenly, shucking off his wet jacket and tossing it over my dresser. Grabbing the edge of his shirt, he yanked it up over his head, pretty much undressing himself in my bedroom. "Maybe this will help."

His bare, glistening chest stared back at me like a steamy scene straight out of my daydreams.

"Um, help with what exactly?" Despite my outrage, my cheeks were burning hot. "If you're trying to distract me, it's not going to work," I said, though my mouth was still unhinged, and I felt pretty damn distracted.

His dimples appeared as he sprouted a smile. "Is this proof enough for you?" he asked and then lifted his arm up over his head, exposing the entire left side of his torso.

I couldn't believe what my eyes were seeing. Right down his ribcage, from his armpit to hipbone, was my name tattooed in elegant, black ink. Bold, thorny vines weaved in and around each letter and then disappeared around the side, presumably to another tattoo that continued on his back.

"Oh. My. God." I shook my head as I struggled to make sense out of what I was looking at—at what it all meant.

"Like I said, I'm not from this Timeline," he repeated, dropping his arm. "I came back for the Amulet five days ago."

"You're actually telling the truth."

The ink was dry. There was no denying it. I finally had my proof—I finally knew for certain that present-day Trace wasn't lying. Every word he'd said to me was the truth and it only made my feelings for him soar to indescribable heights.

Unfortunately, the same couldn't be said for the Trace standing in front of me.

I narrowed my eyes at him like two angry missiles. "So it was *you*. You're the one who left me for dead."

"It had to be believable, Jemma," he explained though his words seemed shrouded in regret. "If Dominic even suspected we were working together, he would have killed Taylor."

"And me? What about me?"

"I knew he wouldn't hurt you."

"You couldn't have known that."

"He's as obsessed with you now as he was then." He slipped his shirt back on and flexed his jaw muscle. "Engel was the only risk, but I knew as long as he tasted your blood, you were safe." He ran his hands through his damp hair, clearing the view to his beautiful face. "I knew I could slip in, get the Amulet, and then slip back out without putting you in any real danger."

"What do you know about real danger?" All the hurt and anger I felt that night came bubbling back to the surface like a boiling cauldron. "You didn't stick around long enough to see it! You just left me there."

"I had to—"

"Why?" I cut in, my voice shaking from inside. "What was so important that you would do that to me? Was it for Linley?"

His eyes steeled. "Linley's gone, Jemma."

"I know, but..." Wait. Had he given up on bringing Linley back? If that was true, something must have drastically changed his course, and as scary as it was, I needed to know what that was. "If it wasn't for Linley, then why did you do it?"

"I had to stop you from giving the Amulet to Engel."

"What are you talking about? I didn't give the Amulet to Engel." Of that I was sure.

"You would have." He said it matter-of-factly and then began recounting a history I'd probably never live through myself. "You gave it to him to save Taylor's life, and with your blood in his veins, and the Amulet in his hands, Engel became invincible. There was no stopping him." He sat down on the chair by my desk and pushed his hands through his midnight-black hair.

I thought back to what Dominic said about Engel's plans for the Amulet. That he wanted to control the undead and come out of the shadows. I shivered at the thought of him being successful; at the very notion that I might have had a hand in it.

"So what happened?" I asked, swallowing the choking ball at the back of my throat, my head throbbing from the merry-go-round I couldn't seem to get off of.

"The *Uprising* happened." He moved his chair in closer, and I couldn't help but notice the dark circles under his eyes. He looked tired—worn out. "It was the beginning of Hell on earth," he explained as grim as a Reaper could be. "Revenants roamed the streets freely, feeding off of humans in the open like it was nothing. There wasn't anything anyone could do about it and it was just the beginning of what was coming."

"What about the Council?"

"Gone. The entire Order was overthrown," he said, shaking his head in disgust. "The factions were at war over power and couldn't get it together long enough to setup a new leader."

A wave of nausea swiveled through my stomach as I pictured this alternate world I wanted no part of. "That's horrible."

"You have no idea." He ran his hand down his face as though trying to erase the images. "Everything was a mess, Jemma, and it was only getting worse. They were taking over. I *had* to do something. I had to stop them and this was the only way."

"I understand. I get it." I nodded into it, finally understanding why he did what he did. The picture had become crystal clear to me, and it was hideous to look at.

"Once I stopped the Uprising, the High Casters got wind of what I was doing and Bound me."

"Why? Why would they do that?"

"To stop me from changing...anything else."

"Like what?" I asked, starving to know more—to know all of it. "If you stopped the Uprising and everything is okay now, why would they think you'd want to change anything else?"

"Because not everything is okay, Jemma." He seemed hesitant, unsure of how much he should say. It was clear he was still hiding something from me; something he was afraid of telling me. "It's far from okay."

My body trembled as I filled in the missing pieces. "You didn't just come back to warn me about what would happen if Engel got the Amulet, did you?"

He shook his head and his eyes glimmered as they caught the light. Sadly, there was no spark left in them, no sign of life.

"You came back because I'm not okay, am I?"

He shook his head again, and my heart sank.

"Am I alive?" I asked quietly, watching him as he dropped his telling eyes to the ground. I knew the answer even before he said it.

"No, Jemma. You're not alive."

15. DEAD GIRL WALKING

The rain battered down hard against the window as Trace and I sat across from each other in my bedroom. I had so many questions to ask him, so many things I wanted to know about the future—about my death—but I didn't know where to start. It was too much to stomach; too much to process in one short lifetime.

"Taking the Amulet that night stopped the Uprising," said Trace as a clap of thunder reverberated outside my bedroom window. "But it cost me you. Everything we went through together. Every kiss, every conversation, every moment, it was all wiped away as if it never happened." The devastation in his words was almost palpable. "The world was back to normal but everything that ever mattered to me was gone. *You* were gone."

Hearing him speak about *me* that way—about our life together—steered my heart to an unrecognizable place. I had yet to know this place for myself, yet somehow, I felt the loss right along with him. I wanted so bad to live there with him, to feel it for myself, but I couldn't help but wonder if I was still meant to.

"What if that's the way it's supposed to be now?" I asked him, my voice shaking as each word made its way out. "There's only one Amulet. What if we can't have it both ways?"

"Then I'll unleash Hell on earth again to bring you back."

"Don't say that," I hissed, afraid the outside world would hear his promise and turn on us.

"Why not? It's the truth." He pushed forward until his knee was touching mine. "I can't live in a world where you don't exist, Jemma. I'll raise the dead myself if it means I can have you back. I swear I will."

"No! God, no." I shook my head, afraid of his words—of the lengths he would go to keep me alive. "You can't do that, Trace. Don't even joke about it."

"Does it look like I'm joking?" There wasn't the slightest hesitation in his eyes.

"Listen to me, Trace. I don't want this. Promise me that if it comes down to it, you'll make the *right* decision. You'll let me go and do what's right."

"I can't make you that promise. I won't."

"I don't want to be the reason that everything good in this world ends. I wouldn't want to live in that world."

"Then take this back," he urged, digging the Amulet out of his pocket. "Put it back on and *never* take it off. Never let Engel get his hands on it. If you keep it on like you were supposed to, everything will be okay. I know it will," he said, but I could hear the uncertainty in his voice. It was as though he were trying to convince himself right along with me.

He was as unsure of the future as I was and coming back here only made it more ambivalent. There was no telling what kind of world he would find when he returned to his Timeline.

I slipped the Amulet back on. I wasn't sure why but it felt right around my neck, like I was always meant to be its wearer.

"You can never let Engel know what you are." His voice resonated in my ears like a promise no one else was supposed to hear. "Your blood is the key to everything, Jemma."

"I don't understand."

He picked up my hand as if to soften the blow. My skin hummed from the contact, instantly pacifying me.

"You're not just a Slayer, Jemma. You're different—*special*. You can do things that other Anakim can't."

I pulled my hand away. "What do you mean I can *do* things?"

"I mean you have abilities that are not natural to Slayers." His eyes softened as he took me in. "And it's going to put you in danger over and over again. The Order, Dominic, Engel—people just like him, they're going to try to use you for their own benefit. You can't trust anyone."

"Do you know what I am?" I asked him, my voice a terrified whisper of hope.

Regret clouded his eyes as he shook his head.

I tried not to let my disappointment deter me from what I had to do. "How do I stop this from happening again?"

"You have to kill Engel," he said and then reached out to stroke my cheek with the back of his hand. His touch sent a warm, lingering shiver down my back. "I tried to do it for you, Jemma. I tried so many times, and I'd keep trying if it meant you would be safe, but I can't change it. It's not my destiny—"

"It's mine," I finished for him. I was the one meant to do this. I was meant to save Taylor and stop Engel. Something inside of me stirred, rattled, shook me to my very core.

My palm burned. I looked down at it expecting to see a Rune blazing through my skin, but there was nothing there.

Still no Mark of the Anakim.

I rubbed my palm and nodded at Trace. "I think I can do this," I announced. I wasn't sure why or how, but blind faith was whispering inside me, telling me I was meant to be the one.

"I *know* you can do it," he corrected, his eyes a stirring blend of emotions I couldn't fully decode. "You have no idea how strong you are, Jemma. How strong you *could* be." He smiled lovingly as he tucked a strand of my hair behind my ear. "You amazed me every single day that we were together."

He seemed so much older now, so sure of himself, and of me. I could almost see the love in his eyes when he looked at me. It was pure, and genuine, and heartwarming, and even though I was a mess and still struggled to put one foot in front of the other on most days, he didn't see any of that when he looked at me.

"So, I guess you're like totally in love with me in the future, huh?" I asked, trying to lighten the mood a little. All teasing aside, I was dying to hear the answer.

His dimples exploded on both sides. "Something like that."

"You're not going to tell me anything about it, are you?"

"Nope."

I tried not to roll my eyes at him but it was beyond my control. "I guess some things never change."

"What's that supposed to mean?"

"That it's still impossible to get a straight answer out of you." I studied this newer, more mature version of Trace. So much of him was different now, yet there was so much that was still the same. "No matter how hard I try, I always find myself on the outside when it comes to you."

Reaching over, he took my hand in his and yanked me off the bed and onto his lap in one quick move. My heart raced in my chest as the good vibrations canon-balled through my body.

"You want to know why I pushed you away?" he asked, his brilliant blue eyes soaring out at me, opening up like a portal to a secret world I longed to be a part of.

"Yes," I said, my tenor barely above a whisper.

"Because I was afraid." His strong, confident gaze never wavered from mine. "I was afraid to let myself love you because I didn't think I could handle losing you. But you know what?"

"What?" I asked with bated breath.

"I'm not afraid anymore."

Heat emanated from my body like steam, fogging up my vision and blurring out my thoughts as my heart ping-ponged in my chest.

"I love you, Jemma." His hand slid through my hair, slow and unhurried like we had all the time in the world to be together. "I love you with the kind of love that isn't even love anymore. It's more than love. It's my entire soul. It's everything that I am or will ever be, and nothing will ever change that—not even Hell on earth."

Oh. My. God.

I thought my heart was going to burst. Like it had literally been filled up right to the top and was about to split wide open. Every fiber of my being was awakened, on alert, trembling from a surge of emotions that shook me to my very core.

"You're everything to me, Jemma. *Everything.*" He touched his forehead to mine and closed his eyes, pulling in a long, jagged breath as he breathed me into himself.

My eyes slipped shut as I submersed myself in his words, in the simplistic perfection of this moment.

"Is this how it always was with us?" I asked him, hopeful that a fairytale awaited me at the end of this nightmare.

His beautiful azure eyes, framed by thick, sooty lashes, opened again, and I instantly felt at peace gazing into them. "Better." He smiled, his dimples igniting again.

His hands slipped down my shoulders and settled around my waist, pulling me in closer to him—as close as our physical bodies would allow us to get. I didn't have to read his mind to know what he was thinking. What he wanted.

My eyes dropped to the hungry smile that played on his lips, and in one sweet breath, those very lips were pressing fiercely into mine, plunging me headfirst into a dizzying kiss that was as vast and deep as the ocean itself.

I didn't think it was possible for Trace's kisses to get any better, yet somehow, they had.

16. INVOCATION

My steamy glimpse into the future by way of Trace's mouth was abruptly halted when I heard my uncle calling out my name from downstairs. I asked Trace to wait for me (pretty much begged him to) but alas, he didn't belong here. The future was waiting for him and he had to be on his way.

"Why are you not in school?" asked my uncle as I came down the stairs still in a daze from my afternoon escapades.

"Huh?" *Oh, right. Crap.* "I, um, didn't feel good," I said, apparently deciding to go with the lamest excuse in the book. "My stomach hurt." Jeez, could I get any worse at this?

"You seem well enough."

I shrugged. "I feel better now."

He nodded, seemingly disinterested in probing my alleged stomach ailment. He waited until my foot touched the landing before asking, "May I have a word with you?"

Crap. Having *words* was almost always *never* a good thing. Despite my instinct to decline his invitation, I nodded my defeat and followed him into the kitchen where he sat down in his usual seat by the bay window.

"Is your training with Gabriel advancing well?" he asked,

taking off his reading glasses and placing them neatly in front of him on the kitchen table.

"Yeah, it's going good." Unless you counted Julian. "Why? Did you hear something?"

"I'm simply catching up on your progress," he offered, doing his best to sound nonchalant though it was clear his question was a loaded one.

"Okay. So...is that it?"

He looked at me disapprovingly. "It's imperative that you take this seriously, Jemma—"

"I am."

He furrowed his eyebrows. "The Magister tells me that you're having issues with your assigned Guardian."

"Yeah, but only because he's a total asshat." I flicked a piece of lint from my shirt, quietly pretending it was Julian's oversized forehead.

"Jemma." He appeared unimpressed with my choice of words.

"What? It's true! He's making it impossible to get through training with the constant jabs and sideline commentary!"

"You have to rise above it."

"Easy for you to say," I mumbled. Clearly, he wasn't grasping the scope of my painstakingly annoying problem.

"You will face far greater challenges and distractions. If you cannot find a way to work with someone who is on the same side as you, how will you prevail out there," he said, gesturing out the window ambiguously, "on enemy territory?"

I didn't exactly like what I was hearing but I knew he had a point. I had to find a way to mute out the irritating giant and stay focused on what I needed to do. "You're right. I get it," I said as I stood up from the table. "I'll try harder."

His posture turned rigid, letting me know there were more words to come, and I probably wasn't going to like them.

I sat back down.

"It's terribly important that you do your best to prioritize your training, Jemma. With *Invocation* a growing possibility, you must be prepared to rise to the challenge—to all challenges you encounter."

"Invo-*what*?" This was the first I heard of this, and already I didn't like the sound of it.

"Invocation—one of the Order's most sacred rituals."

Ritual? I swallowed the word like a lump of coal. "A ritual for what?" One mention of *virgin blood* or *animal sacrifice* and I was taking the first bus out of crazy-town.

"To invoke your Anakim abilities, of course." He said it as though I should have already known this. Like I wasn't paying attention during the homeroom announcement or something. "Invocation goes back centuries," he went on, delving deeper into a history lesson that would never be taught in school, "and was often used in times of war when numbers were scarce and Descendant children were required to mature sooner."

Oh my God, was it starting already? "Is the Order at war?" I asked in total panic. "Are the factions at war?"

"Are the factions at—good grief, Jemma. Of course not," he said with a hint of ridicule.

I exhaled my relief, though the feeling was short-lived due to my numerous lingering questions. "Okay, so then why is Invocation a 'growing possibility'?" I asked, air-quotes and all.

"Well, simply put, it's the only way to break the Cloaking spell without the talisman. Unless you invoke on your own."

"You mean by training?" I vaguely remembered Gabriel saying something about waking up my Slayer abilities.

"Yes, by training. Though even in the best of cases, that isn't very likely, and certainly not within our short time frame."

My suspicion piqued. "What's the sudden rush?"

His gaze broke away from mine as he placed his hands back

on the table, splaying them as though buying himself time. There was something evasive about his eyes, something that caused me to take notice and sit up a little straighter. "Well, as I said last time, the spell is fading. We're still unsure what the repercussions are of a partial Cloak so the Council felt it would be best not to prolong that risk if we don't need to."

"Right." I nodded even though I wasn't fully convinced he was giving me the entire story. After what Trace's Alt told me about not trusting the Council, I was even more committed to getting to the truth. "Any news on those blood tests?" I asked him offhand, hoping to catch him off guard.

It had been weeks since he asked for a sample of my blood to ensure my bloodline wasn't affected by the spell. I had yet to hear anything about it. I couldn't help but wonder if he and the Council knew something that would explain what happened in the church with Engel after he fed on me.

"Unfortunately, the results were inconclusive." His eyes shifted every which way but in my direction.

"Inconclusive? What does that mean?"

"There's nothing to be alarmed about. It's surely just the spell doing what it was designed to do. We'll know more once the Cloak is removed."

I pulled in a long, aggravated breath. "So how much time do I have exactly? Until Invocation?"

"A few weeks." He shook his head grimly. "At the very most. It's best not to delay it any longer than need be."

"Right." The good news just kept on coming.

I had yet to talk to Trace since I had left him at school earlier today. I needed to tell him about my unexpected visitor from the future, and since his phone kept going straight to voicemail, I decided to skip the phone-tag and head over to All Saints where we could talk face to face.

The rain had simmered down to a light drizzle by the time I got there, the earthy smell still heavy in my nose as I shuffled through the front door. Trace was already well into his evening shift, busy talking with Zane, the head bartender, over at the main bar. I wiped the rain from my arms and walked over to meet them.

"You can't stay away from this place, can you?" gibed Zane, smirking at me with a wine glass in one hand and a dishrag in the other.

"I'm practically a workaholic."

He broke out in a fit of laughter. Apparently, the idea of it was hilarious to him.

"It's not *that* funny," I said, trying not to be offended.

"What are you doing here?" asked Trace. He wasn't laughing, nor was he smiling for that matter. I guess he was still upset about how we had left things off this afternoon.

"I tried calling you but your phone was off."

No response.

Oh-kay. "Can we talk?"

He ticked his chin towards the backroom and then pushed off the counter. I followed quietly behind him as we moved our standoff to the Manager's office.

Closing the door behind us, he leaned against the edge of the desk and crossed his feet at his ankles. In this state, with the light hitting his face just as it was, he looked like the marble statue of some beautiful Greek god.

A pissed-off Greek god, that is.

"I'm sorry about today." I buried my hands in the pockets of my jeans to keep from fidgeting. I wanted to tell him that I was sorry about everything—about not believing him—but I couldn't seem to find the words to say it.

"Where did you go?" he asked evenly. It looked like he was working hard to hide the hurt from his voice.

"Back to my uncle's." I took a step towards him and offered a smile. "I had a visitor today...from the future."

He sat up straighter, his interest piqued. "My Alt?"

I nodded.

"What happened?"

I pulled in a breath and went on to tell him about everything that happened earlier that day. I told him about the Amulet and why future Trace needed it, about Engel and the Uprising. I even told him about why he risked coming back one last time after being Bound by the Council.

He took it all in strides. All except the news about my future state of well-being, or lack thereof.

"I don't get it," he said, shaking his head. "How could *you* be dead? Morgan saw us in her vision—she saw *me* die."

"Maybe she's lying," I offered.

"She wouldn't lie to me." He seemed certain of this.

I, on the other hand, was not. She was Nikki's best friend after all. Maybe Nikki got her to concoct this vision to keep us apart—you know, scare him into thinking that if he got too close to me, he was going to end up dead because of it. It's not like they weren't twisted enough to do something like that.

"I hope you're right." Not because I wanted either of us to be dead, obviously, but because her lying about her visions would only further complicate an already *really* complicated situation. We wouldn't just be navigating this thing blindly; we'd be navigating it with an upside-down map.

"So that was it? My Alt just handed over the Amulet?" he verified, eyebrows drawn together. "Just like that?"

I lifted it up as proof, zip-lining the ruby pendant back and forth on the chain.

"And you have no idea who I traveled back with?" he asked, checking off each of his questions as he tried to fill in the missing pieces.

"He didn't give me any names."

He rubbed his jaw as he thought it over. "There aren't too many Reapers around here willing to break Council rules," he noted and then focused back in on me. "Did you get a look at them at all?"

I shook my head. "I wasn't in the room when he left."

He raised his brow, intrigued. "Where did you go?"

"My uncle came home in the middle of our kiss. I got freaked out and didn't bother sticking around to see—"

"You kissed him?" he asked, ticking his head back.

"Yeah." I shrugged it off like it was no big deal even though I could practically still feel his lips on mine. "It all happened so fast."

"Why?"

"Why did it happen fast?"

"Why did you kiss him?" he asked curtly, lifting off the desk. He had a weird look on his face. Something like anger.

"*He* kissed *me*," I responded defensively.

"Did you kiss him back?"

"Well, yeah."

His jaw tightened—he was definitely angry about this.

"You can't seriously be jealous of yourself right now?" I mocked, shaking my head in disbelief.

"I'm not jealous of myself," he snapped, clearly pissed off. "I don't get it. I don't get *you*."

"What do you mean?"

"Nothing." Pumping his jaw, he dropped his head and frowned. "Forget it. It doesn't matter."

"It matters to me. Talk to—"

"Look, I have to get back to work," he said suddenly, cutting off the conversation like he had zero interest in anything I had to say. He mumbled something on the way to the door, but I couldn't make out the words.

I tried to go after him but the door abruptly slammed shut in my face before I could finish calling out his name.

17. SEARCH PARTY

The search effort for Taylor was already well underway by the time I made it to the town square park later that day. The rain had finally stopped, leaving in its place thin trails of fog that drifted over the grounds like a haze. It felt wrong being here amongst the flock of worried townsmen; searching for Taylor when I knew good and well that she wasn't here. But I had to keep up appearances; I had to play my part until I was ready to go after Engel.

We walked in lines, combing over every inch of Hollow and all of its borders until there wasn't any more ground to cover, and then we headed back the way we'd come, retracing our footprints for any missed steps or unturned rocks. All I could do was think about Taylor and what she was going through. I prayed she wasn't afraid. I prayed she was warm. I prayed she was blissfully unaware of everything that was going on.

"Hello, angel." Dominic moved up beside me, falling in line as I walked the edge of the fog-kissed park.

"Dominic," I greeted him coolly.

"Any luck with your search?" he asked, his hands crossed behind his back.

"What kind of a sick joke is that?"

"I was referring to the Amulet," he whispered, craning his head in my direction.

"Oh." I released the breath I'd been holding in. "Sorry about that."

"I take it you have no good news to share."

A grin appeared on my face. "Actually, I do," I said without meeting his eyes. "I have the Amulet."

His eyes snapped to me. "You jest?"

I shook my head proudly. "Nope."

"How did you get it back?"

"It's kind of a long story. What matters is, I got it back." I had no more time to waste. We were on a need to know basis and what he needed to know was I wasn't playing games anymore. "When are we meeting up to figure out how we're doing this?"

"My schedule is always clear for you, love."

"I want Taylor home, Dominic, and I want Engel *dead*. He needs to be stopped before it's too late, and I'm doing it with or without you." I stopped walking and turned to him. "If you want out, now is your chance."

The smirk on his smooth face let me know he was up for the challenge—excited even. "Duly noted."

"And note this," I said, jabbing my finger in his chest. "If you turn on me again, in any way, so help me God I'm going to make sure it's the last thing you ever do."

"I have no intentions of crossing enemy lines," he said, covering my finger with his hand and lowering it. "We're on the same side now, angel. My goal is the same as yours."

"And the Amulet?"

"I would be lying if I said I wouldn't prefer to possess it; however, your lovely hands are a satisfactory second," he said, turning my hand over as if to inspect the evidence.

I pulled my hand back. "You better not be lying to me."

"I assure you, the only lying I wish to do with you is of the horizontal variety," he whispered, leaning in as a group of searchers walked by us.

My cheeks heated up. "In your freaking dreams."

"Indeed." His grin hiked up at the corners as his eyes twinkled with salacious want. "And yours."

For God's sake. "Bye, Dominic." I turned on my heel and started walking off, but he was right there beside me—moving in tandem as if we'd been tied together by some cursed-from-hell rope.

"I met with Engel today," he said without looking down at me. Obviously, he knew that would get my attention.

I stopped walking again. "You did *what?*"

"Simmer down, angel." His eyes focused on some unknown marker ahead of us. "We have to keep up the facade. In case you've forgotten, I'm supposed to be assisting him in the recovery of the Amulet."

"Right." It was becoming impossible to keep up with all the crap, lies, and alibis. "So, what did you find out?"

"The Amulet, of course, is still top priority. However, he does appear to be quite tickled at the prospect of seeing you again," he said, glancing down at me. "You seem to have that effect on my kind."

"Lucky me," I said bitterly. I was pretty much a Revenant magnet at this point. I could only imagine my fate once the Cloaking spell was broken and all barriers were removed.

"He's certainly vested in discovering what you really are. He thinks you could be the one to bring his plans into fruition," he explained and then licked his lips. "Your blood, that is."

A chill ran down my back. I already knew my blood was the key because of what future Trace had told me, but I certainly didn't think Engel would already be looking in my direction.

"After all, it did appear to be the reason why he was unable to be slayed that night. I, myself, am also rather interested in this anomaly and whether or not it was just a fluke." He peered down at me, his eyes as dark as a bottomless well. "And I suggest we figure it out before Engel does."

"He's not getting within a mile of my blood," I assured him, fists balled up at my sides as if I had any actual control over the situation. "The only person who needs to know what I am is me." Not Engel, my uncle, the Council or anyone else for that matter. "I'll figure it out on my own."

"And how exactly are you going to do that?" he challenged. "Do you have a secret lab of scientists somewhere that are equipped to test out the immortality component of your blood?"

"No."

"Perhaps Gabriel offered to be your subject?" he asked mockingly. "Is he going to taste your blood and then repeatedly stake himself in the heart—though I'm sure the martyr would revel in the opportunity," he added under his breath.

"Don't be ridiculous, Dominic."

"Then tell me, love, how pray tell are you going to figure this out on your own?"

"I haven't ironed out all the details yet."

"You don't say?" he said, feigning surprise.

I shot him an irritated look as I shifted my weight.

"If you quit being so stubborn, you may just realize that I'm the answer to your problem. I can help you, angel."

"Help me, or help yourself to me?" I crossed my arms over my chest and braved a step forward. "I bet you're just dying to have yourself another bite. Well, you can forget it, pal! It's not going to happen."

His mouth twitched into a smile. "I don't have to bite you to taste your blood, temptress. There are other ways," he reminded.

I guess he kind of had a point there. I didn't bother giving him the satisfaction of saying it out loud, though.

"We can make this as platonic and scientific as you like."

I bit my lip as I mulled it over.

"I wish you wouldn't do that," he said, his eyes zeroing in on my mouth as though completely intrigued by what I was doing.

I released my lip and narrowed my eyes at him. I'd seen that look in his eyes before—right before he bit me.

"Are you even capable of having a conversation with me without thinking about food?"

"*Food* is the very last thing on my mind." His lazy, lopsided grin let me know where his mind had gone

"I'm not sure which one is worse."

"They're both equally good, angel."

My cheeks burned as the blood rushed up to my face.

"You're welcome to take me up on it anytime. And my offer to help you is still withstanding, of course."

"Right." I shook away the distraction. "I need to think about it," I said and then quickly corrected myself, "about your offer to help me figure things out! Not the other thing. Obviously." I blushed again.

"Yes, obviously," he reiterated, a knowing smirk on his lips. "The choice is yours, angel, though I do hope you make the right one. You ought to know the truth about yourself," he said as he glanced over my shoulder and scowled. "I'm more than willing to help you."

"Help her with what?"

I jumped at the sound of the unexpected voice. Covering my racing heart, I spun around to find Gabriel walking towards us, dressed in his usual dark jeans, black leather jacket, and signature frown.

Shit. "Gabriel! Hey. Wow. Where did you come from?" I asked, hoping my inquiry would derail his own questions.

His mouth tightened into a line. "What's going on?" he

asked, his face draped in suspicion.

"We were just talking about the search perimeters. Dominic offered to split up the area," I said, flinging my arm out as if a demonstration would help solidify the lie.

Gabriel's stare turned to ice as he focused in on his half-brother. "What the hell are you up to now, Dominic?"

"Whatever do you mean, brother?"

"You know exactly what I mean," answered Gabriel, his voice as cool, calm, and collected as he always *appeared* to be.

"I'm not up to anything. I'm simply lending a hand."

He bounced his eyes back and forth between the two of us as though we'd just been caught with our hands in the proverbial cookie jar. "What are you doing out here with him?"

"Nothing," I said, my tone unnaturally high. "He's just helping me."

Gabriel scoffed. "We both know Dominic doesn't help anyone but himself." He bore his worried eyes into me. "You can't trust him, Jemma. You know this."

"Apparently, she can," answered Dominic with a smirk on his lips. He was obviously working hard to provoke his brother, and seemed to be enjoying every minute of it. "Apparently, *you're* the one she doesn't trust."

Gabriel's jaw muscles tightened; his hands clenched by his side. He looked like a dormant volcano that could blow at any minute.

"He's just trying to get a rise out of you," I said, giving his arm a reassuring squeeze. "Don't listen to him."

He looked at me and frowned. "I don't know what he's filling your head with, but you know better than this. He's a liar. It's what he is—what he's always been."

"I know," I said under my breath.

"Is he threatening you?"

"No, of course not. We're just trying to find Taylor."

"There. You heard it from her own lovely mouth," said Dominic smugly from the sidelines. "Now run along, brother."

"Would you seriously just shut up?" I snapped, turning back to Dominic. He was making this a hundred times worse than it had to be, and I wanted to kick him for it.

Gabriel snagged my hand and drew me away from where Dominic was standing, though he was definitely still in earshot of us. "What's going on, Jemma?" His olive-green eyes were etched with concern. "You can tell me. You don't have to be afraid of him."

"I'm not afraid of him, Gabriel." Surprisingly, my voice didn't falter when I said it. "Nothing is going on, I promise. You worry too much. Everything is fine."

I could tell he didn't believe me, and although it broke my heart to lie to Gabriel, I knew that telling him would only lead to Tessa's involvement in this, and I couldn't have that. She wouldn't listen to reason; she wouldn't listen to *me*. I was her little sister after all—what did I know?

I couldn't take the risk; not when Taylor's life was at stake. Not when my own life was on the line.

This is the way it had to be.

18. GRUDGE MATCH

Trace avoided me at school the next day for most of the morning. At least that's how it felt. By the time the lunch bell rolled around, I was determined to confront him about his sudden change in demeanor towards me. Unfortunately, Nikki had beat me to the punch and was already at his locker, eating up all his time and personal space with her big mouth and designer perfume I could smell halfway down the hall.

She obviously never heard of the whole "less is more" thing.

For a split second, I had the urge to walk over to her and tell her all about it, but I quickly retracted my cat-claws knowing I didn't get nearly enough sleep last night to handle twelve rounds with Nikki Parker.

Before either of them saw me, I spun on my heel and headed back the other way towards the cafeteria, where the rest of the group was already sitting down at the usual table.

"Hey, Blackburn," smiled Caleb, his arm strung over the chair beside him. "I saved you a seat."

"Thanks," I said, plopping down in the chair with my paper brown lunch bag in hand. Having completely lost my appetite, I didn't bother opening it.

"What's up, Jem?" said Ben, who was sitting on the other side of the table with Hannah and Carly. There was a somberness in his voice lately, a sadness in his eyes that was impossible to ignore. I couldn't help but think it had everything to do with missing Taylor. Not even Carly (who was working hard to liven up his mood by talking to him about some new Sci-Fi show on TV) had any luck turning around his gloomy disposition.

And, as per usual, Morgan didn't even bother looking up from her phone.

"No shadow today?" asked Caleb, glancing over my shoulder as though searching for something.

"Huh?"

"That six-foot something half-blood that's been following you around everywhere lately." There was more than a hint of irritation in his voice.

"Last I saw him, he was with Nikki at his locker."

"Figures," he said, looking downright aggravated now.

"They're just working on something together." I wasn't sure who I was trying to convince more, myself or Caleb.

"I bet they are."

I gave him a warning look. I didn't need him fanning the flames in my head any more than they already were.

"Are you coming to the game tonight?" he asked, plucking a french fry from the top of his plate. "Brand new *tendy* just came up from Whistler. It's gonna be a *gongshow*."

I laughed. "I don't even know what that means."

"It means you need to start coming to my games," he said, tweaking his eyebrows. "Seriously, you should be there. We're dedicating the whole thing to Taylor."

Ben stopped listening mid-sentence and looked up at me. I could see the loss in his eyes; the concern for Taylor. It was as though he knew her life was sitting in the palm of my hands, and worse, he didn't think I had a chance in hell of bringing her home alive.

I looked back at Caleb and shook my head. "I have a family thing tonight. I don't think I can get out of it."

The truth was, I was going to see Dominic. After tossing and turning in my bed for most of the night, I had decided that Dominic was right. I needed to know exactly what my blood was capable of doing and the effect it had on Revenants. And I needed to figure it out before Engel did. Living in the dark corners of denial with self-inflicted blinders on was no longer an option for me. And I didn't want it to be one.

"That sucks," he said, looking down in disappointment. His head bounced back up a moment later. "You're coming to my party on Saturday though, right?"

Trace appeared at the table just as I was about to answer Caleb. His dark hair was brushed back from his face, and his shoulders were high and wide, like he was coming up on enemy territory. There was no smile on his lips but they looked beautiful and inviting just the same.

"I, um" —*was apparently extremely distracted by said lips*—I turned back to Caleb, blank-faced. "What was the question again?"

"He wants to know if you're going to his party," answered Trace, eyeing the two of us before taking a seat next to me.

"Right." I looked at Caleb again and shrugged. "I'm not sure. Probably. I mean, I think so," I offered, though at this point, I had no idea if I'd even still be alive by Saturday.

Caleb's gaze veered to Trace, who was slumped back in his chair with his feet kicked out in front him and his eyes pinned straight ahead, glaring at some unknown marker.

"How about you?" asked Caleb. "You coming Saturday?"

"Nah, man. I'm busy." Trace didn't bother making eye contact with him when he answered.

"Yeah. Busy doing what?" Caleb's tone was noticeably more aggressive. He lifted his chin a little as though he wanted to add some height to his frame. "Or should I say *who*?"

This was quickly going nowhere good.

Trace turned slowly, his beautiful eyes cold and hard and damn-near unrecognizable. "Don't worry about it, jockstrap. I'll handle my business. You handle yours."

"Your business?" challenged Caleb and then leaned in like he wanted to drop a secret. "Are you talking about Nikki? Or is this Jemma's week?"

The chair screeched back across the floor as Trace jumped up to his feet. "You got something you want to say to me?"

"I thought I just did," said Caleb, knocking his own chair back as he stood up to join Trace.

"Stop it, both of you!" I popped up with my arms spread out on each side, and consequently, landed myself square in the middle of their standstill. "I thought you were friends."

"Obviously not," spat Caleb.

"Yeah, because if you were, you wouldn't be trying to snake in on my girlfriend behind my back."

"Which girlfriend are we talking about again?"

Trace's fist snapped out so fast I barely had time to register the movement. Caleb was on the floor, dazed from the hit, but only for a second before he bounced back to his feet and rushed Trace like a linebacker.

"Stop it!" I yelled, but it was too late. They were already ripping into each other in front of half the school population.

Ben quickly slid across the table and threw himself in the middle of the scrap. His shoes screeched against the floor as he ducked and dodged while trying to separate the two of them.

I heard someone yell out to call the principal but they were quickly shot down with a roar of boos from the crowd.

"Relax, dude. Relax!" grunted Ben as he struggled to stay in between them. It took everything he had to push them apart and he was quickly losing ground.

"Fight! Fight! Fight! Fight!" chanted the crowd.

"Jemma, get him out of here!" ordered Ben as he hung onto each of them by the collar of their shirts.

I rushed up and grabbed Trace's arm, pulling him backwards towards me with all my might as Ben pushed Caleb in the opposite direction. The cafeteria erupted in a fit of disappointment as the afternoon entertainment came to an abrupt end.

"We'll finish this later," threatened Caleb over the noise.

Trace's dimples appeared on both sides. "I'm looking forward to it, jockstrap."

The biting wind slashed through my hair, whipping it around my cheeks and neck as I followed Trace outside. The ground was still wet from this afternoon's rain, the clouds still gray and swollen with angry tears. A clap of thunder exploded in the distance, but I barely registered the sound. I was far too preoccupied keeping up with the raging Reaper in front of me.

"What the hell was that about?" I asked him, chasing him through the student parking lot.

He didn't answer.

"Trace!" I grabbed his arm to get his attention.

"Leave it alone, Jemma. It's nothing." He pulled his arm free and continued walking.

I practically had to jog just to keep up with his stride. "It didn't sound like nothing."

No answer.

Goddamn his stubborn ass! I planted my feet in the ground and stopped. "Who were you talking about before?" I shouted.

I wasn't sure if it was the tone of my question or the fact that my footsteps had stilled behind him, but he finally came to a rest. Shoulders squared, he didn't bother turning around.

"When you said he was trying to snake in on your girlfriend," I clarified even though I knew we were already on the same page.

"Who do you think?" he answered, turning to face me. His expression fell heavy on me like he was offended that I was even asking him the question. "*You*, Jemma. I was talking about you."

"But I'm not—"

"It's just a word," he quickly said, taking a slow step towards me. "I know you're not my girlfriend." His eyes, full of desire and want, moved down the length of my body and then up again. "But you will be."

The wind picked up, rustling his ebony hair as he stared down at me in the parking lot. He was so certain of us—of our fate, like he knew what was going to happen before it even had a chance to come to fruition. Why? Because of what Morgan saw? Because of what she told him? All of that could change in the blink of an eye—evaporate into absolute nonexistence. Nothing was certain in this world. Nothing. Not love or friendship or happy endings.

Sometimes, not even death.

"Why do you always have to be so sure of yourself?" I tried to demand the answer out of him, but it came out meek and afraid like I didn't have the courage to let myself feel any hope and didn't want him doing it for the both of us.

"I'm not," he said, walking up to me slowly. "I'm sure about you."

"Well, maybe you shouldn't be," I said clumsily. I wasn't sure why I said that to him. Maybe it was because I knew what was coming—the darkness that was skirting along the horizon. Who knew if I was going to survive any of it; if I would even live long enough to be his girlfriend someday? In future Trace's world, I was already a goner. Toast. Persona non grata. Maybe all of this was just a prelude to that.

The only thing I knew for sure was what I *had* to do. The outcome of it all was as slippery as an oil slick. The harder I tried to hang on to it, the more it fumbled out of my hands.

"I'm going to see Dominic tonight," I told him, silently resigning myself to the only fate I currently knew.

"Dominic?" His face twisted in anger. "For what?"

"He offered to help me" —I swallowed down the nervous lump at the back of my throat— "test my blood."

"Is that right? And how is he going to do that?" The way he said it, all snide and cynical, made it clear he already knew the answer and didn't approve.

"I'm going to give him some of my blood and then—"

"That's not happening," he cut in before I could finish the rest of the sentence. Crossing his arms over his chest, he walked up to me and stopped just inches from where I stood, his jaw ticking furiously as he bent down towards me. "He's not putting a finger on you and that's the end of it."

"That's not your decision to make," I said carefully, holding his gaze as steadily as I could. "I need to be prepared. I need know what my blood can do, and I have to do it before Engel or the Council does."

"Then we'll figure it out another way."

"There isn't another way." I had already ran through my entire list of options more times than I cared to admit, and quite frankly, it was a pretty short list. Outside of grabbing some random Rev off the street, Dominic was my only good option. "I have to do this, Trace. It's the only way to know for sure."

Realizing he wasn't going to change my mind, he shook his head and then dropped it in defeat.

"I need to know the truth."

"I'm not okay with this."

"I know."

"But you're doing it anyway," he answered for me.

I nodded, my eyes and heart filled with regret.

"Then I'm coming with you." The urgency in his voice from earlier had returned with a vengeance. "You're not going there alone. If anything happens—if he even steps an inch out of line, I'm sending him straight to Sanguinarium myself."

"Do you really think that's the best idea?" I asked, picturing an ex-Keeper locked in a room with a vampire who would be testing my blood (and, consequently, his own limits) while the former watched on, powerless to stop it.

Wetting his lips, he tipped in closer to me, bringing his mouth within a dangerous reach of mine. "I think it's the best decision I've made all week." He closed the tiny gap between our mouths and pressed his lips into mine.

My breath caught.

With just one kiss, Trace could melt my body like butter, clear out my mind like I had reached nirvana. The only worry I had when I was in his arms was if my shaky legs would be able to keep me up long enough to enjoy it.

And therein lay my problem.

I put my hand out and pressed it against his chest, bringing the kiss to a cold, dead stop.

His eyebrows rutted in confusion.

"Trace, I can't do this right now," I said, shaking my head. I couldn't let myself get distracted; sidetracked. Taylor was depending on me and I owed it to her to give this everything I had. "I need to stay focused—"

"Save it, Jemma. I get it," he said, pulling back like a rubber band. Fury filled his scrutinizing eyes as he backed away from me and then bolted for his car.

"Woah. Wait a minute!" I shouted after him as he pulled out his keys and unlocked the doors. "Don't you dare walk away from me like that!"

He stopped cold in his tracks, his back to me and his hand still gripping the door handle. When he finally turned around to face me, I could see him clenching his teeth so hard I thought his jaw might bust.

"What the hell was that?" I demanded.

"I don't get it," he said, shaking his head. "You had no problem kissing him, yet you won't kiss me?"

"I didn't kiss Caleb!" I said indignantly.

"Not Caleb. My Alt."

I quickly realized what this was about. "You're the same person, Trace."

"No, we're not," he said, taking a small step towards me. "*He* screwed you over. *I* didn't. You can't even look me in the eye half the time because of what he did to you that night, yet you kiss him?" he said, outraged by it.

"It's not like that," I said, shaking my head at his summary. "You're twisting everything around."

"Then tell me how it is, Jemma. Untwist it," he said sarcastically as he marched over to where I stood. Crossing his arms over his chest, he tipped forward so we were closer to eye level. "I want to know what was so different about him."

"I don't know, he just was."

"Why?"

"Because," I said, searching desperately for the words that would explain this all away. All my searching amounted to four small words. "Because he loves me."

He didn't flinch. "How do you know?"

"He told me he did. And I felt it."

"How? What did he say to you?" he probed deeper, his eyebrows rutted with curiosity as though our very future depended on it.

I shook my head at him. I didn't want to tell him about the

promises of tomorrow, about what future Trace had professed to me. I didn't want to sway his feelings for me in any direction other than the direction they were *meant* to go.

Realizing I wasn't going to elaborate, he shifted gears. "And what about me now?"

"What do you mean?"

"Do you think I love you?"

I hesitated before answering. "I think you want to love me," I answered as honestly as I could. "I think Morgan's vision convinced you that you're going to love me, but I think you're still confused."

"Confused about what?"

"About how you feel. About Nikki," I added, cursing her name as it cut through my lips. "You have history, that much is obvious, but for some reason or another, you keep going back to her and I think that says a lot."

"She's a friend, nothing else. You're reading too much into it."

"Maybe." I shrugged. "Maybe not. All I know is that's the way I feel about it, and I can't change that."

"I don't know what to say to get it through to you. I *don't* have feelings for Nikki." His gaze shifted to the school building behind us. "I'm not sure I ever did," he added with a slow, regretful blink.

"What do you mean?"

"What do you think I mean?" he shot back, uncrossing his arms. "What I feel for you—right here, right now—I didn't feel even half of that the entire time I was with her." He took a purposeful step towards me, putting himself in my line of fire so that I had nowhere to aim my eyes but at him.

My breath caught in my throat.

"I want to be with *you*, Jemma. Only you," he said with enough heat in his eyes to melt an ice age. "If it's time you want, then I'll give it to you, but sooner or later, you're going to run out of excuses."

He words resonated in my ears as he took a slow step backwards and then took off for his car, leaving me in the parking lot with an echo of his words in my head, and a raging fire in my heart.

19. THE BREAKFAST CLUB

The rain picked up where it left off this afternoon, slicing across Trace's windshield like plummeting axes as we pulled up to Huntington Manor later that evening. I felt my pulse hasten at the sight of the looming house and what awaited me inside, and even though that small voice at the back of my mind kept screaming for me to turn around and go home, I didn't dare utter the words aloud.

The truth was right there within my reach and I was determined to grab it with both hands no matter how thorny or agonizing it may be.

We climbed out of his Mustang and hurried up the water-slicked front steps. Fearing he would change his mind, I decided *not* to call Dominic ahead of time and let him know that there'd been a change in the guest list. Of course, now that we were here, it only made me more nervous to face him.

"Are you sure he's home?" asked Trace as he pounded his fist against the front door. He crossed his arms over his chest and waited. "He's probably out chasing down a snack."

"Shush," I said, worried that Dominic, with his near-perfect hearing, would overhear him and end this before it even had a chance to get started.

The door swung open just as Trace was about to bang on it for a third time.

"That'll suffice, *Romeo*. Thank you for alerting my entire neighborhood to your presence."

"What did you just call me?"

"Which begs the question," continued Dominic, ignoring Trace as he turned to me, "what pray tell is *he* doing here?"

"What do you think I'm doing here?" answered Trace. "Did you seriously think I would let you get within a mile of her without me there?"

"Heavens no," mocked Dominic, knowing we'd been alone together on more than one occasion already. He turned to me and smirked. "I wouldn't dream of it."

"Dominic," I warned.

"Yes, love?"

"Can we get this started please? It's pouring rain out here," I said, hugging my arms for warmth.

"Of course, angel. Come in," he said, stepping aside so that I could enter. As soon as I passed him, he quickly placed himself back in the doorway. "Unfortunately for you, this is a two-person party and you're not invited."

"Unfortunately for *you*," said Trace, shoving him out of the way. "I'm not a bloodsucker so I don't need any invitations." He walked right on in like he owned the place.

A low rumble escaped the back of Dominic's throat. It sounded a lot like a growl.

"Down, dog," said Trace absentmindedly as he inspected his surroundings. It was clear that he'd never been here before but it didn't seem to make him nervous in the least. He shucked off his jacket and tossed it on the settee before grabbing a hold of my hand and leading us into the dimly lit house.

Dominic glared at him as he picked up Trace's jacket and

hung it on the coat rack.

We followed the flickering light from the fireplace and walked into the study; the same room Dominic and I had previously convened in to discuss our plans. I didn't bother mentioning that part to Trace and hoped that Dominic wouldn't bring it up either.

"Real romantic," scoffed Trace, flicking on a light switch.

"Well, I do have a reputation to uphold," answered Dominic as he poured himself a drink—probably a double.

"As what?" laughed Trace, taking a seat on the sofa closest to the fireplace. "A douchebag?"

"Trace, don't," I warned.

"I'm fairly certain you already have that category covered," replied Dominic.

"I'm fairly certain you should watch your mouth if you know what's good for you."

"Tsk, tsk. Threatening a Revenant in his own home," sneered Dominic. "I suppose your premature age and subpar aptitude prevent you from knowing any better."

"But it doesn't prevent me from shoving my foot up your ass," retorted Trace.

"Ugh!" I threw my head back and flopped down onto the sofa. This was going even worse than I anticipated.

"You look stressed, angel. Would you care for a drink?" asked Dominic, turning his attention to me.

"Enough with the pet names," warned Trace, clearly irritated by Dominic's terms of endearment for me.

Undaunted, Dominic's stare remained fixed on me. "Love?" he asked again, and I quickly shook my head.

"I said stop calling her that shit."

"Or what?" Dominic chuckled as he picked up his drink and walked over to where we were sitting, his eyes darkening with menacing shadows. "I could dismember your body in two flat seconds," he informed, his lips curling up on one side as he sat down in the chair across from us.

Trace leaned forward, propping his elbows on his knees as he stared him down. "I'd *really* like to see you try, dead boy."

"Alright, enough!" I yelled, shooting up to my feet like a pop tart. "Both of you need to just shut up!"

Caught off guard by my eruption, they both sunk back into their seats and stared up at me in surprise.

"I came here for one reason and it's not to listen to the two of you bicker back and forth with each other!"

With furrowed brows, Trace stretched his arm along the back of the sofa and looked up at me intensely—almost as though he were seeing me for the first time. Dominic swiveled his drink around his glass, a mindless gesture, though his eyes were also pinned on me with great interest.

Apparently, the floor was mine.

"Look, we're on the same side," I started, bouncing glances between the two of them. "We all want to know what I am— what my blood can do—so either we work together and get this done, or you two can stay here and argue and I'll go figure this out on my own."

"That needn't be necessary, angel," said Dominic, taking a sip of his drink. "I'm sure we can find a way to work in peace."

"Good." I turned to Trace expectantly.

He held my gaze for a few seconds, his jaw muscles ticking as he considered my request, and then tipped his head once in agreement. "Whatever you want."

"Great." I nodded, pleased with my efforts. "Now that it's settled, let's move on to what we came here to do."

"Alright," agreed Trace.

"Excellent," said Dominic with a devious smile playing across his lips. "I think that's a fine suggestion."

My eyes veered to his mouth. Mesmerized by the shiny glint

of his teeth, a rush of anxiety barreled through me as I realized those very same teeth would soon be piercing holes through my skin. Any minute now, I was going to willingly feed my blood to a murderous Revenant, offering myself up to him like some cheap date, and then hope to God that he didn't tear my head clean off my neck as a thank you.

There was absolutely no turning back now, and all I could think was, what the hell did I just get myself into?

20. DEATH WISH

"I propose we do this precisely as it occurred with Engel," suggested Dominic.

"No way," said Trace vehemently. "You're not putting your fangs anywhere near her." His body arched forward in a threatening way as he narrowed his eyes at Dominic. "I *know* what you're trying to do and it's not going to happen."

"What are you talking about?" My gaze bounced to Dominic and then back to Trace. "What is he trying to do?"

"He's trying to strengthen the bloodbond—the connection you have." Trace's jaw muscles pumped in frustration as he glared at Dominic. "He has to bite you to do that."

I didn't know much about how bloodbonds worked, only that it took longer for the connection to form between Revenants and Descendants, as opposed to Humans and Revenants, which was almost an instantaneous connection.

"Nonsense," said Dominic. "I simply want to make the trial as effective as possible." He slumped back in his chair and crossed his legs. "We need to recreate that night using the same exact variables, otherwise the outcome could potentially be skewed and this whole thing will be for nothing."

"It won't be skewed," answered Trace, turning to me. "We'll make a small incision on your hand and let the blood drip out from there. He can drink it from a glass or whatever the hell he drinks his blood from."

I shook my head. "He's right, Trace. Engel didn't drink my blood from a cup. He bit me. We have to recreate that night exactly as it happened." Fear trickled into my bloodstream as I said the words, but I refused to let it affect me. I was determined to find out the truth, no matter how scary or unsettling it was.

He started to protest, but I quickly overruled him. "It's not your choice, Trace. This is the way I want it."

He exhaled his frustration and rose to his feet. Reaching into his back pocket, he pulled out a sharp, wooden stake, placed it down on the table and then glowered across at Dominic. "One wrong move and this isn't coming out," he warned him, his eyes darkening into a deeper shade of blue.

As steady as his voice had been, I could see the trepidation in his eyes. It was written all over his face. I couldn't imagine having to sit by and watch the person you cared about try their luck at a dance with the devil himself.

"Sure thing, Romeo." Dominic rested his drink down on the coffee table and stood up. A wicked grin played on his lips as he walked over to where I was standing.

Contrary to Trace, he appeared to be the pillar of calmness when he stopped in front of me and titled his head to the side. "Do you have any preference, love?" he asked, his eyes filled with desire as they traveled down the length of my neck.

My mouth had gotten so dry I wasn't even sure I could talk. So I didn't.

"Perhaps a spot you prefer?" he continued when I didn't answer. His dark eyes gleamed as they met mine.

I shook my head rigidly. "I don't care where you do it. Just do it." I reached back and gathered my hair, pulling it to the side as my eyes remained fixed on his.

"As you please," he said, bowing his head as though he were about to bestow the greatest gift I'd ever received. His hand came up to my neck and gently moved a leftover strand of hair from my neck, causing a strange tingle to slide down my back.

I quickly straightened my back, toughening my resolve.

His grin widened as though he knew his touch had affected me. Circling his arm around my waist, he tugged me forward, and I gasped as my hips collided with his.

Trace made a displeased grunt from over Dominic's shoulder but I couldn't see his face from where I stood, and I didn't want to. I didn't want to have to face the hurt and worry and melancholy I knew I would find there.

Dominic's other hand came back up along my arm, slowing down when he reached my neckline and then coming to a full stop at my face. Turning his hand over, he brushed the back of his knuckles against my cheek, soft and unhurried as though he wanted to savor every moment.

My eyes slipped shut. As quickly as I resigned myself to the darkness, I was forced to face the light again at the sound of his fangs protracting. He paused for a split second, almost as though he were giving me a chance to change my mind, or maybe he was just waiting for the fear to start coursing through my blood. Maybe he liked it better that way.

Gripping my jaw, he turned my head to the side and mapped his path to my neck. My heart was pounding hard in my chest now, my mind screaming at me to abort this baleful quest, but I didn't move a single muscle. I had already made the decision long before I ventured out here.

Hold on tight, my love, he said, speaking to my mind.

I closed my eyes and braced myself.

21. LOVE BITES

The scorching ache I felt from Dominic's teeth piercing through my skin left me almost as quickly as it came, leaving in its place feelings of a placated euphoria. Everything that had been plaguing my mind, all the grief and fear and burden, seemed to just crumble away to a place I was no longer connected to.

In the back of my mind, I knew it was wrong to feel this way. I knew I should have been trying harder to fight against the takeover, but the contempt I felt for myself quickly slipped away to the same place where all my other bad thoughts had gone.

His venom coursed through my blood like an antidote, remedying everything that it touched. He'd become my medicine, my newfound cure, and I held onto him tighter because of it. It didn't matter that my thoughts were spinning almost as fast as the room was, or that my knees felt as though they would buckle beneath me. I needed to give more. Not because he needed it, which I knew by the fervor of which he drank from me that he did, but because *I* needed it. I needed to be in Dominic's arms for as long as my body could stand it.

He bit down harder into my neck, sinking his fangs as deep as they could go, drawing my blood out in heaps that could not be naturally replenished, but none of that mattered to me anymore. All I could think about was *more* as I whimpered into him with want.

"That's enough," I heard Trace say from a distance, but it only made me clasp onto Dominic harder.

I knew he wasn't going to stop—he couldn't, and this time, I didn't want him to.

Black spots began filling my vision and I welcomed the blackness with open arms. Whatever it took to stay in this rapture—to stay in his arms, I was willing to embrace it.

"I said that's enough!" snapped Trace as he yanked Dominic off of me and thrust him back several steps.

He stumbled into the coffee table.

"Wait!" I cried, trying to reach out to him, to reach out for more, but my legs quickly gave out on me, causing me to tumble forward into Trace's arms instead.

Dominic sighed as he dropped back onto the sofa with his arms and legs spread out wide and his mouth painted in shades of my blood. "You are heaven incarnate, angel."

I could almost smell the salty, metallic taste of blood in the air—my blood—and it made my head swim.

Trace tightened his hold on me. "Are you alright?" he asked, his intense blue eyes running rampant all over my face as he inspected me.

My eyes fluttered open. I couldn't seem to focus.

"You need to lie down," said Trace, scooping me up into his arms and then carrying me over to the sofa where Dominic was sprawled out. "Move," he ordered him.

Dominic got up clumsily and staggered across to the other side of the room before flopping down into the chair he'd been sitting on earlier.

"Talk to me, Jemma. Are you okay?" Trace asked me again, but I didn't answer. I couldn't seem to put words together anymore. All I could think about was the emptiness I now felt without Dominic's vitriol.

"You took too much!" thundered Trace, his eyes reduced to angry slits of vengeance.

In the blink of an eye, he was gone from my sight, vanishing and then reappearing in front of Dominic with the wooden stake in his hand and one goal in his mind.

Grabbing at the sofa, I tried to pull myself up to see—to stop him—but I was too weak to hold myself up. In the split second that it took for me to tumble back into my resting place, Trace's arm was in the air, slicing through it like a bat out of Hell as he plunged the stake into Dominic's chest.

It all happened so fast, and then just like that, everything came to a screeching halt. The seconds ticked by maddeningly as I struggled to see the aftermath.

"I don't believe it," said Trace, taking two slow steps back as he looked down at Dominic in horror.

My eyes snapped to Dominic. He was sitting contently, smiling up at Trace with the wooden stake still protruding from his chest like some macabre fashion accessory.

"How the hell is this possible?" asked Trace, his scrutinizing eyes never leaving Dominic. It was clear he'd never seen anything like this before.

"It appears our little temptress here is quite special," said Dominic as he pulled the stake out of his heart and tossed it onto the coffee table. He smiled over at me like I was God's gift to the world—the Revenant world, that is.

Trace's face contorted with apprehension. I couldn't even begin to imagine what he was thinking; what he was feeling. Would he still look at me the same after what he saw, or would he now see me as some abomination that needed to be exterminated?

Trace picked up the stake from the table and inspected it.

After a short pause, he shook his head. "It's not wood. It has to be synthetic," he decided, even though he was the one who brought it here. He was grasping at straws now, trying to make sense out of the nonsensical. And who could blame him?

"It's wood," said Dominic confidently and then stood up. "Find yourself another one if you need to, but I assure you, the result will be the same," he added, dusting off his pants and then inspecting the thin tear in his shirt from where the stake had entered. His eyes snapped to me. "I wouldn't do that just yet, angel."

Trace's eyes darted over to me as I tried righting myself on the couch. "Jemma, you need to lie down," he said, rushing to my side. He tried to force me back into a reclining position, but I pushed his hands away.

"I'm fine," I said, sitting myself up. Okay, so I wasn't exactly *fine*, but good health was a luxury I didn't have right now. I needed to snap out of this daze and start gathering information.

"You're looking a little pallid, love. Would you care for a sip of my blood?" offered Dominic with a puckish smile on his lips. "I'm told it's a wonderful pick-me-up."

"Yeah, I'm sure it's peaches and cream. I'll pass," I said, rubbing my temples with my fingers as if to coax away the disturbing image. I couldn't even stomach tasting my own blood, let alone someone else's.

"Very well. It's your loss."

Trace said something back to him, but I wasn't paying attention to either of them anymore.

Everything was starting to come back to me now, including the part of myself that had slipped away from me. My head was still pounding harder than a tribal drum, but I knew I had to keep going. I had to stay focused. I sucked in a breath and buried my discomfort. "We need to move on to the next part of the plan."

"And what would that be exactly?" asked Trace, his eyes never straying from mine. He looked down at me strangely, his eyebrows pulled together in curiosity like I was some odd, new species from a faraway Realm.

"We need to find out how long this lasts and what it's protecting him from. You know more than I do about what can harm a Revenant—sun, fire, holy water, silver? Whatever we can get our hands on. We need to test all of it," I explained, tucking my hair behind my ears. "And we need to do it again and again until the effects wear off."

I needed to know exactly what kind of a timeframe we were working with, especially since I was about to go up against Engel, who had previously ingested a fairly large amount of my blood.

Both of them stared at me, speechless.

"Well? What are you waiting for?" I asked, looking at both of them expectantly. "We don't have all night."

As if on cue, they both looked at each other and then did exactly as I told them, heading off in different directions to retrieve the objects needed.

Pulling myself up from the sofa, I glanced around the room at what my life had become. Vampires, wooden stakes, blood, carnage, death. It was nothing like what I'd dreamed of when I was a little girl—what I had hoped for myself growing up.

But it was the only life I had, and it was *mine*. The days of waiting around for someone else to ride in and save the day for me were over. People couldn't be trusted. They lied. They cheated. And then, when everything you were and hoped to be shattered apart into a million pieces, they left.

But not this time. This time, I was going to save myself, and maybe, just maybe, the world too.

We spent the rest of the night running countless experiments on Dominic, which basically consisted of stabbing him in the heart with wooden stakes, dousing his body in a slew of fluids, and branding his skin with different metals. All of which brought an immense amount of pleasure to Trace.

It took several hours of repeating the same tests over and over again before Dominic was finally incapacitated.

"Think we should leave him like that?" suggested Trace. A mischievous grin appeared on his lips.

"Very funny," I said as I walked over to Dominic's dormant body. The snowy white tint to his skin had evaporated from his face, leaving in its place a desiccated shade of gray as dull and gloomy as the Hollow Hills firmament. I reached down and pulled the stake out.

Within seconds, the sickly gray color dissipated from his face and the smooth, milky texture returned. I held my breath and waited, releasing it only when his eyes snapped open.

"Welcome back," I said wryly.

"Thank you, angel," he said, shifting in the lounge chair. He reached up and rubbed his palm over the entry wound. "Time?"

I glanced at the clock on the wall and calculated how long it took to incapacitate him. "A little over two hours."

Trace joined us. "So what now?" he asked, crossing his arms over his chest. "Is that it?"

"We have to repeat the test," answered Dominic.

"For what?" bellowed Trace, his disapproval written all over his face.

"We need to discern whether the amount of blood I drank played a role in how long I remained indestructible," he said, reaching forward for his drink.

I swallowed hard at the thought of having to go another round with Dominic. Not because I was afraid I wouldn't be able to withstand it (which was a pretty good possibility), but because I was afraid of further strengthening the bloodbond between us. Already as it was, I felt an uncomfortable pull towards him—a softening of my heart where he was concerned. I didn't want to feel this way, but it seemed to be out of my control, and letting Dominic drink from me again would only further loosen the flailing grip I had over myself.

I pulled in a sobering breath and reminded myself that this wasn't about what I wanted or what I was afraid of. I had to find out if the amount of blood consumed was a factor or not, even if it was at the expense of myself, and there was only one way to do that.

"He's right," I said, nodding my head in agreement with Dominic as I buried the doubt and hesitation deeper inside of me. "We have to keep going."

"It's not happening," said Trace, steadfast. His eyes were hard and unwavering, daring one of us to try and change his mind. "You've had enough for one night. I'm taking you home," he continued, picking up my hand like I belonged to him.

"We can't stop now, Trace. We're too close—"

"No. We're done," he quickly cut in over me. "We did this your way all night, Jemma, and now it's time to go." Remarking the crossed look on my face, he softened his tone and tried to reason with me. "Look, you already lost a lot of blood. You need to rest. You're no good to anyone if you're dead. We can finish this another day."

I suppose he had a point, what with him being all level-headed and whatnot. "Maybe you're right," I said with a shrug and then turned back to Dominic. A peculiar pang of disappointment passed through me. "We'll finish this tomorrow, okay?"

His dark eyes were fixed on me in a baring way, a way that made it seem as if he knew my inner thoughts, my newfound cravings. "As you wish, angel," he said, bowing his head.

Had his voice always sounded so smooth?

"I'll come back later for my car," announced Trace, though Dominic didn't take his eyes off me, nor did I take mine from his. "Come on," said Trace, his voice a quiet struggle against the connection. He squeezed my hand and began drawing me closer to him, slow and uneven, like dragging a block of concrete.

My eyes shifted back to Trace's and I winced at what I found in them. Hurt and worry coated his features like a new skin as he stared down at me questioningly. He felt the hesitation, the pullback, and God only knows what he saw and heard tonight.

My heart throbbed with guilt.

A forced smile sprouted on his lips as he softly shook his head as if to tell me it wasn't my fault.

But I knew that it was.

"Oh, and Jemma," called Dominic as Trace circled his arms around my waist.

"Yeah?" I answered, my eyes finding him easily.

"Sweet dreams," he purred.

And with that, Trace and I were gone.

22. HEART TO HEART

The familiar setting of my room materialized around me as the frigid cold slowly dissipated from my bones. Trace's arms were still wrapped tightly around my waist, encasing me in the warmth of his body as we stood there holding each other, neither one of us moving an inch. In that moment, it was exactly what I needed. I needed his warmth to bring me back from the brink—to remind me of who I was again.

"I'll always be here to bring you back," he said, his words resonating with layered meaning. He dropped a kiss on the top of my head and stepped back from me tentatively.

I looked down at my shoes because, honestly, after tonight, I was too ashamed to look him in the eye.

"How are you feeling?" he asked after a little while, his poignant eyes sweeping over me like cobalt stardust.

"Tired," I said, shrugging my shoulder. "My mind feels like it's racing a hundred miles a minute." Taking a few steps back, I sat down on the edge of my bed and combed my fingers through my hair. "I doubt I'm going to get much sleep tonight." And it probably wasn't such a bad thing either, I thought.

He looked uneasy. "Is there anything I can do?"

I shook my head and smiled at him. "You've already done more than enough. Thank you for everything tonight."

Smiling, he buried his hands in his pockets and glanced over his shoulder. "I guess I should take off then," he said, ticking his chin towards the door. "Let you get some rest."

Dread rolled through my stomach at the thought of being alone with myself.

"Wait!" I said, springing to my feet as he turned for the door, afraid of what—or *whom*—I would see tonight once I closed my eyes. "Don't go yet."

His eyes ran down the length of my body and then back up again, assessing me, trying to figure me out.

"Please."

"Okay," he said softly, nodding as understanding flickered through his eyes. "I'll stay as long as you want me to." He pulled out the desk chair and took a seat across from me as if to prove his promise was more than just words.

Feeling reassured that he wasn't going anywhere, I released my breath and sat back down on my bed. "I won't keep you long. I just...I don't want to be alone right now."

His eyebrows pulled together in quiet reflection. It made me nervous when he looked at me that way, like he could see right through to the core of who I really was.

"It's just the bloodbond," he said after a short pause. It was as though he could read what was plaguing my mind without having to touch me. "Whatever you're feeling for him—it isn't real, Jemma."

"I know," I said, but it was weak and unconvincing. I stared down at the wooden floor, sweeping my feet back and forth like an antsy child.

"Hey." He leaned over and picked up my chin. "It'll fade with time. I promise."

"I know," I said again. But the truth was, I wasn't sure of

anything anymore, least of all bloodbonds and how they worked.

"Do you want to talk about it?"

I shook my head, unsure of where to begin. "I don't even know who I am anymore. I don't even know if the things I'm feeling are *my* feelings or...something else."

"Like the bloodbond," he said, watching me carefully.

I nodded. "I think it's starting to mess with my head."

Slipping into the spot beside me on my bed, he stared forward, thinking. "Is it messing with *us?*" he asked quietly without meeting my gaze.

"No, of course not." I didn't hesitate because it was the truth. The feelings I had for Trace were real, and they hadn't changed. He was a permanent fixture in my mind, an eternal staple of my heart.

But, somehow, Dominic had begun to creep through the reedy borders of my subconscious, scratching at the walls to find a place, and even though I knew what I was feeling for him wasn't real—that it was fleeting and fabricated and forced upon me—it still didn't stop it from being so.

"I miss you, you know," he said, turning to meet my eyes. His jaw tightened as though he were working hard to keep all the things he wanted to say at bay.

"I'm sitting right here."

"That's not what I meant."

There was a tortured sadness in his eyes that hadn't always been there. It broke my heart to think that I had a hand in putting it there, that I caused him this hurt.

My small smile faded away.

As much as I wanted to give myself to him, to throw myself down at his Alter, I wasn't entirely sure I had anything good to offer him anymore. So much of who I was had become lost, diluted, fragmented. I was being pulled and stretched in every which way, dragged in a million directions with the expectations of the world sitting heavy on my center like a concrete paperweight I couldn't shake off.

What exactly did I have to offer him? A bloodbond? A missing best friend? A troubled past? A hopeless future? Engel?

Everything that touched me was necrotic. Everything that came into my life withered away and died.

I didn't want to do that to him. He was ineffably perfect just the way he was, an enigma filled with both fire and ice that could send my heart into freefall with a simple shift of his eyes. He was the sun and the earth and everything beautiful in between them. I couldn't take the risk of destroying even a sliver of that the way I destroyed everything else.

I lowered my head in defeat. "I don't want to hurt you."

"Then don't hurt me," he said calmly as though it were that simple.

"It's not always something I can control," I pointed out, meeting his curious eyes. "I'm like some big, horrible plague that just infects everything it touches."

He laughed as though I'd said something funny. "You're not a plague, Jemma."

"I'm serious, Trace. I bring death and destruction wherever I go. I need to be exterminated," I blurted out, tears distorting my vision as they threatened to spill over in spite of me. I was fighting them back so hard it was making my chin quiver. "Even my stupid blood is defective."

"Come on, don't say that," he said, wrapping his arm around my shoulder. "We don't know anything yet. I'll be okay."

"How do you figure? I don't exactly have the best track record for things working out in my favor." I shook my head in despair. "I'm an abomination, Trace. It's as simple as that."

"No, you're not. We might not have all the answers yet, but I know there isn't a bad bone inside of you." He picked up my chin again, forcing me to look at him when I tried to turn away. "You're not an abomination, Jemma. Not even close."

"What would you call it then, huh? What the hell am I?" I asked, water trickling down my cheeks in fat, pitiful streaks.

"You're everything that's right in this world," he answered without hesitation. "You're kind and beautiful and selfless. You're the only reason I fight for my future," he added quietly, wiping away my tears with his thumb. "Kind of like the rainbow that comes after a storm."

"Yeah, right," I said, snorting through my sobs.

How he was able to find any semblance of good in this was beyond me.

"If you could see what I see, you would know the answer to that," he replied, his voice a heart-warming murmur.

"I don't deserve to hear you say these things to me. All I've done is push you away." I closed my eyes, guilt-ridden by the way I've been treating him lately.

"Lucky for you I don't give up that easy." His dimples blinked at me like a promise of eternal love. "Besides, I know where your heart is."

"Yeah? And where is that?" I tested.

"With me." His voice was deep and brimming with confidence. "And with Taylor."

Hearing her name strangled my heart.

"I know you don't want to let yourself feel happiness while she's still out there hurting. It's who you are, Jemma, and I wouldn't change it for a second. No matter how hard it is for me to hold back sometimes, I do get it."

In all my despair, it occurred to me that I must've done *something* right in my life to deserve him. With wilted, slow-dying petals and gruesome thorns, to him, I was still a beautiful rose worth saving—worth fighting for.

I rested my head on his chest and held on to the only

semblance of sun I had left in my life. The wonderful humming sensation that I'd come to know and love set sail under my skin, soothing my body and my mind as it charged through my blood.

Yawning, I felt myself drift away, falling closer and closer to a dreamlike state until my exhaustion finally closed in on me.

23. RUNNING SCARED

The blood skies stretched into the horizon like an omen of death; of carnage. I stood alone in a small clearing in the woods, my mind racing almost as fast as my heart was. There was something I was supposed to do, something I had to remember, but I couldn't work out the equation in my head no matter how hard I tried to piece it together.

A menacing shadow mingled with mine as Dominic took his place beside me. He always seemed to have a starring role in my nightmares and this one was no exception. He stood facing the horizon with his arm touching mine, wearing only a pair of black pants and an impish smirk on his mouth. His blond curls looked as though they'd been dusted in pink powder, reflections from the strange red sky that poured down on us like a bloody warning.

"Come now, angel. It's almost time," he said and then walked out of the clearing and into the darkened forest, melting with the shadows and trees as skeletal branches reached out to wrap him in their ominous embrace.

I followed after him without any question, first running to catch up with him, and then watching hungrily as he weaved his way in and out of the brushwood, leading me deeper and deeper into the woods. I followed ravenously, hungrily, craving him and everything he may have been offering.

The red sky darkened as we moved deeper into the forest, almost as though it were frowning down on our trespasses. I reached out to stop him from walking, from venturing deeper into the forbidden lands, but he mistook my gesture and spun on me. With fire in his eyes, his hands reached out for my hips, my body, holding, clutching, digging into my skin as he pulled me into the space between his arms. Icy cold kisses peppered my neck as a rush of excitement barreled through my blood. I instantly knew what was coming.

I tipped my head back, surrendering all my restraint and hope, and then, just like I knew it would, the sharp, scorching pain quickly came for me. Harrowing and infinite like death itself, it consumed my being from the deepest part of my soul right down to the flesh he was tearing into.

"Your blood is the wine."

A murder of crows cut across the red sky as blood spit out from my neck like a fiery volcano that knew no bounds, and I instantly knew...

Death was knocking.

I shot upright in my bed and let out a guttural scream, though the sound was quickly muffled by a hand that clamped down over my mouth.

"It's just a dream," whispered Trace, consoling me in the dark. "I got you." He slipped his arm around my back and gently laid me back down against my pillow.

The room was consumed by shadows. Only a sliver of light peeked in from a slit in the curtains, but it was enough light to see Trace's face and make my hammering heart simmer down. His beautiful eyes gazed down at me, reassuring me, and instantly making everything better again; instantly, making it easy for me to forget the terror.

I *needed* to forget.

I reached up through the darkness and wrapped my arms around his neck, clasping onto him in desperation as I sealed my mouth over his and pulled him back down with me.

"Jemma," he groaned against my mouth as though he thought this was a bad idea, as though he thought we should stop, but it only made me kiss him harder.

He braced himself, fisting the sheets on either side of me as I deepened the kiss for the both of us. His lips were moving with mine, kissing me back, but I could feel the restraint behind them. I could taste the control he was trying to keep over himself.

I moved my hands down from his face to his neck, roaming freely over the expanse of his chest and the swells of his arms. The more I touched him, the more he responded, and the more my body sizzled with electricity. I didn't want it to stop. I wanted more of it—all of it—to burn like an asteroid blazing through the atmosphere.

I parted my lips and gently swept my tongue along his, daring him to let go—to give into me. His breathing instantly turned sharper, faster, his kisses growing more urgent with every immeasurable second that ticked by us.

He drew back suddenly, hovering above me as he fought to hold onto what little self-control he had left. His jaw flexed furiously, hungrily, as his eyes filled up with unbridled want.

And then, as easy as flicking off a light switch, the restraint was gone.

I felt him shift above me as his knee came up and eased my legs apart, his gaze never leaving mine. My breath caught in my throat as he laid himself back down on me, resting his body in the uncharted space between my hips.

His mouth found mine again and he kissed me fiercely, filling me with a surge of emotions that made my body tremor in response. Excitement, fear, anticipation, exhilaration, curiosity, each one hitting me in waves as they funneled through my body like exotic spices I'd never tasted.

There was something in the air, something between us, like a tonic that neither one of us could turn down. And I didn't want to turn it down. I wanted to indulge in its sap and let it take me to that beautiful place where only he and I existed. He was the antidote to my deepest, darkest nightmare. The answer to my prayers. Nothing could touch me here. Not my pain or heartbreak or inadequacy, not the Council or uncle or Engel...not even Dominic and his daunting bloodbond could reach me here.

Here, I was untouchable.

I held onto him tighter, digging my nails into his skin as he trailed a stream of kisses along my jaw and then down to the space below my ear. His hands moved to my side, clutching my hips and then my waist as his thumbs grazed along the flimsy hem of my shirt. Taking the fabric in his hands, he pulled it up slowly, achingly slow, memorizing the lands of my body as he explored every hill and groove beneath my shirt. His warm hands and soft lips brushed against my abdomen in tandem, peppering my skin with caresses that made my stomach tighten and my toes curl.

He was a god fit for a throne and every touch reaffirmed his status as he skirted me closer and closer to the brink. I arched my head back and called out his name like a prayer.

He quickly slid back up my body, pressing his lips against mine to keep me contained, to keep me from freefalling into oblivion. I couldn't get enough of him, of his lips, his hands, the way his body molded itself against mine.

I was teetering on the edge of insanity and every cell in my body was screaming for me to jump.

"I'm crazy about you, Jemma." His breath was as silky and sweet as melted sugar. "I can't get you out of my head. You're the only thing I think about anymore."

And now, I was freefalling.

I pulled his shirt up over his head, surprising myself at how easily I accomplished the feat. His skin was scorching-hot to the touch, his chest rising and falling almost as quickly as mine was. Our want for each other had reached new levels. It was palpable, undeniable.

Cupping my face, he lowered his head again and pressed his lips against mine, only this time, his kisses were softer, slower, measured touches that made me ignite from within—made my entire body shake with an appetite I couldn't define or describe or decipher. It was all too much yet nowhere near being enough. I'd never felt anything like this in my entire life, and it made me tremble from the inside out.

He pulled back suddenly and looked down at me. His eyes were filled with so much fire that, for a second, I thought surely it was my own reflection being mirrored back to me.

"You've done this before, right?" he asked me, gazing down at me as he studied my reaction.

My heart started beating faster, louder, so loud that I was sure he could hear it too.

I shook my head.

The mere seconds felt like hours before he said anything. "Are you sure you want to do this?" he asked, his eyes gleaming as they stripped me down to my soul—discovering, uncovering, listening in for the smallest hint of uncertainty.

Tomorrow was promised to no one, least of all to me. All I had was this moment with Trace, and in this moment, everything was perfect. I couldn't bear to let it go; to fall back into my living nightmare.

"Yes," I rasped as I swallowed the finality of it all—the no-going-back*ness*. "I want to."

Silence.

"Don't *you* want to?"

He laughed quietly, all deep and gruff and sexy. The sound of it sent a shiver through my body. "You have no idea how bad I want to," he said, teasing me with his perfectly timed dimples.

"So, *you* want to, and *I* want to..." I started to pull him back down to me, but he stopped us again.

More silence.

"What's wrong? Why do you keep stopping?" I asked, confused by his obvious reluctance.

He hesitated before answering. "I just want it to be...you know." He licked his lips as he stared down at mine.

My eyebrows rose. "Good? You're scared it won't be good?"

He laughed again. "No. I'm not worried about that," he said with the kind of cockiness that made me want to put him to the test. "I meant *special*. I want it to be special."

"Oh." I smiled up at him, at his sweetness. "It will be," I decided, circling my arms around his neck. "It's me and you, Trace."

He nodded as though he agreed, yet he still wasn't moving.

"Something else?" I asked, growing increasingly impatient with his extended time-outs.

"I don't know," he said, shrugging as though it weren't weighing heavily on him, but his pensive eyes told an entirely different story. "Shouldn't there be like flowers or candles or something?"

"For me or you?"

"Jemma."

I laughed. "I don't know, is that the rule?" I asked sarcastically, though he didn't find it amusing. "I'm not really a flowers and chocolate kind of girl, Trace. I don't need all that stuff." Besides, who knew if I would get another chance? I wanted to seize the day, the moment—*carpe diem* and all that crap.

"No one *needs* that stuff," he said softly, "but I still think you deserve it." I could see the struggle in his face, the warring emotions in his eyes, and then the forfeiture as he pulled away completely and sat back down on the edge of my bed...just out of my reach.

Well, that deescalated quickly.

I yanked up my sheet and covered myself before propping my back against the headboard.

"I want to do this right, Jemma." He pushed his fingers through his ebony hair and looked down at me. "And I want to do it for the right reason."

Something about the way he said it made me pause. "What is the right reason?"

"Because you love me. Not because you're scared you might not get another chance or because you want to prove the bloodbond isn't affecting you."

I lowered my eyes, realizing he'd heard me. "It's not the only reason," I defended.

"I know, but it's a part of it, and I guess I'm not okay with that."

"I didn't mean for it to seem that way." I turned away from the heaviness of his downcast eyes. "I just wanted to feel like myself again, to have one *normal* night where the weight of the world wasn't sitting on my shoulders."

He placed his hand on my leg, calling back my attention. "It won't always be that way."

I gave him a doubtful look.

"I'll make sure of it," he promised. "I'll take the world apart for you and put it back together again if I have to."

I smiled at him as I remembered what future Trace had said.

The vow he made to me that day in my room.

He reached over and grabbed a hold of my hips, pulling me across the bed to him. "Besides, when we do decide to do it," he said, moving a strand of hair from my eyes, "it'll be a lot of things, but *normal* won't be one of them."

I felt the heat rush up to my cheeks as he leaned down and brushed his lips against mine.

Something told me that nothing with Trace would ever feel as mundane and uneventful as *normal*.

We spent the rest of the night alone in my room, holding each other as though we didn't know how to exist without the other, and while we both flirted on the edge of our forever, neither one of us crossed over that line again.

24. BLOODSPORT

I spent most of Friday evening training with Gabriel at Temple. Although I could probably think of a hundred things I'd rather be doing on any given Friday night, I knew it was what I needed to be doing. The harder I trained, the better my chances were at facing off against Engel and anything else out there that meant to cause me or the people I loved harm.

Gabriel seemed to be impressed with how well things were progressing. I could tell that he sensed a shift in my attitude and that I was finally taking my training seriously.

"Nice takedown," he said, complimenting me after I kicked his feet out from under him and knocked him to the ground. He was sprawled out on the sparring mat and never looked prouder.

"Thanks." I smiled proudly and offered him my hand.

He took it and hopped back up to his feet quickly, a small smile sprouting on the corner of his mouth. "You're getting stronger every day, Jemma. It's only a matter of time now."

"Before what?" I asked, retying my ponytail.

"Before you no longer need me." He tipped his head once like an exclamation mark to his statement.

A pang of sadness seeped into my heart at the thought of no longer having this time with Gabriel. He'd become so much more to me than just my temporary Handler. He was my mentor, my friend, someone I could always count on to look out for me—to throw me over their shoulder and carry me home when I'd had too much to drink.

"I'm not sure I'm ready for that."

"You will be," he said with certainty. "This is what you were meant to do. Once the spell is fully broken, you will feel the pull—the call to service."

"My uncle doesn't think they'll be able to break the spell without the talisman," I said, watching his expression for any clues as to what he was thinking. "He said something about an ancient ritual."

"Invocation." His olive-colored eyes seemed to dim at the uttering of the word.

"That bad?"

"I haven't witnessed it personally, but I have heard...rumors."

"And?" I was certain none of them were good. His hesitation to answer only further confirmed it for me.

"From what I've heard, it's dangerous and archaic," he finally said sans emotion. "Frankly, I'm surprised it was even mentioned. Invocation is supposed to be a last resort."

"A last resort? Archaic?" My face contorted at his strange choice of words. "What the hell kind of ritual is this?"

"The only way to invoke your abilities would be to bring you as close to death as possible," he explained calmly, like he was teaching me how to flip a freakin' pancake. "By removing the safety net entirely."

"And how exactly are they going to do that?"

Gabriel struggled to answer.

"Think one ravaged beast, one Slayer-to-be and a fight to the death in an arena for our personal enjoyment," answered Julian as he tossed the magazine he was reading onto the bench.

My eyes snapped back to Gabriel. "He's' joking, right?"

"Unfortunately not."

"That's absurd, and I'm pretty sure it's illegal."

"Human law doesn't apply to us, Jemma. Not in that way."

"They don't call it an *ancient* ritual for nothing," said Julian, smirking. He was getting way to much enjoyment out of this. I bet he was just dying to get himself a front-row seat, hoping that maybe, just maybe, I'd get my head torn off.

"There's no way I'm doing that," I said, deciding to just reject the whole idea in its entirety. "We need to start training harder. My uncle said it's possible to invoke my abilities on my own so that's what we're going to do," I informed, deciding to leave out the part where he said that it wasn't very likely to happen.

"Yes, it's possible," said Gabriel, his steadfast eyes fixed on me. "We'd have to up the threat level significantly."

"Maybe we can start training outside of Temple," I suggested. The only real way to raise the threat level was to put myself in an uncontrolled environment. I knew Gabriel would never hurt me, and that was great for our friendship and all, but it did nothing for scaring my Slayer abilities out of me.

"The Council would have to approve it first," he said, running a hand through his dark hair.

"They'll never allow that," sneered Julian, pleased by the rock and hard place I'd just found myself in.

"Well maybe I'm not going to ask them for their permission." I turned back to Gabriel, my eyes burning with wild determination. "They're not the one that has to go into the Arena—I am, so shouldn't *I* get to make the call on this? You yourself said the whole thing was archaic."

He didn't say anything but I could see the agreement in his eyes. "It may not have to come to that," he offered instead, doing his best to keep things on a positive, rule-abiding note. "The Cloak *is* fading. Your essence is breaking through more and more every day."

"My essence?"

"Your *scent*. If I can sense you, it's only a matter of time before you can sense me as well."

"Really?" I felt a small ray of hope ignite inside me.

"It's slow moving, yes, but it *is* working."

I thought about it. "All the more reason to step-up my training then, right?" Unfortunately for me, I was quickly running out of time and no longer had the luxury of letting things naturally run their course.

"That does appear to be the best course of action."

"So you'll talk to the Council then? You'll make them see it our way, right?"

"I'll get us an audience with the Magister," he conceded after a short pause. "We'll present our request and take it one day at a time."

If by one day at a time, he meant that we were doing this with or without them, then I was totally on board. I wasn't entirely sure Gabriel would be willing to step out of line when it came to Council orders, but one thing I knew for sure, I wasn't stepping foot in that arena.

I would do this myself if I had to.

All I needed was one feral Revenant and someone to back me up in case things went really, *really* wrong. Trace was a scratch right off the bat. He was too invested in me to ever let a hair on my head be moved. Knowing this, I would instantly feel at ease with him watching over me, which would do nothing for raising my personal threat level.

That only left one person...

Dominic.

Somehow it always came back to Dominic. After all, he was

the obvious choice. Firstly, he didn't care about me—not in any real way anyway. He was strong, available, and twisted enough to agree to it. Heck, he'd probably even get a kick out of watching me fall to my knees at the mercy of some untamed Rev.

All I needed was a little *incentive* to win him over, a little something to make it worthwhile for him. And I had just the right thing pumping through my veins. Only question was, would I be willing to give it to him?

25. THE PLAN

Trace picked me up later that evening after Gabriel and I finished training, and together we headed over to Dominic's for round two of our experiment. My uncle Karl had no problem letting me stay out late on account of it not being a school night, though I'm sure it had more to do with the fact that I was with Trace. We'd left him under the false pretense that Trace was taking me out for a late-night dinner and movie. Frankly, he seemed rather ecstatic about the whole idea. I still couldn't figure out why he and Peter Macarthur seemed so adamant on me and Trace spending time together, but I knew something *had* to be up with that.

Of course, there was the obvious reason: they hoped that it would tempt Trace to rejoin the Order and take his rightful place as my Keeper. But was that all there was to it? Something told me I was only scratching the surface when it came to the secrets my uncle and Trace's father were keeping.

"Care for a drink, love?" asked Dominic as Trace stepped out of the room to take a phone call. "It'll help take the edge off."

I looked down at his assortment of dark liquor and shook my head. I could still taste the vomit at the back of my throat from the last time I "took the edge off".

A crooked grin danced across his lips as though I'd done something *cute* or amusing to him. "You really should learn to loosen up, angel."

"I think I'm loose enough." I cringed at my own poor choice of words as Dominic chuckled softly. "I meant that I don't need to be relaxed. In fact, I need to be exactly the opposite of relaxed."

"You ought not to take life so seriously." He walked over to the sofa and took a seat next to the raging fire. "It's not like any of us are going to make it out alive. Well, unless you're immortal like me, that is."

"Deep," I said, flopping down into the chair across from him. My wooden stake dug into the back of my leg, prompting me to spring back up. I pulled out the stake from my back pocket and tossed it onto the coffee table.

"I see your training is progressing delightfully," he said, picking up my weapon and examining it. "You know they mean business when they give you your very own stick," he said mockingly, his silky voice laced with contempt.

"Yeah, and I know how to use it too," I warned him. Even though my aim still wasn't perfect, it had significantly improved over the course of my training and I was fairly certain I could hit my mark on the first shot. Second at the most. "Now I just need to figure out how to carry the stupid thing. It keeps cutting into my leg every time I sit down," I added, irritated by the inconvenience. I'd come dangerously close to tearing myself a new one on more than one occasion.

He got up and casually strode over to the bookshelf. Opening a small box, he pulled out a narrow leather case with a strap attached and threw it over to me.

"What is it?"

"A sheath," he said plainly as I fumbled with it in my hands.

"It goes around your ankle, love."

"I knew that." I turned it right-side up and then smiled up at him. "Thank you."

Sitting back down on the sofa, he crossed his leg and watched as I pulled up my pant leg up and angled the holster against my calf.

"I met with Engel again this evening," he informed, his eyes still fixed on my exposed leg.

My eyes cut to him.

"I attempted to syphon some information from him," he continued and then licked his lips, "about that temptress bloodline of yours."

"And?"

"I'd say things have taken a turn for the worse." His dark eyes met mine lazily. "He was asking a lot more questions, and offering a lot less answers."

"What kind of questions?" I asked, quirking a brow at him.

"About your habits, your friends, places you frequent. He seems rather preoccupied with you—with discovering what you really are." He spoke evenly, like he was discussing the menu at a restaurant and not my goddamned life. "My guess is, he already knows something but he hasn't put all the pieces together yet. Either way, it's not particularly looking good for you, angel."

That noose-like chokehold was back with a vengeance.

"What about the Amulet? Do you think he's planning on going back on our deal? The Amulet for Taylor?" Not that I had any intention of following through with it, but it would certainly make it harder for us to guess his next move if he had his own plans in mind.

"I can't say for sure, though he certainly appears to have shifted gears."

"We can't leave anything to chance." I tightened the strap on my sheath and then lowered my pant leg. "We need to make the first move—catch him off guard."

"Like an ambush?" verified Dominic as he sipped his drink.

"Exactly." I sat back in my chair and thought it over. "I don't want him to see us coming. It has to be before Friday, otherwise he'll be ready for us. We'll be playing right into whatever he might have planned." I glanced over my shoulder at the entrance to make sure Trace wasn't heading back our way.

Dominic's eyes followed mine. "I think it's about time we involve the Reaper. I'd venture that he isn't good for much, but we could certainly use a few extra bodies on our side."

Bodies.

That was exactly what I was afraid of. There was no way I was going to allow Trace to go to his death trying to protect me—to save me. I could only expunge one life-threat at a time and this wasn't Trace's day. Even though I had my suspicions about the validity of Morgan's vision, not to mention her intentions, I still wasn't sure what to believe and I wasn't willing to bet Trace's life on an uncertainty. "I don't want him involved," I said firmly.

"That's not your decision to make," said a deep, edgy voice from the entrance way.

My eyes snapped up to Trace. He was leaning with his shoulder against the wall and a displeased expression on his exquisitely chiseled face.

"I don't need you to protect me, Jemma. I'm supposed to protect you."

"Well I'm not the one that has the death omen looming over my head," I countered. "You shouldn't be there, Trace. It's too dangerous, and probably suicide. I couldn't live with myself if something happened to you knowing it was all my fault."

"And if something happens to you instead?" He plodded across the room with purpose. "Do you think I want to live with myself knowing I wasn't there to protect you?"

"You're both making me ill," interceded Dominic, grimacing at the both of us.

"This isn't going anywhere." I rubbed my temples for relief from the migraine that was beginning to set in.

"That's because you're too busy secretly trying to protect each other rather than working together. You're going to get yourselves killed, and probably me in the process," he added dryly. "Stick to the plan, play your role smartly, and each of us will come out of this with what we want."

"Yeah, and what is it that we want?" verified Trace, eyeing Dominic suspiciously.

"The Amulet. The blond. And Engel dead, of course."

Trace didn't appear to be entirely convinced that Dominic's intentions were pure, and if I was being completely honest with myself, I wasn't entirely sure of it either.

"So what *is* the plan?" I asked him, deciding to get a feel for where his head was before making any outright accusations. "How are we doing this?"

His stare darkened as the diabolic wheels in his mind began to churn. "It's fairly simple in theory. You and I go after Engel, Romeo finds the girl and ports her out of there, and when it's all done and over with, we meet up for milk and cookies to celebrate."

"Where are they keeping her?" asked Trace, ignoring Dominic's blithe comment.

"She's on the premises though I'm unsure of her exact whereabouts," he said casually as though it hardly affected our plan.

"Then we're going to need a tracker."

"Is that like a GPS?" I asked dimly.

"Less technical, more biological," answered Trace. "Someone who can hunt her down by her scent." He ticked his chin in Dominic's direction. "A shifter."

"Like Ben," I said and then thought of something. "Does he know what's going on?"

Trace shook his head. "You know how he feels about Taylor. He would've tried to do something stupid if I told him."

"Maybe it's time to clue him in," I suggested. "He probably knows her scent better than anyone else, and he's a Shifter."

Trace nodded once. "I'll get him in."

"Good. And while we're on the topic of fragrances," I began, a troubling thought having just occurred to me, "what about mine? If we're going to ambush them, won't they sense me coming? Gabriel said the Cloak is fading."

"Yes, I did notice that as well." Dominic smiled as though he were catching a whiff of it now.

I waited for him to catch up.

The smile quickly dropped off. "It would certainly pose a problem if they caught your scent beforehand."

"Right. So, what do we do about it?"

He took a slow sip of his drink, his expression unwavering. "I may have to make the first strike alone."

"That's too dangerous. We don't know how many of his men will be with him."

His grin reappeared. "I can take care of myself, love. You needn't worry about me."

"Don't flatter yourself, Dominic." I pinned him under a hard glare. "I need you to help me take him down, and obviously, you can't do that if you're dead—or deader than you already are."

"Charming." He stretched his arm along the back of the sofa and settled in. "You could, of course, infuse me with your blood. It may give me the necessary edge to withstand the initial onslaught."

I nodded at his quick thinking. With the Amulet around my neck, and my blood in his veins, we'd pretty much be unbeatable. I was really starting to like our odds. "So, Ben tracks Taylor, Trace ports them out, and Dominic and I go after Engel."

"We'll meet beforehand to get our affairs in order. Make sure you come armed. You'll need more than that one stick, love," he said, ticking his chin to my ankle and then turning to Trace. "And a whole lot of Cinderdust."

"Already on it," said Trace as he pulled out his phone and padded out the room.

"Call me crazy but I think this just might work," I affirmed, and surprisingly, my voice didn't waver when I said it.

Dominic leaned back, looking satisfied with himself. After a brief stint of silence, he looked across at me pointedly. "You know, love, you'd miss me if I were gone," he cautioned, though it sounded more like a threat than a warning.

"I'm sure I would recover." I shifted uneasily in my chair under his penetrating gaze.

There was something knowing about his eyes, something dark and haunting, and as much as it sent cold chills down my spine, it also intrigued me—beckoned me in a way I didn't quite understand. Somehow, I couldn't seem to turn my back on the darkness and that scared me even more than Dominic did.

26. DANCE OF THE DEAD

My decision to go to Caleb's party Saturday night was an easy one, though not one completely void of ulterior motives. I needed to ask Caleb for a favor; a favor that required his particular brand of magic. Trace, of course, had his own reasons for deciding to tag along with me. I secretly hoped it was only because he wanted to spend more time with me and not because he was looking for a second round with Caleb.

The bass reverberated through the house as Trace and I walked into the party together. As massive as Caleb and Carly's house was, the space always felt small and crammed at these parties, like there wasn't enough quality oxygen to go around—probably because more than half of Weston's student body was usually in attendance, and that wasn't even counting the busloads from Easton Prep. Rivalry or not, booze and the possibility of a random hookup was all that was needed for everyone to put down their arms and school spirit.

I relaxed back against the kitchen counter as Trace and Ben poured themselves a drink over at the make-shift bar. Otherwise known as the kitchen table. Lost in my own thoughts, I ran my finger over the spot on my palm where we'd made the incision last night. It was almost fully healed. After one too many unwanted dreams about Dominic, I decided to skip the direct bite and go with the no-contact version instead. I didn't want to risk strengthening the bloodbond any more than it already was, and while this pleased Trace to no ends, Dominic was singing a completely different tune.

Even still, there was an underlining satisfaction in his eyes that made me uneasy, like he knew the bloodbond was beginning to have an effect on me, and he was reveling in it.

"Looking good, Blackburn," said Caleb as he leaned into the empty spot beside me.

"Thanks." I smiled, dropping my hands. "Nice turnout."

"Yeah. Not bad." He frowned as his gaze shifted across the room. "It would've been nicer if you left the shadow at home though," he muttered.

Obviously, he had yet to kiss and make up with Trace.

"How long are you two planning on keeping this up?" I wondered. "You've both made your point. It's getting old."

"Feels pretty fresh to me." His sand dune colored eyes narrowed like he was itching to start something.

"Well, it's not. It's *stupid*," I added tactlessly. "You guys don't even like the same girl. He isn't interested in Nikki, Caleb. Trust me." My eyes bounced to Trace, who was stuck in the corner, getting his ear talked off by Hannah.

"What makes you so sure it's about her?" he asked, apparently trying to deflect my comment by getting his flirt-on.

"Because I know when a boy likes a girl. And you like a girl, Caleb. But it's not me."

His cockiness seemed to fade a little as he looked down at me. It definitely felt like we had a moment, though it was abruptly obliterated when a naked sophomore ran through the kitchen, screaming, *Go Bulldogs*, wearing nothing but a hockey helmet in front of his crotch.

"I really hope I didn't look anything like that at Nikki's party last week." You know, stupid and drunk.

"I think that might have been my goalie," said Caleb, shaking his head "And, no, you didn't. You looked pretty hot actually. Well, up until you started blowing chunks anyway," he amended without thinking it through.

"Right. Thanks for reminding me."

He flashed his pearly whites. "Any chance I can get another dance with you later, or is he claiming you for the night?" he asked, ticking his chin in Trace's direction.

"Well, we came together so..." I shrugged it off, unsure of how to finish the sentence. "So, where's Nikki tonight anyway? Shouldn't you be putting in some time with her, earning those brownie points and whatnot?"

"That's not likely." He crossed his arms over his chest and shifted his gaze to the crowd as if searching for her. "I haven't really spoken to her since her party."

"I'm sorry. I didn't mean to mess things up for you." I definitely didn't regret exposing her two-timing ways in front of everyone, though I wished it wouldn't have been at Caleb's expense.

"Nah. It was messed up long before that," he said and then squared his shoulders as though he'd just revealed more than he was comfortable with.

"You deserve better than what she gives you."

He nodded weakly, still staring ahead.

I studied him for a moment and then decided to leave it alone. He'd come around when he was ready to and hopefully realize that he deserved more than the scraps Nikki was giving him.

"Hey, you think we could meet up tomorrow?" I asked, biting the inside of my cheek. "I need a favor but it kind of has to stay between the two of us."

His eyebrows rose with intrigue. "What kind of favor?"

"One that requires your special brand of *talent*."

"I'm guessing this isn't hockey related."

I laughed. "No, not hockey related."

"Alright, I can dig that. I have practice tomorrow night, but I'm free all afternoon," he offered.

"I'll take it."

"So, still no chance on that dance, huh?" he asked as Trace and Ben headed back our way; drinks in hand.

"Unlike some people, I can only handle one guy at a time." I gave him a pointed stare. "Raincheck maybe?"

"Yeah, alright." He smiled sincerely. "I'm holding you to it though. And, Blackburn," he said, calling my attention back as my gaze shifted away to Trace. "I hope he knows how lucky he is."

My cheeks warmed.

"What's poppin', Owens." Ben put his fist out to Caleb as Trace moved in beside me and handed me my drink.

"Pratt," greeted Caleb, happily bumping his fist. "Hope that's a virgin," teased Caleb, ticking his chin to my drink as I took a swig.

"Ha. Ha." I rolled my eyes at him and then quickly looked up at Trace. "It is, right?" I verified. I really, *really* didn't want to have a repeat of Nikki's bitch-bash.

"Yeah, it's just a coke," he said, wrapping his arm around my waist and dropping a kiss on the top of my head.

"Woah. Looks like it's getting serious over here," razzed Ben, tweaking his sandy eyebrows at Trace and me. "Are you two official now? Is team *Tremma* a thing yet?"

"Oh, my God." I dropped my head and tried to disappear into my own shirt. "Could you be any more embarrassing?"

"I could try." He winked.

"Try being less of an ass instead," chided Trace as he placed our drinks on the counter.

"What can I say, man? I'm an ass man."

I couldn't help but laugh. Even if it was at my expense, it was nice seeing Ben smiling and joking around again. It was such a rare occurrence these days, I nearly forgot what it looked like. I glanced up at Trace to see if he was laughing too and caught him staring down at me with a soft, adoring look in his eyes.

"Dance with me," he said, and it wasn't a question.

I was about to sass him about ordering me around, but then he took my hand in his and smiled at me—a smile that reached all the way to his stunning eyes and instantly made me want to follow him anywhere.

"Okay," I said, and decided to leave out the part about how I'd walk into a raging fire if he asked me to.

Clasping my hand, he led us into the low-lit living room and through the crowd, maneuvering his way around the mess of bodies like he'd run this track hundreds of times before, until he found a quiet spot by the back window. Turning to me, he reached out and wrapped his arms around my waist, pulling me into the shadowy corner with him; away from prying eyes and callous whispers. My heart sputtered an erratic beat as he ran his hands down my back and began moving us in a slow-burning tempo that sent tremors of electricity shooting across my skin.

"Are you trying to keep me distracted to avoid talking to Caleb?" I asked, trying not to get too swept up in him. It was futile though, because the minute I looked up and met his eyes, I was freefalling right into them.

"Maybe." He stepped in closer to me, his black boots planted on each side of my feet, caging me in. "Or maybe I just wanted to kiss you." He licked his lips and smiled, revealing his perfect set of dimples.

My temperature spiked just looking at him.

I pushed up on my toes and pulled his mouth to mine. I

couldn't help myself even if I tried. He smiled against my lips and then immediately kissed me back, tugging my hips forward as he greeted me with the warmth of his tongue. A pulsating current shot through my veins as he deepened the kiss, and I nearly toppled over from the buzz.

Stunned, I pulled back and looked up at him, wondering if he'd felt that too.

"What *is* that?" I asked him breathlessly.

"What is *what*?" He moved my hair over my shoulder and leaned in, grazing his lips against my neck.

The charge intensified. "It's like my skin vibrates every time you touch me." Lately, it didn't even need to be skin-to-skin contact anymore. It seemed to buzz right through my clothes now.

He pulled back and looked at me without saying anything.

Oh, God. "Is it just me?" I asked, feeling all the heat in my body rush up to my cheeks.

He ran his thumb along my blushing cheek as though he wanted to feel the color. "No. I feel it too."

"Is it one of the *things* you do?" I whispered, not wanting to outright ask him about his abilities in mixed company.

He shook his head. "I only feel it when I'm with you."

"Oh." I pulled in my bottom lip as I thought it over. "So, what is it then?" I asked him, coming up empty of my own explanations. "What does it mean?"

He hesitated before answering like he wasn't sure what to say. "I don't know what it means."

"Yes, you do." I narrowed my eyes at him.

He leaned in again, running his jaw along my cheek, and then moved to my ear. "I think it just means our souls are happy when they're near each other," he whispered in that husky baritone voice that was all his.

My heart did a backflip in my chest. "What, like soulmates

or something?" I asked, watching as he flexed his jaw.

"Maybe." He pulled back and gazed down at me, his own eyes unreadable.

"Do you really believe in that?"

"That our souls can recognize their other half?"

I nodded.

"That people are placed in each other's lives for reason—that it's not purely coincidence?" he continued, getting *really* specific about it.

I swallowed my anticipation and nodded again.

"Yeah, I believe in it." His eyes never wavered from mine. "I believe in a lot of things."

"Yeah? Like what?" I smiled, completely enamored by him. Suddenly, I wanted to know all about it. I wanted to keep him talking until every last word in the English language had been used up.

"I believe in *you*." He kissed me again, harder this time. "That you're going to be a force to be reckoned with."

"Me?" I puffed out a laugh, certain that he was placating me. "I'm practically afraid of my own shadow."

"Doesn't make a difference if you are or aren't." He shrugged like it was inconsequential. "It doesn't stop you from doing what you have to do. Everyone's afraid of something, Jemma. It doesn't mean you're weak. It means you're alive. It takes real courage to feel that fear and do it anyway."

"You think so?" I hadn't really thought of it that way.

"I know so." He tucked a strand of my hair behind my ear and then grazed my cheek with his thumb.

I could easily fall in love with the way he was looking at me. Like I was something special; something worth fighting for.

"You are," he answered with absolute conviction. He lowered his mouth to mine and pulled a kiss from my lips, soft as an angel's feather. "It's like you have all this light inside of you, but you can't see it. It chases away the darkness in people and draws them in closer to you. It's one of things I love most about you," he whispered, sending shivers down my arms, "but it's also one of the things that scares me the most."

"Why does that scare you?" I asked, confused by his quiet confession.

"Seeing the affect you have on people—people like Dominic." He blinked slowly, his eyebrows pulled together in concern. "I'd be lying if I said it didn't make me nervous."

"I can handle Dominic."

"And if you can't?" His jaw ticked as something unpleasant passed before his eyes. "I'd kill him if he ever hurt you. If anyone ever hurt you—"

"No one's going to hurt me," I quickly cut in, forcing the conversation back to a happier, safer place. It didn't matter that neither one of us believed me; it felt wrong hearing him say it out loud, like the heavens might hear our words and make them so.

Trace grimaced. "I wish I could take this all away for you. Give you the life you really deserve."

I held onto him tighter, wishing the same for him; for both of us.

"Maybe when this is all over, we can go somewhere nice. Somewhere far away from here where no one knows us and the sun never sets." The twinkle in his blue eyes made my heart flutter.

"You know a place like that?"

"If I did, would you go with me?" he asked, his majestic eyes filled with the kind of unbridled hope and vulnerability I was rarely permitted to witness from him.

"I'd go anywhere with you, Trace." And it was the truth.

Probably the truest words I ever uttered.

27. DRAGON'S BLOOD

Less than twenty-four hours later, I was back at Caleb's house—sans Trace—standing on his front porch as I waited for him to answer the door. I was about to give up and leave when he finally answered, wearing nothing but a white bath towel and water beads cascading down from his wet, tousled hair. My mouth fell open at the sight of it.

Apparently, he was quite an athlete.

"Hey, Blackburn." He stepped back from the threshold to let me in. "Just give me a minute to change. I just got out of the shower."

I tried to tell him, "sure thing," but what came out sounded a lot more like a gibberish mumble. Heck, it could've been pig-Latin for all I knew. I gave up and nodded instead.

Once inside, I headed into the kitchen and pulled out a chair at the table—the same table that was covered with kegs and plastic red cups just a few short hours ago was now adorned in textbooks and homework assignments. There was no way he cleaned this place up all by himself, especially in such a short time frame. He probably had a maid...or a magic wand.

Five short minutes later, Caleb reappeared—fully clothed in

pair of blue jeans and a matching Henley shirt.

"So, what's this favor you want to ask me?" He sat down on the chair across from me and tapped his hands on the table as he waited for me to solve the mystery.

"I need you to do a spell for me."

His eyebrows shot up, intrigued. "What kind of spell?"

"A Cloaking spell." If we were going to ambush Engel, I needed to make sure they couldn't sense me coming.

His head ticked back a notch, expressing his confusion. "Aren't you already Cloaked?"

I didn't bother going into the details about the current state of my wavering Cloak. "I need something more powerful," I explained. "Something that would mask me from Revs. Are you able to do that?"

He laughed smugly. "I've been casting since before I could walk. Pretty sure I could handle it." He winked.

"Good. And, I need it to be attached to a talisman," I clarified. "I have to be able to break the spell when I'm done with it." I wasn't interested in having that whole can't-break-the-Cloak issue all over again.

"Not a problem." He tilted his head to the side. "So, do you just want to eliminate any Slayer essence or do you want to replace it with something else? Like a human scent, or maybe some other Sup?"

"Sup?"

"Supernatural."

My eyebrows rose in surprise. "You can do that?"

"I can just about do anything," he said with a cocky grin splayed from ear-to-ear.

"Even replicate a Revenant's essence?"

He snorted like there was nothing to it. "Just say the word." He grinned.

I was so impressed I didn't even bother trying to knock his

arrogance down a peg. "Oh, and I need something else from you. A protection spell...for Trace."

His sunny disposition quickly evaporated.

"I know you're not talking to him right now, but he was your friend at some point, wasn't he?" I tried pleading to his sentimental side though I wasn't sure he had one. "He's going to help me get Taylor back, and it's going to be stupid dangerous. If something happens to him…" I shook my head, chasing away the thought of it. "I wouldn't be able to live with myself. Could you?"

He grimaced as I cornered him with guilt. "I'm not sure what I could do," he began cautiously. "Protection spells are pretty limited. The business of life and death isn't exactly the kind of spells the Order gives us access to."

"Well, what *can* you do? There has to be something."

He ran his hand along his slight five-o'clock shadow and then pinned his eyes on me. "Dragon's blood."

"Come again?"

"Dragon's blood," he repeated as though I were hard of hearing. "I guess you haven't gotten that far in your lectures at Temple. He only needs a few drops. It'll make him faster, stronger, and a lot more resilient to pain." He shrugged. "It's probably the best I can do."

"I'll take it."

I had a text from Caleb first thing Monday morning, asking me to meet him in the art room before class. I stopped at my locker to drop of my schoolbag and lunch, and then hurried down the east hall to the Art room.

Cracking the door open, I peered inside to make sure the coast was clear. Caleb was already there, sitting on one of the tables, waiting for me.

"Fancy seeing you here," he said as I closed the door behind myself and joined him where he sat.

"Did you get it?"

He opened his schoolbag and pulled out a black suede satchel. "Did you doubt me?"

"First and last time. You're amazing!" I took the bag from him and untied the string, eager to catch my first real-life glimpse at this so-called Dragon's blood.

"I keep trying to tell you that, but somehow you're still immune to my charm."

I laughed as I inspected the strange vial of blood, noting the thick, ink-red color before shoving it into my purse. The last thing I wanted was someone walking into the class and catching me with *that* in my hands. I had enough rumors going around about me—I didn't want to add blood-drinking-witchy-freak to the mix.

"And your talisman, my lady." He handed me a silver ring with a strange, circular symbol I'd never seen before engraved at the center. "Just toss it into a fire when you're done with it."

I slipped it onto my index finger and gave my hand a quick once over. "I owe you for this, Caleb. Seriously. You're a lifesaver." I reached over and wrapped my arms around his neck in a hug.

The door crashed open, startling me off of Caleb. I whipped around towards the commotion and found Trace standing at the threshold, his arms crossed over his husky chest and an angry glare in his eyes. He took one quick look at us and then stormed out the room, throwing the door back so hard that it knocked the stopper clear off the wall.

"Trace!" I grabbed my bag and started after him, nearly running head-first into Nikki and Morgan, who were standing just outside the door with a matching pair of snotty grins on their faces. No doubt this had their catty names written all over it.

"I told you this town was too small for her," sniped Nikki, her callous eyes falling hard on me.

"Keep talking, Nikki. Maybe you'll say something interesting enough for him to notice you someday."

I shoved my way past them and took off down the hall after Trace, racing to catch up to him. He was merely walking, but I still had to jog just to keep up with him.

"I know it looks bad, Trace, but it was innocent. I was just thanking him for helping me."

"Helping you with what?" The skepticism dripped off his tongue like tar.

I reached over and touched his arm. *With a spell.*

He stopped short and turned, causing me to nearly face-plant into him. He snatched up my hand and pulled me across the hall into an empty classroom. The dusty gray light dripped in from the windows, making the room feel as dreary and bleak as our lives had become.

"What spell?" he asked, slamming the door shut behind himself.

"A Cloaking spell."

"You're already Cloaked." He spat it out as though it were another lie I was trying to force-feed him.

"I know." I leaned back against one of the desks. "But Gabriel said it's fading, and Dominic confirmed it. You were there, remember? You heard him."

"So what? Isn't that what you wanted? Didn't you want to be able to sense them and see them coming?" he asked, moving a little closer to me as he tried to make sense of my story. "Wasn't that the whole point of training with Gabriel?"

"Yeah, but not like this. Not with Engel out there hunting me..." I let out a strangled breath and shook my head. "I don't need another target on my back. I have to make sure he doesn't see me coming."

His eyes filled up with a mixture of worry and sadness and it only made the gravity of the situation weigh heavier on me.

"I don't know if I'm ready for it, Trace. For any of it." It rocked my body saying the words aloud. Destiny was coming at me full speed and I hadn't even graduated high school yet.

His knowing eyes softened as he pulled me off the desk and dragged me into his warm, waiting arms. "It'll be okay," he said, lulling me with his words. "I'm not going to let anything happen to you, Jemma."

In that moment, with his arms around me as they were, I actually believed him.

"I'll always be here to bring you back," he whispered in my ear like an affirmation.

"And what about you, Trace? Who's going to bring you back, huh? Who's going to make sure nothing happens to you?"

"That's my problem, Jemma."

"Well, it's mine now too."

He pulled back a little and looked down at me with questioning eyes.

"I asked Caleb for some Dragon's blood," I explained softly. "For you."

His confused countenance quickly morphed into full-blown anger. "You did what?" He stepped back and I instantly felt a chill from the loss.

"I had to make sure you would be safe."

"I told you to stop trying to protect me!" he barked, his jaw ticking like a time bomb.

"I was just trying to help."

"I don't need your help and I sure as shit don't need Caleb's help either! Dammit, Jemma."

My eyes slammed shut at his words, unable to stomach seeing the sting in his eyes. It wasn't just that I'd done this behind his back. It was that I'd made him feel weak—unable to protect me or even himself. The realization made me shrink inwardly.

All I wanted to do was keep him safe, but it seemed like the more I tried to do that, the more I ended up hurting him.

"I'm sorry," I said, reaching out.

He tried to step away from me when I moved in closer, but I stepped with him this time, refusing to let him shut me out of his world again.

"I'm sorry I went behind your back, Trace, I am," I started, forcing him to look at me. "But I won't apologize for caring about you enough to do it. You're not the only one that's falling in love. I'm falling in love with you too, and the thought of something bad happening to you scares me to death, and if that makes me a bad person then—"

His lips crashed against mine, knocking the wind right out of my entire world.

I faintly remembered the sound of the earth quaking in the background, though it could've just as easily been the desk screeching as he moved me back against it.

His hands gripped my hips and lifted me onto the desk. There was no room for thought, no time to slow things down. There was only me and him and the undeniable charge that sent us crashing into each other, time and time again.

His mouth easily found mine again and he deepened the kiss, scorching my mouth with his tongue and my heart with his intensity. His hands broke away from my face and moved down my legs, searing my skin like an electric shock and then moving back up the other way, under my skirt and over my hips. My blood ran hot, humming, burning up with every touch of his hand. Weaving my hands through his hair, I urged him closer to me and he responded by squeezing my hips and tugging me forward.

"Ahem," said a soft voice from behind us.

Everything halted.

I pulled back from Trace and carefully peered over his shoulder. Hannah and four other students were straggling around the door, waiting for us to notice them.

The bell sounded just as I scooted forward and dropped my feet to the ground. Neither one of us said a word to our spectators as we adjusted our uniforms and then cleared out of the room like nothing happened.

"Well, that was embarrassing," I muttered in the hallway.

He didn't seem bothered by it. "Did you mean what you said in there?" he asked, his voice a cautious whisper of hope.

I stepped into him and dropped a soft kiss on his lips. "Every word."

A smile sprouted on his lips. "I've been waiting a long time to hear you say that."

"I guess I finally ran out of excuses."

The moment the words left my mouth, a horrible feeling came over me as Morgan's words reverberated in my head like the echoes of a death threat I couldn't shut off.

You told him you loved him and then he was dead.

An icy chill sliced its way down my back as my stomach twisted with anxiety. What if she was telling the truth? What if her vision was real?

Had I just taken Trace one step closer to his own gruesome end?

28. PREMONITIONS

A dewy fog wafted over the landscape as I walked up the front steps to the Huntington Manor Tuesday night after my training with Gabriel. I quickly texted my uncle and let him know that I would be staying over at Hannah's house to study, and then let myself in. Everyone was already inside by the time I arrived, with Ben and Dominic sitting by the fire, and Trace pacing back and forth like a caged animal. There was a heaviness in the air that hit me as soon as I entered the room. It choked my lungs and made my skin crawl with trepidation.

"Welcome to the festivities," said Ben. He was smiling but there was no sign of his usual jovialness in any of his features. His eyes were hard and angry, yet somehow still controlled. It was exactly the kind of motivated determination we needed.

I smiled back at him and then turned my attention to Trace.

"We need to talk," he said before I could say anything to him. "In private."

"Oh-kay." I nodded and then followed behind him as he marched out of the study and cut straight through the house.

Without looking back, he pulled open the front door and stepped outside into the mist.

"What's going on?" I asked as he turned around to face me.

The look on his face stopped my heart cold.

"You can't be there tonight." His jaw was ticking feverishly—urgently. "You need to go home."

"Excuse me?"

"This isn't up for debate."

I stepped towards him, refusing to let him intimidate me. "You're right. It isn't up for debate because I'm going. This isn't your call to make," I reminded him.

"Well I'm making it anyway."

I narrowed my eyes at him. "No, you're not."

"Watch me."

"This is ridiculous. I'm going back inside." I started towards the door, but he jumped in my path, blocking me.

I gaped at him. "Move, Trace."

"No. I can't let you go, Jemma." His nostrils flared as he held his stance like some otherworldly bodyguard. "It's too dangerous."

I tried to step around him but he moved with me, refusing to give me even an inch of space to work with. "Stop trying to Tarzan me, Trace. This is my fight. I got her involved in this and I'm going to get her out of it."

"I can't let you do that," he said again. His tone was more pleading now and filled with something else; something that hadn't been there earlier. *Fear.* Pure, primal fear.

I felt a chill run down my back. I glanced over my shoulder into the darkened front yard, gathering my bearings. It was pitch black but for the thin sliver of moonlight casting its eerie glow into the listless fog.

"What's going on?" I asked, turning back to his worry-filled eyes. "What aren't you telling me?"

His jaw ticked again as an ephemeral battle raged behind his eyes. "Morgan had a vision."

"And?" I asked evenly.

"It's a trap, Jemma. She saw it."

"Oh, she saw it, did she?" I scoffed at his utter trust of her *holey* visions. "Was I at least dead this time? Because she missed that part last time."

"This isn't a joke, Jemma. She's a Seer."

"Well, she isn't a very good one. The girl obviously can't foresee her own breakfast." I crossed my arms over my chest, rejecting the misinformation I wanted no part of.

"You're not going to make it out of there alive." He stepped into me, slow and cautious, as though walking up to a cornered lioness that might pounce at any moment. "He's too powerful, and it's not just about the Amulet anymore. He's out for blood. Going there is suicide and I can't let you do that."

"Are you telling me she saw all that?" I asked disbelievingly. *What happened to her 'I only see bits and pieces' bull-crap?*

"She saw enough." He shook his head. "You're not ready yet. You're outnumbered, outgunned. He's going to see you coming a mile away."

"He's not going to see me coming," I countered, feeling confident with our plan and all the precautions I took. "I'm Cloaked, remember?" Doubly, actually.

"It doesn't matter." The fear and frustration was twisting in his eyes like a whirlwind. "Don't you get it? It wasn't my blood in the vision. It was yours! It was yours all along."

I tried to swallow but my throat seemed to be drying up.

"We need to leave town," he said suddenly as though the idea just dawned on him. "We can go to my dad's cabin. If we leave now, we'll make it there before midnight."

"I'm not going to your dad's cabin, Trace. I'm not just going to bail on Taylor. He'll kill her."

"Then let me and Dominic handle this. You don't need to be there. We'll get Taylor back, and we'll waste Engel and every last one of them and you won't have to get within a mile of any of them." His chest was rising and falling so fast, I could almost see the frantic adrenaline coursing through his veins.

I had to calm him down before he went full-Tarzan and dragged me out of here over his shoulder.

"You can't expect me to hide for the rest of my life, Trace. We both know that's not possible. As long as we stick to the plan, everything's going to be fine."

He was about to say something back but I quickly cut him off. "Look, I know you're worried about me but you don't have to be. I was meant to do this, and more than that, I *know* I can do it. And I'm protected, so if you truly don't believe I'm ready to face him, then at least believe in the Amulet."

His eyebrows rutted together as he listened to me plead my case.

"They can't hurt me as long as I'm wearing this," I reminded him, pulling the enchanted necklace out from under my shirt. "And I'm not going to take it off."

He released a ragged breath. It was working.

"I'm literally indestructible as long as I have this on."

His jaw muscles flexed as he thought it over. "Then promise me you won't take it off for anything or *anyone*." His eyes were a symphony of desperation that begged for my compliance. "I need to hear you say it."

"I promise," I said, touching my hand to his cheek.

He turned into it and kissed my palm. His fierce eyes met mine again as he pulled me to him. "I swear to God, Jemma, if you so much as move your hand towards that necklace, I'm porting you out of there—with or without Taylor." His eyes burned with ferocity, attesting to his words. "I can't lose you. Do you understand what I'm saying?"

"Yes, I understand perfectly." And I did. Because I felt the same way about him. I reached up and punctuated it with a kiss.

"It's not coming off."

The fire was still burning wildly when Trace and I rejoined the rest of our party in the study. Thick flames licked out at the firewood, decorating the room in morbid shades of orange and red. Something about their dance mesmerized me, like they knew what was coming and wanted to bask in the bloodshed.

"Everything all patched up?" asked Dominic with more than a hint of irritation. He was sitting nearest the mantel with his legs crossed and a goblet of brown liquid in his hands.

"All good." I sat down on the sofa and tied my hair back.

"I propose we hit them right before sunrise," begun Dominic, eager to get this massacre underway. "They'll be at a great disadvantage with the threat of sunrise over their heads, not to mention, preventing their escape."

"That's a good idea, actually."

"Uh, isn't he a bloodsucker too, though?" asked Ben, thumbing Dominic. "Won't he go all stir-fry in the sun?"

"He's got a temporary day pass," I said, not wanting to elaborate. The less people that knew about my *irregular* blood, the better. I turned to Trace. "Did you get everything we need?"

He tossed a burlap bag on the coffee table. "Cinderdust, daggers, stakes, and a few explosives in case things get a little too dicey."

Ben leaned across the table and started inspecting the arsenal as Dominic awarded himself another sip.

"You might want to slow down with that," I suggested. "It's probably not the best time to get trashed."

Dominic's laughter hissed at me like an insult. "I can handle my liquor, love. In fact, I hear you're in need of instruction. I'd be more than happy to lend a hand."

My eyes narrowed at him.

"Lend this," said Trace, giving him the finger.

"You're not my type, Romeo."

"Seriously?" I snapped at their bickering. "Not tonight!"

Ben looked up at me with furrowed brows but I just shook my head at him, dejected. I didn't have enough energy to explain the strange frenemy dynamics between Trace and Dominic.

Shrugging, he turned his attention back to the artillery. I dug my hand into my pocket and pulled out the vial of Dragon's blood Caleb had graciously provided me with and tossed it over to Trace as Dominic cleared the coffee table and spread out a map. Trace caught the vial in the air and clenched his jaw, apparently still trying to fight me on it. He wouldn't win this one. I stared him down until he flicked the cap off and dropped the contents into his mouth.

"They're staying at the abandoned factory on Old Miller road," started Dominic, pointing to a circled section on the map. "There's approximately twenty or so of them, though they rarely ever congregate at the same time." He pulled out some kind of blueprint and flattened it over the map. "This is where Jemma and I will be entering the premise. The two of you need to hold up the back end. My guess is they're keeping the blond one right around here—"

"She has a name," interrupted Ben, his sandy eyebrows pulled together in an angry point. "Her name is Taylor."

"*Taylor* then," said Dominic through pursed lips, "is most likely being retained in one of the offices over here. I'd venture there's only one or two guards watching her at the most. I'm assuming you two knuckleheads could handle two Revenants on your own, yes?"

Trace looked as though he were about to reach over and rip Dominic's larynx out of his throat.

"Yeah, they got this," I jumped in, trying to keep things moving along. "What's next?" I asked, leaning over the blueprint.

"Once they locate *Taylor*," he continued, exaggerating her name again, "Romeo will port the three of them out of there."

"And us?" I asked hoarsely, my voice rasping from the sandpaper that had now become my throat.

His onyx eyes glowed with mischief. "Our only goal, love, is to take down Engel and to do so as swiftly as possible. Kill as many of his men as you need to in order to get to him, but make no mistake. The longer it takes to reach him, the harder he will be to take down."

My hands were starting to shake now but I refused to let any of them see it. I buried them deep in my pocket and steeled my backbone. "Anything else?"

"Yes, angel," simpered Dominic. "Don't get killed."

29. A TIME TO KILL

The rain came down slow like dripping blood—a prophetic embodiment of the bloodbath that awaited us. We parked several blocks from the factory in an unmarked car and waited impatiently for dusk to slip away from us. When the time finally came, the four of us stepped out of the car in silence and made our way towards the abandoned building.

"Last stop on the Hell train," said Dominic as we approached our first mark—a parking lot across the street from the factory. "If anyone wants to get off, now is your chance."

"We're good, leech. Hurry up and do your thing."

We'd already staked out the building an hour earlier, familiarizing ourselves with the grounds and layout. There were four entries into the building, though only the front and back ones were accessible, and consequently, being guarded. Across the street from the building, there was a deserted parking lot shrouded in overgrowth and shadows; a perfect place for shapeshifting.

"Alright, people, stand back," said Ben lifting his arms dramatically. "I need some space here."

"Amateur," snorted Dominic as he cracked his neck and

lowered himself onto his knee. He looked regal in that pose, like a dark knight awaiting his honor.

A pulsation quickly overtook his body, blurring his form into an indistinguishable dark shadow that no longer bore any resemblance to the enigmatic Revenant that haunted my dreams. His black wolf form quickly emerged from the inky haze and then stepped to me, shaking the water from his fur.

"Watch it, dog," warned Trace.

Dominic growled back, low and threatening.

Ben went next, and while his shift wasn't as fast as Dominic's, it was still impossible to see what was truly happening in the dark haze that seemed to be vibrating. Before my mind could put the picture together, a mottled, dark gray wolf materialized with a quick howl to the moon.

"I don't think I'll ever get used to seeing that," I said, hugging my arms for warmth.

"You will," answered Trace, his tone somber and grim. "You'll get used to a lot of things."

Ben's wolf form stalked past me, grazing my leg as he moved to Dominic. The two of them began circling each other like some kind of primal dance I wasn't privy to.

Trace slipped his arm around my waist and pulled me into the warm space between his arms. "Remember what you promised me," he whispered softly in my ear. "Don't make me regret this." He brought his mouth to mine and kissed me hard, instantaneously melting the chill that had begun anesthetizing my bones.

With that, he pulled away and started down the street, his raven hair and dark clothes blending into the night as Ben followed closely behind him.

I turned to the ebony wolf beside me. "Ready to slay some vampires?"

Lead the way, Slayer.

I released my wooden stake from the sheath around my ankle and secured the silver dagger in my other hand. Pulling in a lungful of air, I abandoned my fear where I stood and started down the street parallel to the one Trace and Ben had disappeared into.

There was no going back now, so I didn't even look.

We rounded the side of the building and eased our way towards the front entrance where a dark-haired Rev was loitering under a dilapidated shelter, pulling in a drag from his cigarette and staring off into the barren street. A plume of nicotine from his lungs floated into the rain like a smoke signal to the heavens.

I got this one, love, said Dominic to my mind, but I was already creeping towards Smokey-the-vampire.

The minute his back was to me, I pounced on him from the shadows, ramming my foot into the center of his back. His cigarette flew from his fingers as he hit the wet concrete. Before he could shake the stars from his eyes, I spun him onto his back and jammed my stake into his heart.

The smooth, chalky color and texture quickly left his now desiccated face as he lay motionless on the ground.

Is it odd that I'm slightly aroused right now?

"You would be," I hissed back at him as I dusted Smokey in Cinderdust. A flash of colorful flames ignited over the corpse like a dazzling Aurora Borealis spectacle, before devouring the body completely and leaving nothing in its place but the sound of my wooden stick clinking against the concrete.

I'm impressed, angel. You're a natural.

I picked up my weapon from the ground and moved to the now unmanned entrance. A rusty door sitting half off its hinges was the only thing standing between me and Engel. He was somewhere inside this building, and so was my best friend. And I was going to make him regret the day he ever set eyes on her.

Peering through a small slit in the door, I made sure that the coast was clear before sliding through with Dominic hot on my heels. I waited as he sniffed the air for their scent.

They're in the old warehouse. This way, he said and started heading east through the building.

Black mold and whittled paint covered every inch of the walls, broken up only by the bad graffiti and boarded up windows that hung on the walls like an omen. Water dripped down from the exposed ceilings, slicking my hair and arms as my feet sloshed through the murky slush that blanketed the floor like a sodden carpet. The smell of mildew and stale cigarette smoke turned my stomach as it seeped into the inside of my nose.

They're up ahead, informed Dominic, apparently hearing them, though it took another twenty or so steps before I could hear the faint voices for myself.

As we drew closer, the muffled sounds got louder, as did the pounding of my heart. My mind began assaulting me, plaguing me with doubt and accusations of inadequacy but I refused to let myself listen in. Instead, I tuned it out like a shitty song on the radio and kept putting one foot in front of the other.

I'll take down as many as I can, love, said Dominic. *Don't look back. Find Engel and kill him.*

"You smell that?" asked a gruff voice up ahead. "It smells like a wet dog."

"That's not a wet dog," answered another voice, clearly on edge. "That's a wolf."

Chairs scuffled around in panic as Dominic rounded the corner. Seven sets of wide eyes stared back at us with a mixture of surprise and confusion on their faces. We didn't give them a chance to work out the equation. The minute we entered the room, Dominic thrashed through the air with barred teeth, landing on a blond-haired Rev who barely had time to put his hands up before Dominic slammed him to the ground.

My eyes fell on Engel. He was still seated at the furthest end of the room, watching calmly—waiting. My stomach tightened into a knot as I started running straight for him.

A short, stalky dark-haired Rev jumped out in front of me, blocking my path and bringing my onslaught to a halt. The jagged scar through his top lip twisted awkwardly as he smiled up at me.

I smiled back.

Running on pure adrenaline and basic instincts, I cut through the air with my dagger, slicing his cheek and then using it to gorge out his eyeball. He keeled over, covering his bleeding face just as another Rev jumped into his place.

This one was bigger, at least a foot taller than me, and with a neck almost as thick as his head. His wispy brown hair fell in chunks around his chin, highlighting his offset jaw. With fangs already retracted, he stepped to me quickly, forcing me to take a step back.

"What's the matter, dollface? You scared to play with the big boys?"

Adrenaline shot through my body as I pushed on the balls of my feet and pounced on him. My arm cut through the air, landing a hard punch to his throat and then kneeing him in the face when he leaned down to cover up. Raising my dagger, I swiped at him with the blade, only nicking his left cheek as he quickly jumped back. With a taste for his blood, I pulled back and tried again, though this time he was ready for it. He caught my hand and twisted it back until I dropped the dagger.

Gritting my teeth, I plowed my knee into his crotch and then spun out of his hold. The shrilling cry that escaped his mouth only made the fire inside me burn hotter. I dropped down and twisted my extended leg, kicking his feet from under him just as I'd practiced hundreds of times with Gabriel. He lost his balance and slammed down against the concrete floor just in time to get hit with a fist full of Cinderdust.

I was surprised that the Cinderdust worked without a stake to his heart, but I didn't have time to sit around and ask questions. I picked up my dagger and jumped over his body, not even bothering to stick around for the light show.

I zeroed in on Engel as a man screamed out in agony behind me, but I didn't dare take my eyes off my target, who was now retreating from me.

I followed him cautiously, inspecting his stance, his eyes, gauging his next move.

"I must say, I'm quite impressed," he said calmly as though his entire crew wasn't being maimed and mauled in the shadows behind us. "You truly are a splendid Being."

I didn't respond as I continued stalking his retreat.

"Come to collect your comrade, I imagine?"

"Among other things."

"Ah, I see. You're out for blood then." The smirk on his face elongated. "As am I."

"Well, the blood bank is currently closed," I informed.

"Yes, indeed, and I intend to make that permanent."

My eyes narrowed at his threat. "It's too bad I don't have some kind of Amulet to protect myself," I said innocently, still shadowing his every move. I pulled the necklace out from under my shirt. "Oh, wait. That's right. I do."

I twisted the wooden stake in my hand, adjusting my hold on it as I readied myself for the attack. Engel's eyes snapped to my weapon.

"That's quite unnecessary," he said, shaking his head at me. "The Amulet is yours."

Reaching the end of the room, he halted with no more space to retreat and no place left to hide as I closed in on him.

"I didn't take you for the quitting type, Engel. I have to say, I'm kind of disappointed."

Obviously, he knew he had no chance.

I tightened my grip on the stake and took another step.

"You need it more than I do." Something dark and sinister washed over his pallid face as he glanced down at my hand again. "However, I suspect nothing, not even your precious Amulet, will be able to save you from the evil that's coming. Such, I suppose, is your fate when you're the Princess of Darkness."

I stopped short. "What the hell are you—"

Engel's hand shot out through the air like a knife, seizing me by my neck and spinning me into him before I even had a chance to finish the question. My back hit his chest hard, knocking the wind out of me as I scrambled clumsily to regain my footing.

But it was too late.

He had mm exactly where he wanted me and all I could do was yelp out in pain as his teeth tore into my flesh.

Hot liquid poured down my neck and onto my shirt, staining it with bold crimson streaks. I tried to swing my stake at him, but he caught my hand easily and forced it back down to my side before prying it loose from my fingers.

My feet swung in the air wildly, aimlessly, my fingernails digging and scratching at his arm as I tried to loosen his hold from around my neck. A futile last ditch effort for the venom had already begun settling in, simmering down my body and all of my efforts to escape.

Dominic's keen wolf eyes snapped in my direction. He swiped his claws across his opponent's face and then hurtled over the mess of bodies and broken chairs. Racing towards me, he kicked off from his back legs and dove through the air like a black raven, crashing into the two of us and knocking us both down to the ground. Dominic's teeth clamped down onto Engel's arm, pulling, tugging, tearing at his flesh as he tried to rip the meat clear off the bone. The unrelenting brutality of his attack forced Engel to release his hold on me in an effort to save his own arm.

Run, said Dominic. *He has your blood in him!*

I rolled off of him and tried to stand up, but my legs wouldn't work. It was as though I'd gained a hundred pounds over the last few minutes and no longer had the strength to hold up my own body weight. I grabbed at the floor, trying to gain enough traction to drag myself away, but it was too slick with slush and blood.

Come on, angel, get up!

"I can't," I cried, hopelessness closing in on me.

I tried to will my legs to work, to pray for some kind of miracle, but there wasn't enough blood in my body to support any of my efforts. My thoughts immediately snapped to Trace and the promise I made to him. Dammit! I couldn't let this happen. I couldn't go out like this.

I dug down deep—deeper than I ever had before and summoned all the strength and fight I had left in me.

Sadly, there was only enough to get me up on my hands and knees and start crawling away. I was getting nowhere fast, but at least I was moving now. Engel may have been down, but with my blood in his veins, it was only a matter of time before he would be back on his feet, ready to finish the job.

Dominic circled around me frantically, darting from side to side to inspect me, to calculate the damage. Stopping beside me, he lowered himself to the ground and nudged my arm.

Get on, he ordered.

I reached up and grabbed a hold of his neck. Using his fur for leverage, I pulled myself up and threw my leg over his back. Straddling him, I wrapped my arms around his neck and threw a quick glance back at Engel. He was on the floor and bloodied, but very much alive.

Whatever blood was left in me drained from my head and I collapsed in exhaustion as Dominic raced us out of the warehouse and into the dawn of a new day.

A very, very bad new day.

30. INDECENT PROPOSAL

I awoke alone in an unfamiliar bedroom to hostile voices somewhere outside the door. Though muffled, I could tell the discussion was heated and the participants agitated. *Where the hell am I?* I wondered as I tried to unscramble the thoughts inside my pounding head. Rubbing my temples, I dropped my feet over the edge of the bed and inspected myself. My skin was covered in filthy, black grime and what looked like old, crusted blood.

I glanced around the room, trying to acclimate myself to where I was. My eyes bounced from the bonded-leather headboard to the onyx furniture that blended into the charcoal walls. There was a gray accent rug at the center of the room that matched the thick, black-out curtains. It was a man's room, no doubt. Probably Dominic's.

"What the hell am I doing in—" My hand came up to my mouth. "Oh, God. Oh, God. No, no, no!"

The events of last night bombarded my memory, flooding me with images that stifled the air in my lungs. *I failed.* I failed miserably. Engel was still alive, and it was all my fault.

My mind snapped to Taylor. Where was she? Was she still

alive? Had Trace and Ben been successful in bringing her home? I had a million questions and a whopping zero answers.

I slid off the bed and stumbled to the door in a daze. Desperate for answers, I yanked open the door and staggered out into the hallway, bracing myself against the walls as I moved through the darkened corridor. The voices got louder as I approached the landing at the top of the staircase, prompting me to quicken my steps. My head was still spinning, though I wasn't sure if it was from the blood loss or the full-blown panic attack I seemed to be having. I reached out for the banister and peered over the edge. My eyes immediately fell on Trace and Dominic.

"Jemma." Trace looked up as though sensing I was there. His eyes filled with concern as he rushed up the stairs, taking two at a time. "You need to rest. You neck was ripped wide op—"

"No," I cut in, my hand reflexively rushing up to the bandage around my neck. "Where's Taylor? Please tell me you got her out of there, Trace. Tell me she's okay!"

"She's in the study with Ben." His gaze briefly flickered away from mine. "I think you should wait before going in there."

"Why?" My anxiety was notching up to mountainous proportions. I wasn't sure how much longer I could withstand the torment. "What happened? What's wrong with her?"

"Nothing. I mean, she's okay," he tried to assure me, though it didn't sound even remotely convincing. "She's just a little out of it. Look, I think you both need to rest before you—"

I pushed past him and made a mad dash down the stairs.

"Angel, I think you should heed his advice," cautioned Dominic, his voice rising on the tail-end of his warning, but I had already passed him and was halfway to the den by the time he finished the sentence.

Stopping at the entrance, I peered my head into the study as my heart thumped madly in my chest. My eyes quickly found

Ben. He was sitting quietly in the lounge chair, elbows pressed to his knees in quiet contemplation, watching—guarding. My eyes followed his devoted gaze to the sofa...to Taylor.

She was lying on the couch, propped up with cushions behind her head, and staring into the fire as though it held all the answers and apologies she deserved. Her once-beautiful long, blond hair was matted with mud and dirt and dried blood, and her alabaster skin didn't appear to be in any better shape.

"Taylor," I whispered her name like a birthday wish.

Her head turned slowly towards me.

Tears brimmed from my eyes, trickling down my face without shame as I took all of her in. For the longest time, I wasn't sure I was ever going to see her again. And now, here she was; rundown, tattered and broken, but she was *here* and she was *alive*.

I rushed to her side, dropping to my knees beside her as if to beg at her shrine for forgiveness.

"Jemma." A small smile decorated her mouth as water pooled in her denim-blue eyes. She touched her hand to my face and creased her eyebrows as her eyes traveled over my features. "You look horrible."

I laughed, and then I cried. "So do you," I sobbed, wrapping my arms around her neck and pulling her in so tightly that you would've needed the *Jaws of Life* to come between us. "I'm so sorry, Taylor. It was all my fault."

"Don't you even dare," she rasped. "Trace told me everything. It wasn't your fault. You saved me, babe."

We squeezed each other even tighter, our filth mixing together like a noxious testament of our thriving friendship.

"Ah. Ebony and Ivory," leered Dominic from the entrance way. "My two favorite flavors."

"You're rancid," spat Trace as he walked over to us.

I pulled away from Taylor and glared back at Dominic.

214

He caught my death stare and immediately corrected himself. "I jest, love." His eyes shimmered with sincerity, almost as though he were actually capable of feeling remorse.

I softened my eyes as I recalled what he'd done for me last night. "You saved my life."

"I did."

"Thank you."

His lip hitched up on one side. "Anytime, angel."

Trace cleared his throat, causing me to shift my attention to him. My eyes easily fell on his form, taking in the divine being and all his glory as he stood in front of the crackling fire. The flames seemed to dancing behind him—for him, like they knew the status quo and yearned to worship him.

"And thank *you* for bringing her back home." I turned and smiled at Ben. "Both of you."

"Well, now that the outpouring of love is out of the way, we ought to move on to more pressing matters," chimed in Dominic, the self-appointed bearer of bad news. "Unfortunately, Engel is still alive, which is putting quite a wedge in my merriment."

Taylor whimpered softly beside me. I looked her over and noticed she was trembling. She was shaking at the mere mention of his name. What the hell had he done to her?

I turned to Trace for answers, but he just shook his head, unable to deliver. Ben stood up and moved to the foot of the sofa. Lifting Taylor's feet with one hand, he slid down onto the couch and then placed them back down on his lap.

"Everything's going to be okay, Tay," said Ben. "We're all here. No one's ever going to hurt you again."

A sob choked the back of my throat, screaming to break free from my body, but I refused to let it go. I had to keep it together for Taylor's sake. I looked up at Trace and ticked my head, signaling that I needed to talk to him—in private.

"I'll be right back, okay?" I squeezed Taylor's hand reassuringly. "I'll get you some more blankets, and maybe something to eat? Has she eaten anything?" I glanced around the room at blank faces.

"My stomach's too icky to eat."

"You have to try, Tay, please. How about some soup? It'll warm you up and make you feel better."

She gave a small nod and that was good enough for me. I turned on my heel and zipped out the room, grabbing Dominic's arm on my way out.

Once inside the kitchen and out of Taylor's earshot, I turned to Dominic and Trace with weighty tears spilling from my eyes. "What did he do to her?" I demanded.

"She wouldn't say," said Trace, wrapping an arm around my shoulder. "She doesn't want to talk about it."

I sobbed into his shirt. "This is all my fault!"

"No, it's not. You need to stop blaming yourself, Jemma." He stroked my back with the palm of his hand in small, reassuring circles. "You didn't do this to her. Engel did."

"Yeah, and I let him get away," I said, stepping out of his comforting arms. I didn't deserve them—I deserved to feel this burden of pain. "I screwed up, Trace. I screwed up bad."

"What happened out there?"

I shook my head, glancing from him to Dominic, who was watching me intensely, and then back again.

"I had him cornered. He was as good as dead and we both knew it. He was trying to talk circles around me, pretending like he didn't want the Amulet anymore. But I knew he was just trying to distract me, you know, throw me off my game." I rubbed my sweaty palms against my pants as I recalled the events. "But then he said something about me needing it more than he did—that it wouldn't save me from the evil that was coming, and I hesitated."

"What's he talking about?" Trace asked Dominic as he folded his arms across his chest. "What evil?"

"What makes you think I have the slightest idea?"

"Because you're one of them, aren't you? Don't act like you don't know what's going on!" snapped Trace.

"If I was 'one of them' as you so moronically put it, then I would not have been there tonight, fighting alongside Jemma. Besides, if you think I'm part of the supposed great evil that Engel is referring to, you've gravely overestimated my strength."

Trace pumped his jaw, considering it.

Whatever it was that Engel was talking about, it had to be bigger and badder than both of them combined.

"I screwed up and he was ready for it," I said, lowering my head. "And now he's still out there. Because of me. I let him get away." The fizzing anxiety was back with a vengeance, making my body thwack with fear. "He's going to make me pay for this."

"You don't know that."

Dominic huffed. "Let's not placate the girl with falsities." His gaze shifted to me. "You still have what he needs, love, and worse, you've now royally pissed him off." He didn't bother sugar-coating anything for me.

"We need to go back there tonight. No, *right now*," I said frantically as I tried to head out the kitchen and make a push for the door. *I'll show him a Princess of Darkness!*

Dominic snagged my elbow and pulled me back. "He's long gone, angel. Returning is futile. We need to lay low for a while until I can gather more information on his whereabouts. Luckily, he only saw my wolf form and not me. I'm fairly certain I can still get close to him without alerting him to our motives."

"What about Taylor?" I felt another surge of panic as the air became harder and harder to take in. "What are we supposed to tell her? God only knows what they did to her. She'll never be able to eat or sleep again knowing he's still out there."

"Then we lie to her," suggested Dominic.

"She already heard me admit that he got away." Crestfallen, I turned my eyes to the ground.

I felt utterly powerless in my ability to take the horror away and make everything better for her again. There was nothing I could do short of a complete lobotomy, which—

My mind froze on the thought, and my eyes snapped up to Dominic. "Unless we take her memory away."

"You mean compel her?" asked Trace, eyebrows rutted.

"Exactly." My eyes remained pinned on Dominic, heavy with desperation. "Erase her memory so that these last few days never happened—take it all away and replace it with something better, something beautiful. Can you do that?"

"Do you really think that's a good idea?" asked Trace. I could hear the skepticism in his voice, the grounded rationalism, and I wanted to sucker-punch him for it. "Shouldn't she be prepared if she's going to be around us?"

"She doesn't belong in our world." I shook my head as the sobering reality set in. "If it wasn't for me—for our friendship— none of this would have happened. She wasn't supposed to be a part of this. She was supposed to be home, living her normal life, completely unaware of this horrible world she doesn't belong in."

"Jemma."

"That was her right, Trace. Her gift. And I took it away from her."

"You can't blame yourself for being friends—"

"But I can make it right," I went on, not hearing a word of his argument. "I can give it all back to her."

"What are you talking about?" he asked, unable to keep up with my infinite spiral. "What are you going to do?"

"Not me." I turned to the silent Revenant who was watching me with great interest. "Make her forget *me*, Dominic. Make it so that we were never friends. Make it so that I'm nothing to her." The words twisted bitterly from my mouth and stung my ears as they reverberated in the room.

"Don't you think you should talk to her first?" objected Trace. "Make sure this is what she wants?"

"I can't do that," I said, shaking my head at his perfectly valid point. "She'll never agree to it. She'll fight me on it, and I can't let her change my mind."

Trace ran a hand over his face like he didn't like where any of this was going and wanted to wipe away the entire conversation from his mind. Sadly, his apprehension barely registered with me. The answer to all of Taylor's problems had been uttered, and I refused to turn a deaf ear to it.

"Will you do it, Dominic?" The grit and desperation blended in my heart like a potion that begged to be taken. I was going to make this happen. I had the chance to make her life better, to take away her pain and trauma, and no one was going to stop me.

Not even Taylor herself.

"Certainly." His lip quirked up on the side, pushing up into his smooth, flawless cheek. "For a price, of course."

"Typical," said Trace, flexing his jaw.

"Name it."

His eyes darkened. "I'll do it in exchange for one night with you."

"Are you out of your fucking mind!" snapped Trace, shoving Dominic into the doorway. "I'll kill you right where you stand."

Dominic laughed, amused by Trace's reaction. "What's the matter, Romeo? Are you afraid of a little competition?"

"Competition? You're not even in the race, leech."

"Then what's one date going to change?" challenged

Dominic.

Trace turned to me with rage in his eyes. "You're not seriously considering this, are you?"

"You can always ask Gabriel instead," suggested Dominic, knowing that would never happen. "Though you'd have to explain to him how she came to be in Engel's grip in the first place, and of course, why you've been lying to him this entire time."

"He's manipulating you," spat Trace.

I knew that, but it didn't change anything. He had something I needed—the ability to restore my friend to her former grace and make everything in her life right again. How could I turn away from that?

"Jemma, please. Don't do this."

I couldn't even look him in the eyes. "I have to," I said and then flinched at the sound of Trace punching a hole through the wall.

"You're going to pay for that," bit Dominic, but Trace was already storming out of the room like a caustic hurricane hell-bent on destroying everything in its path.

Water pooled in my eyes, burning under my lids as it fought to be released. No matter how hard I tried to do the right thing, to do what was best for everyone, someone always seemed to get hurt anyway. And it usually ended up being the one I cared about the most. I was damned if I did, damned if I didn't, and damned every other which way in between.

Dominic stepped into my blurry line of vision, hands crossed behind his back as he waited for the verdict. "What do you say, angel? Do we have a deal?"

"You have a deal," I said, nodding my defeat as I swallowed down the remnants of my pride. "One date."

31. THE GIFT OF GONE

I took a few minutes to get myself together before I rejoined Taylor and Ben in the study, carrying a tray of warm chicken soup and a glass of orange juice as promised. Although she wasn't very hungry at first, with a little coaxing from me, she forced herself to take a spoonful, and then another, and before I knew it, she had devoured nearly half the bowl.

While I sat with Taylor, Trace, who had calmed down enough to come back inside, pulled Ben aside and clued him in on what we were planning to do for Taylor. Like Trace, he didn't agree with it and thought that Taylor should be the one to make this decision, but I knew that if I told her, she would have chosen our friendship over her safety, and I couldn't let her do that. She did not belong in this world. She had no ability to see the enemy coming and she was entirely powerless to stop them. It was up to me to do what was best for her, even if that meant saying goodbye to my best friend.

When the time finally came, Dominic strolled in calmly and took his seat next to Taylor while Ben and Trace stood by the fireplace, arms crossed over their chests in matching vexation. Dominic was confident enough to go ahead with his side of the deal, knowing that what he was about to do could easily be undone if I decided to renege on our date.

"He's just going to make sure you're okay," I said to Taylor as Dominic scooted closer to her.

"Look at me," he instructed her, and she did. He began to recite the script I rehearsed with him earlier. "Everything is going to be okay. You had an accident last week and hurt your head. You were confused for a while and couldn't find your way back home, but you are better now. Nothing bad happened to you."

"Nothing bad happened to me," she repeated in a daze-like trance.

"After you leave here today," he continued, his hypnotic eyes captivating her full attention, "you're going to forget this ever happened. You're going to forget Engel and the warehouse, and everything that happened there. You'll remember waking up on the side of the road and heading back into town when Ben happened to drive by and find you." He glanced back at me for a final confirmation.

I nodded for him to continue, refusing to meet Trace or Ben's eyes, already knowing good and well what I would find there. Disapproval. Judgment. Scorn.

"As soon as you leave this house, you're going to forget your friendship with Jemma. She's merely a girl at school with whom you've never interacted. She means nothing to you. Your life is full and you are safe and content." He gently swiped her chin with the pad of his thumb.

Taylor smiled back at him, her eyes beaming with the same carefree happiness she had the day I met her.

Ben moved to her side again, hovering around her like her own personal Guardian. "Come on, Tay. It's time to go home."

"Home," she murmured contently.

Even though it was a school day, I was fairly certain Taylor would not be attending classes today. Probably not for a few days...if her parents ever let her out of the house again, that is.

Taylor stood up and joined Ben. Turning to me, she smiled. My heart swelled as I saw the light reach all the way up into her slate-blue eyes, and I knew I'd made the right decision.

"I love you, Tay," I said, knowing that the moment she left Dominic's house, she would completely forget me and everything we'd gone through together.

"I love you too, babe." She stepped forward and threw her arms around my neck. "Call me later."

"I will," I lied.

"Alright, later peeps. Come on, doofus." She tapped Ben's arm playfully and strutted out of the room.

Ben bounced on the ball of his feet and happily took off after her.

"You ready to go?" asked Trace, his piercing blue eyes slicing into my heart as he stood by the entryway, his shoulders high as though anxious to put this room and everything in it behind him.

I nodded, and then gathered my jacket and bag.

"I'll be seeing you," sang Dominic as I made my way out the room, but I didn't bother looking back this time.

I'd made my bed with Dominic and I was going to have to lie in it, but I was too tired to deal with that right now. All I wanted to do was go home, wash the grime off my body and crawl into my bed.

A light drizzle peppered the windshield as Trace and I pulled up to the Blackburn Estate. My uncle's luxury black sedan was missing from the driveway, confirming that he'd bought my story last night and left for work this morning without a doubt in his mind.

"Do you want to come in?" I asked Trace as he stared out the window in quiet contemplation.

He turned slowly, meeting my gaze with a heaviness in his eyes that ripped my heart to pieces. "Not today," he said, his voice low and somber. "I should probably get home."

I bit the inside of my cheek and scrutinized him. I wanted to tell him I was sorry for hurting him again, for always doing the wrong thing, but I couldn't seem to twist the words out of my mouth. "Will you call me later?" I asked instead.

He nodded but didn't say anything else.

I opened the door and slipped out into the haze. Throwing my jacket over my head, I made a run for the door and then turned back to wave at him, but he was already backing out of the driveway.

My heart splintered.

I was going to have to find a way to make this up to him, to convince him that this date with Dominic was just a means to an end and that he had nothing to worry about. I wasn't sure how I was going to do that, but I knew I had to find a way.

Once inside, I wasted no time shucking off my dirty clothes and jumping into a steaming hot shower. I tried to relax my mind and enjoy the momentary hiatus from mortal danger, but I couldn't seem to get my brain to cooperate. Anxious thoughts whipped out at me like a form of corporal punishment, knocking the wind out of my lungs as they slapped me with the dire circumstances of my newest reality.

After everything I'd gone through to get her back, in the end, I still lost Taylor. Even if it was for her own good, the loss still hurt like hell. And now Trace probably wasn't that far behind her, being that I couldn't seem to stop myself from hurting him like some kind of sick sadist.

And then there was Engel. Deathly, omnipotent Engel who was still out there, out for my blood and madder than ever—waiting, plotting, readying himself for the ultimate payback.

I pushed back on the glass and slid to the ground, crumbling into a ball of tears on the wet, tiled floor. The cascading water pummeled over my sagging body, mixing in with the salty tears I could no longer contain. Every raw emotion I'd ever felt broke free in that moment and I let myself cry harder than I ever had before, relinquishing demons and sadness and sobs that were drowned out by the dissonance of running water. I cried for seconds and minutes and then hours, crying until time blended into an immeasurable mess of weighty despair—until I couldn't cry out a single other tear to save my life. And when I was done, just like flicking off a light switch, I shut it all off again.

Squaring my shoulders, I sucked in the last of my sobs and picked myself off the floor. I turned off the water and stepped out of the shower, wrapping myself in a thick, terry cloth towel. Fully contained, I walked to the sink and ran a hand across the fogged up mirror, staring at the battered girl in the reflection.

My hair was sopping wet, my eyes tired and sagging with defeat.

I ran the tips of my fingers across my bandaged neck and then pulled back the gauze to inspect the damage. Raw, open flesh mocked me like a celebration of what was yet to come. Pulling out the first aid kit, I carefully cleaned the wound and then applied a fresh bandage.

After drying my hair and dressing, I stalked back into my room and climbed into my bed. My body ached and my mind screamed for reprieve, but my heart demanded I wait.

So I did.

I waited for hours for Trace to call me that night, but the phone never did ring.

Eventually, I closed my eyes and slowly drifted off to sleep, fully knowing that the dark angel from my nightmares would once again come for me in my dreams, and that sadly, this time, there would be no light to wake me up from the horror.

32. AND SO IT GOES

Thick, roiling storm clouds gathered low in the sky as I walked into school the next morning. Not surprisingly, Taylor wasn't there, but according to Ben, she was already doing infinitely better than she was the last time we'd seen her. Her parents were both relieved and overjoyed beyond words to have her back home again, convinced that her return was nothing short of a miracle. And, of course, to celebrate said miracle, a black-tie *welcome home* party was already set for Saturday, hosted by her parents on their sprawling acreage.

"So they bought the whole memory loss thing?" I asked Ben quietly as we stood next to Trace's locker discussing the after-events of last night.

"Yup. Her doc suggested she do some rehab to try and jog her memory but her parents pretty much said 'no thanks'." He ran his hand over his buzzed mane. "They think it's better for her if she doesn't remember, but honestly, I think it's more for their sake than hers. I don't think they can handle hearing it if anything bad happened to her."

I nodded, knowing I felt the same exact way.

Now more than ever, I was convinced that I'd made the right

decision for her.

Trace shut his locker and secured the lock. "Any word about Engel?" he asked, barely meeting my eyes as he leaned back against his locker and stared forward across the hall.

"I haven't heard anything." It was all silence on the Engel front and it was making my skin crawl with unease.

"We should probably do some tracking tonight," suggested Ben. "See if we can pick up his scent."

"I can cut my training short and meet up with you guys." I adjusted my schoolbag as I bounced a glance between the two of them.

"Nah, that's alright, Jem. There's not much you can do anyway. Not until you get your full Spidey senses," he added playfully, his voice a secretive whisper.

I nodded and then turned my attention to Trace. He was still avoiding eye contact with me, and the loss was making it hard for me to fill my lungs. Ben inspected him and then me.

"Yeah, so, anyway, I got this thing to do." He fiddled with the barbell in his ear. "I should probably go and do that now. I'll catch you two kids later," he said, obviously sensing the thick tension in the air and wanting to give us some time alone to iron out the issue.

"See you later, Ben."

He smiled at me and then fist bumped Trace before taking off down the hall.

"So I guess you're still mad at me, huh?"

Trace's eyes slid over to me slowly, like they were too heavy with resentment for him to maneuver. "Wouldn't you be?"

If he was going on a date with Nikki? Hell yeah, I'd be furious. Then again, what other option did I have? "There was no one else to wipe her memory."

"Maybe you shouldn't have done it then," he said evenly.

"I had to."

His jaw muscles flexed as he crossed his arms over his chest. "What do you want from me, Jemma? My approval? Because you're not going to get it. I'm not good with this. With any of it."

"It's one date, Trace. It doesn't mean anything. *He* doesn't mean anything. You have to know that."

"That's what you keep saying," he muttered, clearly not believing it anymore. "But every time I turn my back, there he is. I don't like it, and I sure as shit don't like him around *you*." There was no mistaking the jealousy in his voice, the possessiveness in his tone.

"He's just helping us."

"Yeah, he's helping alright," he bit back sarcastically. "More like helping himself to you." He shook his head, his eyes dropping with concern. "At the end of the day, he's still just a Rev. He can't be trusted."

"I know that," I nodded in *semi* agreement. "But I can't just walk away from the deal. He'll take away the compulsion and everything bad that happened to Taylor will come crashing down on her again. I can't do that to her." I would go on a hundred Hell-dates with Dominic before I let that happen. "Besides, it'll give me a chance to feel him out, to see if he figured out what this whole 'great evil' thing is about. It'll be more like a business date."

He didn't appear any less apprehensive about it.

"And, I have my Amulet," I continued, undeterred. "Hell, I'll even bring some Cinderdust in case he really pisses me off." I winked at him playfully, and his eyes softened in response. "You already *know* where my heart is, Trace, so how about you stop worrying about Dominic and start thinking about me and you instead. Like where we're going for our first date." I bounced up on my toes and stole a kiss from his lips.

Heat flashed in his eyes. "Who says I haven't already?"

Reaching out a hand, he grabbed the hem of my blazer and tugged me forward into him.

A soft gasp escaped my mouth as my body crashed into his. He paused to look down at me for a moment and then moved his hand to my head, burying his fingers in my hair and using it as an anchor to draw my mouth to his. Our lips connected, and I welcomed the sparks as they crackled against my skin. I could feel the want in his touch, the need in his kiss, and it only made the charge between us stronger. I pushed myself all the way into him and he groaned in response.

"Nice form, Trace!" heckled someone from behind us.

Trace pulled back from the kiss, but his hold on me never gave. "You like that, Travie?" he called back, his eyes directed somewhere over my shoulder. "I got it from your mom."

Claps of laughter erupted behind us.

"Nothing better than a mom-joke to start the day."

His dimples popped as he smiled down at me. "You busy Saturday night? I need a date for Taylor's party."

"What, Travie's mom isn't available?"

He burst out laughing. "Something like that," he said and then leaned into me. Brushing his lips along my cheek, he made his way to my ear and whispered hotly. "Will you go with me?"

"Yes," I said without thinking twice. Honestly. I'd be his date for the freakin' end of the world if he asked me to.

"I'll pick you up at eight," he said, trailing an even row of kisses along my neck.

I sighed, sinking further into him. "I'm looking forward to seeing you all decked out in your tuxedo again." Especially since the last time was cut short.

"And I'm looking forward to seeing you in pretty much anything." He pulled back and smiled seductively. "Or, better yet, nothing at all."

"Trace!"

He laughed, all throaty and sexy.

"Honestly, it might come to that if I don't find a decent dress to wear in time." Just thinking about dress shopping reminded me of Taylor and how she was there to save the day for me last time. I choked back the memory, afraid I might burst in tears if I didn't keep myself in check.

"You'll find a dress," he said as though he suddenly had the gift of foresight, "and you'll look beautiful in it no matter what," he added, circling his thumb against the small of my back.

It was a small gesture, but it was enough. I lifted onto my toes and kissed him full on the mouth.

The electrifying humming sensation immediately funneled through my body, making me feel as though everything were right in the world again. I knew it was a lie, of course, but I basked in the sweet deception nonetheless.

33. DEMONOLOGY

After three grueling hours of hand to hand combat training followed by an additional hour of practicing takedowns and grappling techniques, Gabriel-the-slayer-driver finally agreed to let me have a break. Twisting the cap off my water bottle, I guzzled down half of it and then collapsed on the sparring mats in a pool of my own sweat. My reprieve, of course, would be short-lived. Demonology 101 was up next and I knew he was about to exhaust my brain twice as much as he did the rest of my body.

"What is a demon?" he asked, kneeling down on the mat without even so much as a lick of sweat on his skin.

Apparently, it was time for a pop quiz of the magical variety.

"A demon is an unclean spirit or otherwise dark soul from Hell that may or may not be in possession of a human body."

"How does one vanquish a demon?" he continued, firing his questions at me without the slightest pause.

"A hell-trap or Exorcism, depending on the demon's form."

"What is a Revenant?"

"An *earth-born* vampiric demon, capable of mind-control and super human strength."

"How do you vanquish a Revenant?"

"A stake to the heart or Cinderdust, preferably both."

"Define lycanthropy."

"The transformation of a human into an animal form, usually a wolf, also known as a werewolf."

"How is a werewolf created?"

"From the bite of a Shifter while in animal form," I answered, wiping the sweat from my forehead.

"How can the werewolf curse be cured?"

"Trick question," I smirked at him. "The werewolf curse is incurable."

"How do you vanquish it?"

"Heart removal or silver bullet to the heart."

"What is the Dark Legion?"

"Descendants that have turned against the Order and pledged themselves to the dark side."

"What is the purpose of the Dark Legion?"

"To, um—" I fumbled with my fingers as I tried to sift through the countless lectures for the correct answer. "To wreak havoc," I answered, though it came out more like a question.

Gabriel blinked his disapproval. "The purpose of the Dark Legion is to bring forth the *Light Bearer*, whom they believe to be the true Savior, and open the Gates of Hell."

"Right."

"Who is the Light Bearer?"

"Lucifer, also known as Satan, also known as the Devil."

"And, as a disciple of The Order of The Rose, your purpose is to do what?"

"To stop them at all costs."

Julian slow-clapped his hands. "You say it, but do you really believe it?"

"Excuse me?" What the heck was that supposed to mean?

"I just don't know if you're up for the challenge, kid."

"How about you worry about yourself, string bean, and I'll worry about me."

"String bean?" He ticked his head back at my insult. "What's that supposed to mean?"

I took a swig from my water bottle and grinned obnoxiously. Two could play his game. "Figure it out, genius."

"Alright, that's enough. On your feet," ordered Gabriel.

Apparently, my break was over and I was convinced it was all Julian's fault. I cut a hard look over at him and shuffled back up to my feet. Gabriel marched offside to the weapons case and pulled out some medieval, double-sided axe that looked like it came in straight out of the Middle Ages.

"This is a battle axe." He swung the weapon in the air, twisting it around his torso, under his arm, and then back again. "There are several different ways to engage your target using this one weapon. The bit," he said, pointing to the glinting iron blade, "the handle, the butt—good for spiking, and the axe-eye—ideal for stabbing." He swung the axe over his shoulder, around his side, and then straight forward, showcasing all the different angles and swinging techniques.

"That doesn't look very user-friendly," I noted. It seemed rather big and clunky. "What exactly am I supposed to do with *that*, and how am I going to kill a Revenant with it?"

"Not every battle you face will be waged on earth, Jemma. You will need different weapons for different battles, and at the end of the day, you need to be skilled in each of them."

"Right." Trace's words about *this world and beyond* whipped around my subconscious, reminding me that I was only scratching the surface when it came to this new world I was living in. "But can we just stick to Revs for now? Like, I still don't know how to evade one if I needed to. Or maybe we can talk about tracking and ambushing them in the event that you can't really fight them outright?" I bit my lip, trying to quell my verbal diarrhea.

"Why would you not be able to outright fight?" asked Gabriel suspiciously.

Crap. Quick, start the back-peddling! "How should I know," I laughed, trying to act ditzy and confused. "I'm just trying to take a more active role. You know, participate, ask questions..."

"Sure."

I couldn't tell if he was buying it or not.

"So, anyway, how do I use that thing?" I asked, ticking my chin to the axe.

Without a warning, he tossed the axe over at me.

Being that I was a normal, seventeen-year-old girl, my natural instinct *should* have been to flinch back or dive out of the way, but instead I threw my arm straight out and caught the handle in my hand, surprising myself and probably everyone else in the room.

The faintest hint of a smile graced Gabriel's mouth. I straightened my back as a wave of pride fluttered through my body. The truth was, I had to work damn hard for those smiles and it was worth it every time.

After a very brief introduction into battle axe yielding, Gabriel was ready to put my new skill to the test. I wasn't nearly as ready but I quickly learned that with Gabriel, you had to move fast or risk getting left behind. Coming at me from every direction, my only objective was to put him down.

He moved quickly, too quickly for me to keep up, although in my defense, *I'd* just finished five hours of non-stop training and *he* was a Revenant who hadn't even broken a sweat. We were clearly on uneven playing fields.

"What's the matter, Jemma? Can't keep up?" said Gabriel, taunting me from behind me as I aimlessly swung the axe around.

"Yeah, I'm a little tired," I huffed, swinging again, and

missing again. "Sue me."

"And now you're a little *dead* too," he answered as he pulled the weapon from my grip and sent me flailing to the ground on my hands and knees. Hard. "Get up," he said sans remorse.

Snarling at him, I forced myself back up and retook my previous stance. He tossed the weapon back at me and started circling again, pushing at my back and knocking my arm down as I tried to bring the axe back into position.

"Not good enough. Try harder."

I spun on him, hooking the axe from around the side, though he easily maneuvered out of my reach and disarmed me once again.

"Dead again." He swung it back to me.

"This stupid thing is useless," I said, adjusting my hold on it as though my grip on it were the problem here.

"Again," he ordered, ignoring my protests.

He was really starting to tick me off.

Holding the axe firmly in my hands, I trailed his every move, turning with him as he tried to weave circles around me, refusing to give up my back to him. As I readied myself for another attempt, so did he.

He moved faster, jabbing me with his fist while continuously changing directions, making it hard for me to predict his next move. The more he jabbed me, the angrier I got, and the angrier I got, the harder it was for me to see anything but red.

Cursing, I pulled back the axe and swung.

Not only did he easily catch the weapon, but this time, he used it to hold me in place as he twisted my arm back and kicked me to the ground.

"Dammit, Gabriel!"

"Again."

"No! Not again!" I threw the axe across the room, watching furiously as it clinked and crashed against the floor. "What the hell is your problem? Why are you being like this?"

"You wanted to step up your training, did you not?"

"Yeah, but this—"

"Well, that's what I'm doing. Do you think your opponents are going to be gentle with you? They won't. They're going to play dirty and say horrible things that a girl like you should never have to hear, but that is the reality of this life. I'm trying to prepare you because if anything happens to you—" He cut himself off, rolling his shoulders as he tried to regain his composure. He softened his eyes and his tone when he continued. "The harder I make it for you in this room, the easier it will be for you out there. You must understand that."

My anger fizzled away into nothingness. "I understand." I did, and I knew he was right. I'd seen it firsthand that night in the warehouse. They were ruthless and heartless and used whatever warfare was at their disposal.

I chased away my disenchantment, pulled in a breath and then dragged myself back to my feet.

Stalking across the room, I bent down and picked up the battle axe from its resting place. All my frustration and exhaustion was gone. Twisting it in my hand, I walked back over to where Gabriel stood on the mat and nodded once, letting him know without words that I wasn't leaving this room until I got it right.

I lifted the axe and smiled. "Alright, Handler, let's do this. Give me everything you got."

And he did. Over and over again until I finally got it right.

Gabriel was unusually quiet on the drive home. I could tell something was plaguing his mind, and as much as I wanted to be there for him, to rummage through his closet of skeletons, I wasn't entirely sure how to even start the conversation. Gabriel wasn't exactly the most talkative guy, and frankly, he was pretty intimidating even on a good day.

I chewed my bottom lip as I tried to wrangle out some moxie.

"Is everything okay?" I finally asked, spitting out the words before my mouth had a chance to chicken out on me. When he looked over at me with creased eyebrows, I added, "You seem kind of upset."

"Yes."

"Yes everything's okay, or yes you're upset?"

He didn't answer, but it was clear that he was bothered by something.

"Do you want to talk about it?" I asked, angling my body towards him.

"I'm not sure there's any benefit in talking to you."

"Ouch." Okay, so I wasn't a clinical psychologist or anything, but I wasn't *that* clueless.

His pale, jade-green eyes fell on me. "What's the point of talking to you if you're just going to lie to me?"

"Who says I'm going to lie to you?"

He arched his brow at me like an insult. "You've already made that quite clear to me the night of the search."

"This is about Dominic," I realized. It wasn't hard to guess since most of my issues with people stemmed from my involvement with Dominic. Not that I was like, involved with Dominic. Obviously.

"I know something is going on, Jemma. I can sense your anxiety. It pains me that you don't trust me enough to come to me." His eyes remained pinned on the road ahead.

"I trust you, Gabriel. I trust you with my life. I just..." I shook my head, unsure of how I could even begin to explain the mess I was in or why I'd kept it from him for so long.

"Is it about the Amulet?" he asked without meeting my stunned gaze. "Are you in trouble?"

"What makes you say that?"

"I noticed a significant change in you right after your sister gave you the Amulet." His grip tightened around the steering wheel. "Is Dominic after it? Is he threatening you?"

"No." I lowered my gaze, staring down at my fingers. "He's actually been protecting me."

"From what?"

I didn't answer.

"Engel." The word sounded like corrosive metal when it came out of his mouth.

I couldn't bring myself to deny it or confirm it, deciding instead to see what kind of a reaction he had to it.

He looked over at me with wise, knowing eyes. "I can't help you if you don't tell me what's going on," he said pleadingly, like my safety—my life—genuinely mattered to him.

I wanted so bad to talk to him, to confide in him, to tell him the truth about what's been going on. He deserved to know the truth. He deserved absolute transparency. He deserved so much more than what I'd been giving him. I couldn't risk it before—I couldn't risk Tessa finding out about it while Taylor was still missing. She would have completely bypassed her for the greater good of all, and there was no way I could allow that to happen.

But Taylor was home now, safe and sound.

What harm could it do?

"He knows I have the Amulet." I felt a huge weight lift off my shoulders as the words passed through my lips. It was as though the shackles around my ankles had been broken and all I could do was run like the wind with it. "He's known since the Spring Fling dance."

"Why didn't you come to me?"

"I was trying to take care of it on my own. I didn't want to involve anyone and risk getting more people hurt."

"Do you have any idea of the danger you're in? How could

you pretend everything was okay all this time?" he asked, looking at me as though I'd just taken off my mask. "How could you lie to *me* all this time?"

"I'm sorry that I lied to you, Gabriel, I am. But I've been pretending everything is okay since the day my father was killed, and today is no exception," I admitted solemnly. "If I don't lie to myself—if I don't find ways to keep living my life in spite of everything, I wouldn't be able to get out of bed in the morning."

He blinked slowly as though taking it in.

"I pretended it was all okay because I *had* to believe that it would be." I didn't meet his eyes when I continued. "But it's not okay. Nothing is."

"Has he come after you?" he asked, trying hard to hide the concern in his voice, but it was right there, looming just under the surface.

I nodded that he had. "I know he can't hurt me while I'm wearing the Amulet, but that won't stop him from going after the people I love to get to me," I explained, trying to keep my emotions steady. "That's why I have to get him first."

"What is with you Blackburns?" he bit out angrily. "If it were that easy to take him out, someone would have already done it. He's powerful, Jemma. Far more powerful and cunning than you can ever imagine. You aren't ready to face a Revenant like Engel. You aren't ready to face *any* Revenant."

"I've already faced him twice and lived to talk about it," I shot back, feeling the burn from his words and his lack of confidence in my abilities.

"That is because you have the Amulet," he said plainly.

"Exactly! I *have* the Amulet. Who better to face off against him than the girl that can't be killed?"

"I can think of several people."

I chose to ignore that. "If I don't do something about it, he's just going to keep coming after me and my friends, picking us off one at a time until he gets what he wants. I can't let him do that, Gabriel. I have to stop him."

"You can't do this on your own. I forbid it."

"I'm not doing it on my own. Trace and Dominic are helping me." I looked over at him before continuing. "You won't have to lift a finger. Just please don't tell Tessa about it."

"I won't be involved in lying to her," said Gabriel firmly. There were no ifs, ands or buts about it.

"Then don't lie to her...just don't tell her about it right away," I said, pretending there was a difference. "Give me some time to fix this, Gabriel. I can do it. I know I can."

"This is a bad idea." He shook his head, still staring out at the road ahead of us. "No good will come out of this."

Something in the back of my mind was telling me he was right, but I quickly batted the irksome thought away.

I was already in way too deep to turn back now.

"I have everything under control. Trust me," I assured him, though I really wasn't sure who I was trying to convince more.

Him, or myself?

34. GREAT TEMPTATIONS

Friday came dressed in gloom with a torrential downpour that smothered the town like a nightmare that couldn't be woken up from. There was a constant hissing in the air, a scratching taunt that gnawed at my insides, almost as though the wind were trying to reach out and caution me, to warn me of what was to come. My skin prickled from the presage.

There was still no news about Engel. Ben, Trace and Dominic had spent the night tracking his scent and following up with leads that led nowhere. There was absolutely no sign of Engel anywhere in town, nor any other Revs for that matter. It was as though they'd all just picked up and disappeared from Hollow Hills.

Of course, I knew better than that. I knew the silence was surely just the quiet before the storm.

Dominic picked me up after my shift at All Saints, ready to cash in on his end of our agreement. I was infinitely less enthused than he was for this date and went into it with the mindset of just wanting to get the whole thing over with. Besides, it would give me a chance to catch up with him and find out if he'd heard anything from the ol' vampire grapevine.

"Where are we going anyway?" I asked him when he turned onto the main highway instead of the throughway that would've taken us to the Huntington Manor.

He turned his smoldering chocolate eyes to me and quirked his lip up on the side. "It's a surprise," he said, refusing to relinquish any clues as to what his plans for me were. "Just sit back and enjoy the ride."

Right. As if that was even a possibility.

I slouched back in my seat and watched the wipers slash back and forth as the slick road became a melted blur of scenic sameness. Seconds turned into minutes and my eyelids became too heavy to keep open.

Angel.

I felt a poke on my arm and opened my eyes, fighting to bring myself out of the sleepy haze I'd drifted into. Realizing the car had stopped, I straightened in my seat and searched my surroundings for telling signs.

"Where are we?" I asked, staring out at an unfamiliar dark-brick building that appeared to be manned by two juice-heads.

"Temptation," he smiled wickedly. "The most sinful drinking hole in all the lands."

"I'm not going in there," I protested, still cranky from having just woken up. "I'm not even legal," I reminded him.

"Need I remind you that this is my date, therefore my rules? Moreover, this isn't that sort of establishment. Your identification is not a prerequisite, angel. In fact, they much prefer you come without it."

"What kind of a club doesn't want you to bring your I.D.?"

"The kind that doesn't want you leaving a trail of trouble."

Oh, sure, because that sounded totally legit. I rolled my eyes. "How long do I have to stay in there?"

"As long as it takes."

"As long as it takes to do *what?*"

"To break you out of your good girl shell." He winked, though something in those dark, sinful eyes of his told me he wasn't joking. "I know there's a bad girl in there simply dying to break out and I've decided to appoint myself as her unofficial freer."

"How very noble of you."

Flashing a grin, he swung his door open and climbed out of the car, adjusting his black jacket and then coming around the front of the car.

When he reached my side, he pulled open my door and held out his hand as though this were an actual date; as though he were some kind of gentleman.

I passed on the offer and stepped out on my own instead. The rain was still falling but I welcomed it, enjoying the cold wetness as it trickled down my skin in cleansing streaks.

He quirked an eyebrow at me. "Are you always this stubborn?"

"Yes, I am," I answered, staring him dead in the eyes. "And I'm also really moody, a hot-head, and a liar."

"Is that so?" He appeared to be smirking at my self-assessment. "You wouldn't be trying to sway my interest, now would you? Because I have to say, those sorts of things turn me on."

Irritated, I rolled my eyes at him again. "Is there anything that doesn't turn you on?"

"Not when it comes to you, temptress." He ran the back of his knuckles against my cheek, searing my skin.

I turned my face away from his touch, quickly breaking the connection. "It's not going to work, you know."

"What's that?"

"Trying to coerce the good out of me."

"Is that a fact?"

"I'm nothing like you, Dominic, and I never will be."

"Never say never, angel." He stepped in closer to me, prompting me to push back against the car door and suck in a breath. "I think you're a lot more like me than you'd ever care to admit. I can see it in those seductive eyes of yours."

"See what?"

"The curious thirst for the darkness." He pushed up against me, commanding yet careful. "It's in your blood."

My hand instantly moved up between us, forcing him to reopen the space. "You don't know the first thing about me," I bit out through gritted teeth. "And you never will as long as I have anything to say about it."

The words had come out far angrier than I had intended them to, and even though it troubled me to see myself react that way, I wasn't yet primed to question it.

"If you say so, angel," he said, chuckling softly as though he knew he'd gotten under my skin. "However, be warned."

"About what?"

"About how much I enjoy a good challenge."

I walked into Temptation with my expectations low and my guard all the way up. The club boasted two floors of fully stocked bars and a purple-lit ambiance that fell over the club like a blanket. Bodies moved wickedly, grinding against each other as they danced to the kind of music that sounded like a prelude to something more. There was sin in the air and everyone appeared to be high on the fumes of it.

I followed Dominic to a private table tucked away behind white organza curtains, feeling increasingly uneasy as I moved deeper into my own personal Hell. There was something off about this place, something wrong, and it was making my skin burn with trepidation. Straightening my back, I put on my best resting bitch face and slid into the booth ahead of Dominic.

"Something to drink, love?" he asked, gesturing over his

shoulder like he was part-owner of the joint.

A blond waitress with hair that reached all the way down to her round hips walked up to our table. "What can I get for you tonight, Dominic?"

She knew him by name. *Figures.*

"I'll have my usual."

"And for your little friend?" she asked him with ridicule in her tone.

"His *little* friend will just have water," I answered her, forcing her eyes to begrudgingly fall on me. "Bottled." I didn't trust this place. God only knows what kind of venereal diseases were floating around in the tap water.

The waitress arched her brows and glanced back at Dominic like he had the final say.

"She'll have the same as me."

"Um, no I won't," I objected, but it was like I wasn't even in the room, let alone at the table.

He gave her a cunning wink and she smiled impishly at him before prowling off, swishing her hips from side to side like some sex-infused pendulum.

I glowered at him. "Are you this courteous with all your dates or am I just the lucky one?"

"I don't have dates, angel. I have liaisons."

"Gross, Dominic. I don't even want to know what that means." Though, I had a fairly good idea.

He laughed, leaning back in the booth and then stretching his arm across the frame behind me. "Well, if you change your mind, I'd be more than willing to show and tell with you."

"I'd rather set myself on fire, but thank you." I gave him a pointed look and then glanced out at the room, gauging our surroundings and company before focusing my attention back in on him. "Have you heard anything from Engel?"

"Must we sour our date with business talk? We have plenty

of time for that later."

"In case you haven't noticed, I'm running out of 'laters'," I said impatiently.

"I haven't heard anything directly, though from what I've gathered thus far, he's vacated Hollow Hills until further notice."

For whatever reason, Engel was still gone and seemed to be keeping it that way. I felt my heart gallop with hope.

"That isn't a good thing," he quickly clarified, busting my bubble of happiness.

"Why not?" I asked, baffled. Frankly, it was the best news I'd heard all month.

"Because Engel doesn't give up. I'd say it means he's gone to gather reinforcements." He placed his free hand on the table, palm down as though rooting himself in the conversation. "Something big is coming, and I'm not sure I want to be around here when it all goes down."

I scoffed at his vow of abandonment. "Thanks for the allegiance, Dominic. It's nice to know that when the going gets tough, you get gone."

"It's a matter of self-preservation, love. You ought to think about getting out of here too. You have the Amulet, the blond is safe and sound. I'd say it's about time you move on to greener pastures."

"I can't just run off and save myself, Dominic. He'll go after the people I love."

"And?"

I glared back at him.

"Ah, yes, of course. Attachments." He tweaked his dark blond eyebrows as though he were above it all. "They're far more trouble than they're worth if you ask me."

"You say that yet here you are," I shot back.

He looked at me strangely, though he didn't grace me with a

rebuttal as the waitress returned with our drinks. She placed two glasses on the table (along with zero water bottles) and then left without a word to either of us. Dominic, like a predator that already had his prey cornered, never took his eyes off me.

I straightened under his stare and trudged on. "So, basically, you think Engel's gone to build his goon brigade because something big is coming, but we have no clue what that might be," I summarized, feeling more bleak than ever before.

"Precisely."

I pushed out a gust of air, sending a lock of my hair fluttering in front of my face.

"Relax, angel." He reached over and tucked the strand behind my ear, and I shivered from the brief contact. Involuntarily.

Damn bloodbond.

"I've already put the word out. Now it's just a matter of waiting to collect."

Again with the waiting game. Was he not getting the urgency of our little problem or did he just not give an actual damn?

Maybe he was onto something with the whole 'not caring about anyone or anything' thing. *Must be nice*, I mused.

Unfortunately, I didn't have that luxury. I shook away the reverie. "Shouldn't we be out there then? Talking to people—to Revs that might have heard something?"

"We aren't just here for the good malt, angel. In case you haven't noticed, this place is a hotbed for Supernaturals."

My eyes quickly darted around the room, surveying the alleged suspects. Maybe that was the reason I had felt uneasy the moment I walked in here. Apparently, I was on enemy territory, and somehow, my body knew it before I did.

I guess the Cloaking spell really was fading after all.

"Balls," said Dominic, his eyes narrowing into slits.

"What is it?" I asked as my pulse quickened. I could tell by the look on his face that something bad was headed our way. I turned around and tried to follow his pointed gaze, searching the room for what surely had to be Engel or his coven of rabid Revs.

What I found was far, far worse.

"Balls," I repeated, turning back to Dominic as Tessa and Gabriel zeroed in on our table, looking *not* surprised and wholly pissed off. How the hell was I going to explain this one away?

The seconds ticked by like tepid tar. A moment later, an overbearing shadow loomed over our table.

"Tessa. Gabriel. You're both looking well."

"Get up, right now," ordered Tessa, ignoring Dominic's greeting. "Both of you."

"What's the hurry? Sit down, take a load off, enjoy a drink with us," answered Dominic, clearly enjoying the nuclear bomb that had just gone off in my life. "You look like you can use a drink. Possibly even two."

"You have two seconds to get up before I feed your ass to that pack of werewolves at the back of the bar," she said without even looking.

Dominic berated her with his laughter and was about to say something when I quickly jumped up from the table.

"Come on, Dominic. Let's just go." I knew my sister well enough to know she wouldn't hesitate to make good on her threat. Plus, I *really* didn't want to face the firing squad on my own.

He looked over at me for a moment and then nodded. "Very well, angel," he said, finishing the rest of his drink and then standing. "The things I do for you.

35. HIGHWAY TO HELL

The tension in the car was thick and suffocating, like the lies between us had manifested into something tangible. Neither Tessa nor Gabriel said anything to me on the drive back to Huntington Manor. I wanted to think that their silent treatment was simply the result of catching me out with Dominic, but something told me this was about far more than their disapproval of the company I'd been choosing to keep.

Dominic's car was already parked in his driveway when we pulled up to the Manor in Gabriel's black SUV. Breathing a sigh of relief that he didn't bail out on me, I got out of the car and followed Gabriel and my sister into the house as my brain conjured up a dozen different reasons why the two of them were here, and exactly how much trouble I was going to be in.

"Sit down," ordered Tessa as we entered the den, her gray eyes as sharp as a sacrificial dagger.

I flopped down on the red sofa and watched as Tessa moved around the room, locking the doors and drawing the curtains together as if to entomb us in our own coffin of privacy.

I looked up at Gabriel, who was standing by the mantel, staring down at me in utter silence. His arms were crossed over his chest and his eyebrows were pulled together in disappointment. It was the same look he'd left me with the last time I saw him.

I threw the disappointed look right back at him. "You promised you wouldn't tell." The sting from his betrayal made my voice crack like a prepubescent kid.

"She had to know," he answered mechanically. "She's your sister, and I'm your Handler. It's our duty and responsibility to keep you safe." The fact that he didn't seem to have any remorse only made me angrier with him.

"I trusted you."

"When are you going to learn, angel?" Dominic took a swig of the drink he'd fixed himself before we arrived. "When it comes to Gabriel, it's always duty above all else. Right, brother?"

"Something you couldn't even begin to understand the meaning of," snapped Tessa, joining Gabriel by the broiling fire, her face draped in shadows as the flames danced behind her thin, athletic frame. "The only person you give a damn about is yourself, you arrogant little—"

"That's ironic coming from you, Miss Missing-In-Action."

Tessa's arm lashed out through the air so quickly that I could have blinked and missed it. Luckily, Gabriel was ready for it, and much faster than her. He quickly clipped her wings mid-air before she had a chance to make contact with Dominic's face.

"Stay focused," cautioned Gabriel. "This is about Jemma."

Shaking out of his hold, she straightened her shirt and regained her composure. Her short, dark hair was pulled back into a ponytail and even though it was hard to make out all her features in the dim light, she was still as beautiful as always. Furious, but still beautiful.

Her thoughts turned inward, darkening her expression.

"Okay, Tess, just come out with it," I said, raising my hands, ready to face her wrath. "Tell me how reckless I was and how much trouble I've gotten myself into. Go on. But just so you know, I'm already aware of it and I feel horrible."

"You feel horrible?" she repeated. The way she said it made it sound like she was insulting me, mocking me with my own words.

"I should have told you about Engel. I made a mistake. I admit that, but I'm fixing it."

"You really have no idea what you've done, do you?"

The severity of her tone made me falter.

"This is so much bigger than Engel." She shook her head at me like I was completely clueless. "They're coming for you, Jemma, and they're not going to stop until they get what they want."

I was already well aware that Engel was gathering reinforcements, and I'd made my peace with it. In fact, I was depending on it. "I'm kind of counting on that, Tess," I said, doing my best to show her I was still in control of this. "I have the Amulet and as long as it stays around my neck, two things are certain—one, I'm protected, and two, Engel will come for me—"

"Jemma."

"—But he's never going to get it, and neither will any of the leeches he sends after me. I know what I have to do. I just need to get close enough to him to—"

"Jemma!" she shouted, startling my mouth shut. "This isn't about Engel or the stupid Amulet anymore. Don't you get that? It stopped being about the Amulet the minute you took it off and let Engel taste your blood," she seethed, obviously knowing a lot more than the watered-down version I gave Gabriel.

Gabriel's eyes snapped to me for confirmation, but I didn't have the nerve to face him. Not with all my lies and dirty laundry dangling so freely in front of everyone.

"I didn't *let* him taste my blood. It just happened," I said quietly without meeting anyone's eyes. "And how do you know about that anyway?"

"You need to be less concerned about what I know and more concerned about what the *Dark Legion* knows."

"The Dark Legion?" Dominic narrowed his eyes at her. "What exactly does the Dark Legion have to do with any of this?"

"They *know* about Jemma," answered Tessa, her expression somber. "They know everything."

"So Engel has some kind of sick obsession with my blood and told all his little friends about it. Big deal. It doesn't change anything," I insisted.

"It changes *everything.*"

"Why? What difference does it make?" I continued, refusing to back away from my mounting pile of denial. "I'm still going to take him out, and anyone else he sends my way, and then all of this will go away! Everything will go back to normal."

"No, Jemma. It won't." Her eyes squeezed shut as though trying to stave off a migraine. "He knows *what* you are now. They all do. You've put something in motion that you can't undo."

Gabriel's eyebrows drew together. He heard that too.

"What do you mean he knows *what* I am?"

"I think you know what I mean," she said woefully.

"The hell I do! What are you talking about?" I demanded. "What aren't you telling me, huh? WHAT AM I?" I shouted, gripping the edge of the sofa as something primal took over inside me.

"I'm sure Tessa misspoke," said Gabriel, his eyes bouncing between me and my sister as he waited for her to confirm it.

Something told me he'd be waiting around until the next Ice Age. Clearly, I wasn't the only one left out of the loop.

"Oh, she only gave you half the story too? Well, here, I'll

catch you up," I said to Gabriel with mock-spunk. "It turns out that my blood is some kind of Revenant elixir that keeps them from being vanquished, and apparently, Tessa knows why that is."

"Jemma," said Gabriel, looking at me like I was a silly kid playing make-believe. "There is nothing in existence that can protect a Revenant from being vanquished."

"Yes, nothing...except her blood," answered Dominic. "We've already tested it every which way and the results are always the same."

An array of emotion flickered across Gabriel's eyes— confusion, concern, horror—and it only prompted my heart to beat faster and my anger to intensify.

"There you have it. So, what's the truth, Tessa?" I glared over at her with more conviction than a congregation of the Lord's most devout. "What's wrong with my blood? What am I?"

"It's not just about you, Jemma. It's our entire bloodline," she said, taking a purposeful step towards me. "The Morningstar bloodline, that is."

"Morningstar? As in *Jacqueline Morningstar*? Our mother?" I verified because, well, I wasn't sure of anything anymore.

She dipped her head in a nod and then took the seat beside me on the sofa. "The Morningstar bloodline is not like other Descendant bloodlines. We descend from a very powerful angel, Jemma—the first ever to be created and the first ever to fall."

"That's not possible," interrupted Dominic. "That bloodline doesn't exist. It's just a bunch of hogwash they put in the books to make their insignificant prophesies sound factual."

"It *is* possible, and it *does* exist," said Tessa emphatically. "You probably shouldn't talk about things you have no actual clue about."

"Is that so?" jeered Dominic.

She looked at him as though he were miles beneath her. "The

Morningstar bloodline is *the* single most powerful bloodline known to our kind. Do you really think they would share something like *that* with someone like *you*?" she asked with venomous contempt. "Think about it."

He appeared to be turning it around in his brain.

"The Order's been protecting the bloodline from the moment it was created, and for good reason. They had to make sure the balance never tipped in the wrong direction, that the Dark Legion never found out about it," explained Tessa, her eyes locked on mine now. "That's why our mates are chosen for us, why we're bred like cattle—to keep *His* blood contained," she said and then glanced away, her eyes going to some faraway place. "And it's worked fine...until now."

"Until now?" I struggled to swallow the ball that was throttling me at the back of my throat. It was taunting me with nightmares and screaming out truths I wasn't ready to hear.

"They've always known there would come a day when a daughter of the heavens would be born in His favor, and she would be the key to unlocking the gates."

"Gates? What gates?" I shook my head in confusion.

"You aren't seriously implying that she's the One in the prophecy?" flouted Dominic. "The Daughter of Hades?"

"The Daughter of *who*?" I exchanged looks with Gabriel who stood as silent as a sentinel. "What prophecy? What's he talking about? None of this is making any sense!" I shouted frantically.

"Try to keep up, angel, will you?"

I jumped up from the sofa, unable to contain the adrenaline shooting through my veins. "Go to hell, Dominic!"

"Well, that's ironic."

"Enough, Dominic!" Gabriel's voice boomed through the room like a judge's gavel.

Rubbing my temples, I tried to focus on what they were telling me. Morningstar bloodline. The First angel. Daughter of

Hades. I couldn't seem to string a set of cohesive thoughts together to save my life. "I. Don't. Understand. Someone needs to start talking plain English because I'm about to lose it," I said, bouncing looks between the three of them.

"Here, let me." Dominic leaned forward with a smirk, his eyes locked on mine like a nuclear missile locked on its target. "She's saying you're a Descendant of Lucifer, love."

"Lucifer?" My eyes bugged out wildly, threatening to pop from the surge of blood that shot to my head. "As in the devil?" There was no way I'd heard him right.

"As in Heaven's first and most powerful angel," clarified Tessa.

"Semantics," said Dominic, chuckling.

I looked over at Gabriel, desperate for him to rebuke this entire conversation, to put the two of them firmly back in their place, but he just stood there in silence, his lips pulled together in a telling line of inability.

"I think I'm going to be sick." I sat back down on the sofa and cradled my head in my hands, trying to stop the world from spinning its vicious web around me.

"His blood is dormant in me as it was in Mom and her mother, and her mother before her. But you're different, Jemma. You've always been different."

"No." It was the only word I could speak.

"The Morningstar bloodline is dominant in you. It's always been dominant and I've spent my entire life trying to protect you from that truth. Just like Mom and Dad did before me—"

"No! Stop it! Don't talk about them!" I couldn't hear this, I couldn't hear any of it. It was too much to take in. She was shattering my world with her words, dropping bombs over the only life I knew and annihilating any semblance of hope I had for a future. "Why are you doing this to me, Tessa? Why are you saying these things?"

"You *have* to hear this, Jemma. It's time you knew the truth. The whole truth." There was no comfort in her words, no softness in her voice. "Mom didn't just leave us—she died protecting your secret, Jemma, and I think Dad did too. He left the Order for a reason and it wasn't just because he didn't want this life for you. He had to keep the truth from them because if they ever found out, they would have killed you."

My head was spinning so far out of control that I could barely sit upright on the couch.

"I think she's heard enough," said Gabriel, running a hand over the length of his face. "She needs time to process this."

"How much time do you figure she needs?" said Dominic sardonically. "An hour? Maybe two? Let's play it safe and give her three just in case. I'm sure she'll be fine then."

"We need to go to the Council and figure out our next move," said Gabriel to Tessa. "Engel obviously tipped off the Dark Legion. They need to be made aware of the threat against her."

"You still don't get it, do you, brother?" Dominic shook his head at Gabriel. "They're going to kill her."

"Yes, and that's precisely why we need to go to the Council. If the Dark Legion is after her—"

"He's not talking about the Dark Legion," whispered Tessa.

"Then who is he talking about?" snapped Gabriel.

Tessa and Dominic exchanged looks as a clap of thunder exploded outside the house. Apparently, they were the only two who were still on the same page.

"The Order," answered Tessa. "He's talking about the Order."

36. NO WAY OUT

The storm tightened its grip over us, pelting rain against the glass like bullets spraying down from Heaven. Bullets that were undoubtedly meant for me.

"Why would the Order want me dead? I thought they were the good guys? I thought they were supposed to protect me?" My head was spinning around information like a wheel of misfortune and every prize I landed on was another bomb going off in my life.

"They *are* the good guys," said Gabriel firmly. He believed it with every cell in his body—it was engraved in him, right there in is DNA.

"Sure. They're they good guys...until they aren't," added Dominic cryptically. "It's quite conditional."

"What does that mean? You're not making any sense!"

"It means you're a weapon, angel. Possibly the most dangerous weapon in existence."

Tessa gave him a surly look and then turned back to me. "Your blood is like a key, Jemma, and that key can open the doors and unravel everything good they're worked to protect and everything bad they've locked away."

"So they're just going to kill me because of some ancient crap written ages ago by God knows who! Since when can blood open up doors anyway?" I shouted, grasping at straws.

"We both know that temptress blood of yours can do a lot of things," reminded Dominic.

"So that's it? Shoot first, ask questions later? Don't I get to defend myself? Don't I get to plead my case?"

"If what your sister is saying is correct, your blood is prophesied to bring on the end of days, love. To unleash Lucifer and open the very Gates of Hell. Permitting you to live means the Order is willing to risk the end of the world, which I assure you, they are not. Duty first, remember?" Dominic took of a swig of his drink and cocked his head over at Gabriel. "Tell us, brother, what are you going to do when you get the order to terminate her? Are you going to be a good little soldier and do as you're told?"

Gabriel's back stiffened.

"No one is killing anyone," said Tessa as though she had any actual control over the situation. She said it with so much conviction that I almost believed her. "All we have to do is find a way to bring down the Dark Legion, and I'll worry about the Council later, if it comes to that."

"If?" scoffed Dominic. "If the Dark Legion's already positioned themselves, as you say, it's only a matter of time before the Council catches on. And that's if they haven't already. I wouldn't be the slightest bit surprised if they already knew exactly what was going on."

"You're not helping," scolded Gabriel upon noticing my horrified expression.

"I beg to differ. I think I'm the *only* one helping here. She ought to know the truth and be prepared for the worse of it." Dominic turned his attention to Tessa. "What makes you so certain they aren't already fully aware of the circumstances? That they're not conducting inquiries into her blood as we speak?"

"I would know it if they were," insisted Tessa. "Jemma would've had to have given them blood. We would've heard something by now."

"Oh, yes, because the Council is certainly known for their outstanding open-book policies," mocked Dominic.

Tessa said something back to him, but I wasn't paying attention anymore. All of my thoughts folded inward, into my own despair, my fear, into the weighty betrayal that was dangling right in front of my eyes in plain sight.

"That's preposterous," scoffed Dominic, glaring at Tessa.

"Uncle Karl asked for a sample." My voice was so low, I wasn't even sure I'd said the words aloud.

"What makes you the expert?" retorted Tessa, glaring right back at him.

"Jemma?" Gabriel called my name through the back and forth bickering between my sister and Dominic. "A sample of what?"

The room fell silent.

"My blood."

"Dammit, angel. Tell me you didn't give it to him!"

"I didn't know."

"When? When did you give it to him?" asked Tessa and then turned to Gabriel as the two of them exchanged silent concerns.

"A few weeks ago." I looked up and meet her eyes. "He said the tests were inconclusive because of the Cloaking spell."

"Which is why they've been pushing for Invocation," realized Gabriel as he folded his arms across his chest. "They need to break the spell in order to test your blood."

"So they say," said Dominic, clearly untrusting of everything and everyone that came out of the Order.

"I'm so completely and utterly screwed," I realized, burying my head into my hands. "I can't fight them, I can't run from them, I can't even hide from them. The Dark Legion's already coming for me, and even if by some miracle I manage to escape them, the Order will be waiting to finish the job just as soon as they get caught up on the truth."

Gabriel's eyes were pained. "Jemma—"

"And that's if they haven't already found out. Maybe the test is just some formality. You know, make sure they dot their i's and cross their t's. Maybe they know all about my demonic blood and are just getting ready to make their move."

"You still have the Amulet," reminded Dominic.

"So freaking what?" I shouted at him. "My life is officially over, Dominic. I'm an abomination! Like an actual curse destined to bring on the end of the world. That's me, Jemma Blackburn, the girl fated to bring on the freaking Apocalypse!"

"It isn't over yet," said Gabriel, but I wasn't even listening anymore.

I could see Tessa's lips moving, spitting out words frantically, but none of them were registering. All I could think about was all the things I wanted to do. All the things I'd never get to become. And the worst part was, I wasn't giving it all up to do something bigger, something grander, like becoming a revered Slayer and saving the world. I was destined to be the end of it. How was I supposed to live with that?

I couldn't.

I *wouldn't*.

That wasn't who I was. I wouldn't allow it to be. "I need to give myself up," I decided, rising from the sofa in a haze of my own despair and twisted reasoning. "I have to tell the Council the truth. They'll know what to do from there."

"They'll kill you, love," said Dominic as if I hadn't already realized that.

"I'm not going to be the reason the world ends. Not again." Trace's Alt had stopped something horrible from happening in the future, but that paled in comparison to what would happen if the Dark Legion got their hands on me. Their only earthly desire was to open the Gates of Hell and raise Lucifer from his tomb. And I was the damn key.

"*Again?* What are you talking about, angel?" asked Dominic before turning to Gabriel and Tess for answers. "She's obviously lost it," he concluded.

"I haven't lost it, Dominic."

"You don't know what you're saying, love."

"I know exactly what I'm saying. I'm not going to sit back and wait for the Dark Legion to find me and use me as a weapon against the world. I might have been born with the wrong blood in my veins, but I'm still in charge of myself. I get to decide who I am, and what I do, not some ancient text written eons ago. And you know what?" I looked at each of them as a quiet fire burned inside my heart. "I choose to make my own destiny. I choose to make my life mean something...even if that means I have to die to do it."

"Look," said Tessa, cautiously moving closer to me as though I were a bomb that might go off if she got too close. "We aren't making this decision tonight. There may be a way to get you out of this without shedding your blood for either side. Dad had the right idea, with the right spell—"

"The right spell, Tess? Come on." I shook my head, knowing where she was going with this. "You can Cloak me until there isn't anything left to Cloak, but they still know who I am. Engel knows and they won't stop until they get what they want. We both know this, and soon, so will the Order."

Neither one said a word, their tongues unable to lift a lie heavy enough to bury the truth.

"Leave us, please," asked Tessa, not taking her eyes off me.

"I'm not going anywhere," said Dominic, "this is my h—"

His protest abruptly died as Gabriel snatched his elbow and

yanked him off the chair.

"This is a three hundred dollar shirt," barked Dominic, shaking his arm free from Gabriel's firm grip.

"We'll be outside," announced Gabriel, forcing Dominic to lead the way into the hall.

Tessa stood silently for a few moments after the room cleared out, waiting for the sound of the front door opening and then closing shut before turning to me. Her eyes were glowing by the light of the fire, and if I didn't know any better, I would have thought there may have even been a tear in there.

"Tess." I wanted to reach out to her, but I wasn't sure how to make the connection.

Squaring her shoulders, a steely look settled over her expression as she swallowed down any semblance of the sadness and fear she might have been feeling a moment ago, and then took a step towards me. I could see the determination in her eyes; the ferocity that told me she wasn't going to give up that easy.

"This isn't over, Jemma. Not by a long shot," she said, her voice filled with firm resolution. She was, after all, the girl with no quit in her, and she was as determined as ever to bring the fighter out of me, whether I wanted it or not.

"Then I hope you have a better plan than some Cloaking spell," I said, folding my arms.

"That's not a bad plan," she defended.

"It's a horrible plan." Shaking my head, I matched her advance. "I'm not going to spend the rest of my life on the run, hiding from everyone and everything I've ever known. It's no way to live, Tessa, and I won't live that way."

She didn't argue the point. Probably because she didn't have one. "If hiding you isn't an option, then there's only one thing left for us to do," she said, her eyes meeting mine in a chilling way. A way that let me know something big was coming;

something astronomical. "We go to Hell and we kill Lucifer ourselves."

37. THE DEVIL INSIDE

The rain fell in sheets outside Huntington Manor, pattering hard against the window as claps of thunder rattled through the glass. Each explosion getting closer and closer as though God's angels were closing in on us, ready and willing to take out Heaven's number one enemy.

"We go to *Hell*?" I repeated, certain that I'd heard her wrong. "Are you out of your freaking mind?"

"Hear me out, Jemma." She put her hands on my shoulders and pulled me down to the sofa with her. "The Dark Legion wants to raise Lucifer from his tomb, and they need your blood to do it. So, it's safe to say they aren't going to stop trying, or stop coming after you, as long as the possibility still exists."

"Right," I said, my lids fluttering nervously as I tried to follow along with everything she was saying.

"So, the only way to stop them for good is to completely eliminate any possibility of ever freeing him."

"By eliminating him," I concluded.

"Exactly." Her eyes flared with determination. "Without a devil to raise, your blood is meaningless to them."

"Okay, but..." I shook my head, unable to work out the

actual details. "*How* exactly are we going to do this? I mean, it sounds great in theory, but is any of this even possible?"

"Everything is possible, Jemma."

"We can't just 'go to Hell' like it's some corner store, can we?" I didn't know much about other Realms, but I was fairly certain that Hell didn't have an open door policy.

"Well, no, not exactly."

"And even if we did find a way to get in that didn't involve a permanent first-class ticket there, how exactly are we going to find him, *kill* him, and then get back out of there without getting caught and tortured for the rest of eternity?"

"I haven't worked out all the specifics yet."

"No shit," I said sarcastically.

"I just need a little more time to figure everything out," she said calmly as though she were planning our spring break vacation and not a suicide trip to Hell. "It's not hopeless, Jemma. Where there's a will, there's a way. We can do this as long as we stick together."

My heart softened at her sheer determination, at her absolute refusal to give up on me. I wasn't sure if she fully believed what she was saying was possible, but if she didn't, she wasn't letting on about it one bit.

"Are you in this with me?" she asked.

The more I thought about it, the less crazy and convoluted it sounded. She *was* right: where there was a will, there would surely be a way. Besides, what did I have to lose anyway? I was going down one way or another, that much was certain, but I wasn't about to make it easy on them to take me out. I wasn't about to go gently into that good ol' night.

They were going to have to take me down kicking and screaming, fists blazing until my very last breath.

"I'm in."

Gabriel drove Tessa back shortly after our talk, leaving me behind again with spiraling thoughts of an uncertain future, and Dominic. The latter rejoined me in the den as soon as the coast was clear, and quickly fixed himself another drink. He seemed rather preoccupied with pouring and stirring and mixing, never once bothering to look up at me.

"You know it's bad when Dominic Huntington can't even face you." There was something tragically ironic about that.

His eyes flicked to me, though the rest of his body didn't move an inch. "I can face you just fine, love. I'm thinking."

"About what?"

"About how I'm going to get you out of this mess."

I waited for the punchline to what was surely a joke, but it never came.

"Did Tessa have anything useful to say?" he asked as he picked up his drink and rejoined me by the fire.

"She's working on something," I offered, aiming for vague. Tessa thought it would be best if we didn't share our plan with anyone just yet. The fewer people that knew about this, the less chance there was for someone getting in the way of it.

"Mostly, she just wanted to bore me to death with her sisterly pep-talk. You know, keep your chin up, don't give up, it could be worse. She really should stick to her day job. Or night job, I should say." Okay, I was rambling now.

Dominic looked at me skeptically. "That's a long time to talk about perseverance."

"Well, she's a wordy girl."

He didn't appear to be buying my story, but he also didn't bother pressing the issue.

"Since when do you care anyway? I thought you were getting out of town the first chance you got?"

"As did I." He unfurled his arm along the back of the sofa.

"So, what changed?"

He blinked lazily as though bored of the question. "I don't have an ulterior motive, if that's what you're thinking."

"I didn't say you did."

"I happen to like the world as it is. It's as simple as that." He put his glass to his lips and took a sip of his drink, avoiding my gaze again.

"It just sounded like maybe there was more to it."

I could have sworn I saw a slight shift in his detached countenance. Something vulnerable, almost afraid, seemed to be peeking through, and it was making me dangerously curious.

"What is it that you're expecting to hear?" he asked dryly. "That I've developed some very marginal feelings for you? That I care about what happens to you?"

Was he mocking me or confessing to me? I honestly couldn't tell.

"Well, no. I mean...do you?" I cleared my throat. "Care about what happens to me?"

"I doubt you want to know the answer to that."

My heart thumped loudly, warning me that I was walking on a very dangerous, thin line. "You're probably right," I said quietly. "I'm honestly not sure which answer would be worse."

"That makes you nervous, doesn't it?" His gaze fell slowly, traveling down from my eyes to my chest, and then further down before turning back up the other way in a slow, even climb.

My body prickled with unwanted heat.

"Not at all," I lied, though I'm not sure why I bothered. He could probably already hear my heart slamming against my chest.

"I think you're lying to yourself again, angel. I think I make you *very* nervous, and I think I know why."

"You don't know anything," I said defensively, refusing to take his bait.

His eyes darkened as he took me in, watching me like a hungry wolf eyeing its prey. "I must admit, though, it does make perfect sense now."

"What does?" I was almost too afraid to ask.

"My attraction to you." A devious smile crept across his lips. "All that darkness I sensed in you..."

The heat quickly evaporated from my blood, leaving frigid ice in its place. "Go to Hell, Dominic." I shot up from the sofa and stormed out towards the nearest exit, desperate to get away from him and the painful reminder of what I really was.

In an instant, he was behind me, his hands gripping my shoulders as he pulled me back against his chest. I gasped. His face dipped down into my hair, his arms circling around my chest as he held me firmly against him.

"Stop running from what you are, temptress." His voice tickled my ear and I shivered involuntarily.

"Let me go, Dominic."

"You ought to learn to embrace it, to use it your advantage."

"I don't want to embrace it. I don't want to have anything to do with it. It's not who I am!"

"The blood doesn't lie, angel, and I think deep down you know that as much as I do."

Something inside me cracked, splintered.

"Perhaps, one day, you'll come to realize that—possibly even welcome that side of yourself."

"That's never going to happen," I promised blindly. My eyes filled up with tears, burning like acid rain drops that ached to fall free. "I'd sooner rip my veins open and let every last drop of it pour out of me before I ever welcomed it into my life." The admission came out of me without my permission.

"That would be a real pity, angel."

"More like a worldwide blessing." I pushed his arms apart and broke out of his hold, causing the tears I'd been trapping to simultaneously break free.

Remembering the last time I cried in front of him, I kept my back to him and wiped them away before he could see.

"I suppose it's a matter of perspective," he said calmly. "It doesn't have to be a bad thing, angel. None of this does."

I spun on him, completely horrified. "How could you see it any other way, Dominic? How could *anyone*? I'm as damned as the damned could get. Anyone with eyes can see that."

Anyone *decent*, that is.

My thoughts immediately went to Trace. He had no idea what was going on; no clue about what I really was. What would he think when he learned the truth? That I was nothing more than the glorified spawn of Lucifer. My stomach twisted and turned with disgust, cutting through to me until I couldn't stand it anymore.

"I'm going to be sick," I said and bolted for the bathroom.

I barely had enough time to drop onto my knees before I began heaving violently, my body spewing all the bile and truth and corruption out of me. Tears continued to spill as the already-broken pieces inside of me shattered over and over again. Shards of brokenness upon shards of brokenness, slicing and ripping at my skin and bones and heart.

Dominic appeared behind me after a few agonizing moments, his footsteps giving me no warning or heads up. I wanted to tell him to go away, to leave me in my sickness and misery, but I couldn't stop vomiting long enough to get the words out.

He crouched down beside me and pulled my hair back. He didn't move or say anything until I was done.

"Better?" he asked after the longest minute of my life.

I flushed the toilet and scooted back, propping myself against the cabinet as I tried to get my body to stop thwacking.

"He's going to leave me." I pulled my knees up to my chest.

"If he leaves you then he never deserved you to begin with," said Dominic, knowing what I was talking about—what I was sick about—without even having to utter the words.

"He deserves so much better than what I am."

I was right the first time—I *was* a plague, and destiny just confirmed it for me. How could I even attempt to stand beside him now? He was a beautiful, loving, godly being, and I was the Daughter of Hades.

Tears sprung from my eyes and fell, running endlessly down my cheeks.

I should just disappear now—run away before he finds out the truth and tosses me out with the trash. And who could blame him? I was worse than trash. I was the walking Apocalypse.

More tears fell.

"Alright. Get up." Dominic's hard tone snapped me out of my downward spiral of self-loathing. "The pity-party's over."

I crinkled my nose at him. "Actually, I'm just getting started."

"Actually," he said as he reached down and grabbed my upper arm, pulling me up to my feet in one swift move, "you're done."

I looked at him indignantly. "I think I'm entitled to a few tears, Dominic. This might be nothing to *you*, being that you're a big black hole of destruction-loving darkness, but for a *normal* person, this is a pretty BIG DEAL!"

"Firstly, you already had your moment. You cried and you retched and now you're done. Secondly, I take offense to that. Thirdly, it is a 'big deal'," he said, using air quotes, "and that's precisely why you need to keep your head on straight and start working on a way to save your neck, because trust me, angel, you're not going to do it drowning in a bucket of your own tears. Are you reading me clearly or should I go on?"

My mouth dropped open to bark something back at him, but I quickly shut it, realizing he was completely right.

"No." I pulled my arm free and then swiped away the last, straggling tear. "I'm done."

"Good. Now, let's fix ourselves a couple of stiff drinks and figure out how we're going to save the world from *you*."

"Dominic!"

He grinned back at me, a soft twinkle playing in his eyes. As blunt and inappropriate and downright infuriating as he was, I couldn't help but smile back at him. What else could I do? The guy had a demented sense of humor.

Curled up on the sofa in the den again, I sat in quiet contemplation, staring into the fire pit as Dominic whipped us up something to take the edge off the dire circumstances. The wheels in my head were churning as determination began taking over. I had to figure out a way to stop this, to stop the prophecy and change my grim fate, and the more I thought about it, the more I realized Tessa was right. Lucifer *was* the key to stopping all of it.

Of course, if I had any chance of bending the prophecy to my will, I first needed to fully understand my role in it. Only then would I be able to do anything about it.

"You're going to chew a hole right through your cheek," said Dominic as he placed two glasses on the coffee table and retook his seat beside me on the couch.

"We need to find out everything we can about the prophecy," I said, continuing my inner dialogue aloud. If we were going to take out Lucifer for good, we needed to figure out where he was being kept, and what exactly was needed to revive him.

"You're plotting, love. I like it."

"If we can find out how this is supposed to go down, maybe

271

we can figure out a way to stop it."

"As far as I know, the Council keeps all their old scriptures and texts down in the *Vaults*. However, you're going to have a difficult time gaining access to it. It's locked up tighter than Fort Knox."

"Do you think Gabriel can get in?"

Dominic laughed as he picked up his glass. "Not since he Turned."

"What about the Dark Legion? If they know about the prophecy then they must have their own text, right? Maybe they have information that the Council doesn't have."

"Such as what?"

"Such as the *when*, or more importantly, the *how*," I said, scooting in closer to him. "They aren't just going to wing it. They need my blood for a reason, probably for some kind of ritual, right? We need to find out exactly what that is."

"And how to you intend on doing that, temptress?"

"Not me, Dominic. *You*."

He laughed as though I weren't being completely and totally serious about it.

"You must have a contact, someone from the inside that can tell us what we need to know."

"What makes you so sure of that?" he wondered.

"Well, you're obviously not with the Order, so..."

"So, if I'm not with the Order, I must be with the Dark Legion?" he surmised.

"Isn't that where all Descendants go when they've turned against the Order?"

"Let's get something clear, angel. I don't work for *anyone*. Not for the Order and not for the Dark Legion."

"So you're an independent contractor then." I thought about it for a moment. "That might actually work in our favor."

"How do you suppose?"

"Well, you don't have ties to either side." I moved in a little closer, holding his gaze as I purposefully placed my hand on his knee. "You're in the perfect position."

His eyes snapped to my hand. "To do what?"

"To play ball with the dark side." It came out far more seductive than I had intended it to. "We need someone on the inside, someone who could gain access and find out what they know, and what they're planning." I leaned in closer to him, holding his gaze. "Who better than you, Dominic?"

"Reaching out to them is risky. I'd be putting myself directly on their map, and I'm not sure I'm prepared to stick my neck out that far." A smug look came over his expression. "The Council's already looking for a reason to dust me. I'm not sure I should be giving them any more reasons."

"No one would have to know but us." I bit my bottom lip.

His eyes instantly glazed over with want as he stared down at my mouth. "That's not fair, angel. You're playing dirty."

"All is fair in love and war, Dominic."

"You truly are going to be the death of me."

"I'm going to be the death of all of us if we don't figure out a way to stop this."

Forcing his eyes back up to mine, he ran his fingers along his smooth jawline.

"You're the only one who can do this," I said, pushing harder. Alarm bells sounded inside me, warning me to tread carefully—to think this through. Thrusting Dominic towards the Dark Legion for recon work probably wasn't the best idea. Frankly, it was downright dangerous, but it was also the only idea I had at this point. "*Please*, Dominic."

"Very well. I'll play ball with the dark side, as you put it." A wicked smile sprouted on his lips, letting me know there was going to be a price to pay.

With Dominic, there always was.

"Just know that you're going to owe me big for this, angel. Bigger than you've ever owed anyone in your life." His onyx eyes took in every inch of me as if to survey his prize. "And I promise you...I *will* collect."

38. WHISPERS IN THE DARK

It was well past midnight by the time I got back home. I tiptoed up the stairs with my shoes in hand, doing my best not to make any sounds that might alert my uncle to my presence. The last thing I wanted to do after everything that happened tonight was see him. I had no idea how much he knew or on which side of the enemy line he stood. Just being in the house made me feel uneasy, like I may have been sleeping under the enemy's roof all along and didn't even know it.

Once inside my room, I carefully closed the door behind myself and released the breath I'd been holding since I got upstairs. I stood there for a moment, letting the quiet and darkness wrap itself around my tattered soul.

A small light flicked on behind me, startling me. Panicked, I whipped around expecting to find an intruder—some unknown face from the Dark Legion ready to make good on the prophecy.

"It's just me," said Trace.

He was sitting at my desk with his arms crossed over his husky chest, and a sexy half-smile on his lips. Lips that made me want to sell my soul for the chance to kiss them again. I smiled back at him and padded across the room.

"I missed you," I said, crawling onto his lap.

He pulled me into his warmth and tightened his arms around my waist. "I missed you more."

"I seriously doubt that."

His dimples appeared and then disappeared. "How did your date go?" he asked as he leaned in and buried his face in my neck, taking in my scent like it was the air he needed to breathe.

"Not good." I ran my fingers through his hair and closed my eyes as he peppered my neck with soft kisses.

"Did he try something?" he asked evenly, his breath tickling my neck as he swept another kiss below my ear.

I sighed as his lips brushed against my skin like a paintbrush blessing a canvas with its masterpiece. "No, he didn't try anything. He was actually pretty decent," I said as my mind unintentionally slipped back to the way he held my hair for me as I spewed my dinner into his toilet.

He pulled back and met my eyes. "You got sick?"

I nodded, wishing so bad that I didn't have to talk about tonight, that I didn't have to obliterate this perfect moment with the cold, sobering truth.

"What happened?" His jaw ticked and I knew he was working hard to keep himself calm.

"Tessa and Gabriel showed up."

"What for?"

"Tessa found out about Engel, about my blood, the Amulet...she knows all of it, and a whole lot more." Tears stung the corners of my eyes as I tried to summon the courage to speak the truth. "It's bad, Trace. Really bad."

"Whatever it is, we'll deal with it together," he said trying to comfort me, but it was no use.

There weren't any words in the English language that could erase the reality of what I really was, of the venom that was coursing through my veins or the target it put on my back.

"We already knew Engel was curious about your blood," he said, answering my thoughts. "It doesn't change anything. We're still going to waste him, one way or another."

"You don't understand." I shook my head and looked away from his penetrating eyes. "It's not just about Engel anymore."

"Then who's it about?" he asked, picking up my chin and forcing me to meet his eyes again. "What's going on, Jemma?"

"The Dark Legion knows about me, Trace. About my blood."

His head ticked back, fear and confusion warring in his eyes for supremacy. "What are you talking about? What does the Dark Legion have to do with this?"

Deep down, I'd hoped I'd never have to utter the words to him, that I'd never have to see him look at me the way he inevitably would, but I knew that wasn't possible. He deserved to know the truth, no matter how ugly it was.

"They think my blood is the key to raising Lucifer," I said without pausing to think twice about it. "That I'm the girl from the prophecy."

"The Daughter of Hades?" he verified, obviously knowing his scripture well. "That prophecy is bullshit."

"It turns out that it isn't. The bloodline exists and the Order's been keeping it a secret for centuries." I had a hard time meeting his eyes, but I forced myself to look up at him. "I'm one of his Descendants, Trace."

He didn't say anything as he stared back at me in utter, soul-shaking silence. As petrified as I was, I had to continue. I had to get it all out before I lost my nerve.

"His blood is dormant in Tessa, like it was in my mother and all the women before her, but it's dominant in me," I explained, trying not to choke on the words as they came out. "My dad tried to hide the truth by taking us away from here, by having me Cloaked, but the minute Engel tasted my blood, he put two and two together and tipped off the Dark Legion. And now they know the truth about me and they're not going to stop until they get what they want...until they fulfill the prophecy."

He stared back at me, still speechless. His mouth opened and closed as though he were going to say something, but decided against it at the last minute.

"There's more." I watched as his eyes flared, like he couldn't possibly comprehend how I could deliver this much bad news at once. "The Council has a sample of my blood and they've been secretly trying to figure out if the bloodline is dormant in me or not. If they don't already know the truth, it's only a matter of time before they do. And when that happens, they're going to come for me too."

He blinked quickly, trying to work through everything I was saying.

"My blood could potentially raise Lucifer from his tomb, and they would never allow that to happen. You understand what that means, right?"

His eyes went from blinking to staring straight ahead like a deer caught in the headlights.

"Say something, Trace."

"I'm trying to," he said, shaking his head. His eyes and voice seemed hollow. "I'm trying to process this."

I could see him struggling to take it in, to accept it. I couldn't imagine what he was thinking, what he was feeling, but I imagined it wasn't anything good.

"I think it might be better if we stay away from each other for a while," I said softly, trying to hold back my tears. The truth was, I wanted to give him an easy out so I wouldn't have to hear him tell me that he couldn't be with me anymore—that I was an abomination and I made him ill.

He winced. "I would never say that to you."

Tears burned under my eyelids. "Never say never."

"Dammit, Jemma. Look at me," he ordered, cupping my face and forcing me to look at him. "I would never say that to you because I would never think it. I don't want to stay away from you—not for a while, or a minute, or ever. Don't you get that?"

Grabbing my hips, he lifted me off him to guide my left leg over his lap and then sat me back down so that I was straddling him. Being this close to him, this intimate, made my pulse quicken and my heart race.

"Nothing else matters to me but this right here," he said, pointing to the two of us, limbs entwined. "I don't care about Nikki, or Engel, or your bloodlines, or some stupid prophecy. I care about *you*, Jemma. I care about making you happy, and keeping you safe. I care about what's in here," he said, running his thumb across my forehead. "And here," he added, placing his hand over my somersaulting heart.

I wrapped my arms around his neck and pressed my lips against his. A gentle hum purred under my skin, making everything seem a little bit better. A little more tolerable.

I wanted to stay this way with him forever, to wrap myself in his love and let all of the bad fall away from me, and even though I knew I should have been trying harder to push him away, I couldn't bring myself to do it. It was dangerous for us like this, I knew that, and keeping him close to me was selfish, but I didn't know how to exist without him anymore.

I didn't know how to let go of the only light I had left in my ever-darkening world.

"Then don't," he answered simply. "I know how you feel about me, and I hope you know how I feel about you, so why don't we just accept the fact that we're going to be together and move on to more important shit?" he suggested, grazing his thumb along my lips and then touching his to mine as if to drive home the point.

When he pulled back, I found myself staring into his eyes,

into his soul, never feeling closer to any one person before in my entire life. I could see the love he had for me—I could feel it right there in my bones—and it burned hotter than the heat of a thousand suns.

"I'm scared, Trace. I'm so scared I don't even know what to do with myself anymore," I confessed, my voice shaking as I spoke.

"Everything's going to be fine. I'm never going to let anything bad happen to you."

"Don't do that. Don't make promises that are impossible to keep." I grazed my thumb over his protesting dimple. "I don't want to pretend anymore. I don't want to pretend everything is going to be okay because it's not. Not unless we find a way to stop the prophecy."

"Then that's what we'll do," he said and then kissed the inside of my hand. "We'll do whatever it takes."

"Do you really mean that?"

"You know I do."

"Good, because I already asked Dominic for his help," I said, watching him carefully for any signs of an impending explosion. "He's going to try to dig up as much information about the Dark Legion as possible...from the inside."

"The *inside?*"

"I need to know what *they* know about the prophecy, and if they have information we don't—like how, when, and where it's supposed to go down."

"Do you really think that's a good idea?"

"What?"

"Sending Dominic in there like that. He's kind of prone to turning on people."

"It's a risk I have to take, Trace. There's no one else."

His eyes shifted away briefly but he didn't say anything. "Alright. What else you got?"

"I'm going to ask Gabriel if he can try to get in the Vaults at Temple. We need to find out as much as we can about the prophecy if we have any chance of manipulating it," I explained, unusually calm. "Dominic thinks the Council might have some information or records in there. It's worth a shot."

"He'll never be able to get in there," said Trace. "He's a Rev. They might let him into the building with a Guardian and whatnot, maybe even let him continue hunting for the Order, but that's it. He won't even make it into the hallway."

"Alright, fine." I exhaled, refusing to let it get me down. "Then I'll think of something else."

"I can do it." His voice was as steady as a rock.

My face squinched up at his outlandish offer. "You're not even with the Order anymore. They'll never let you in there."

"That's not exactly true."

"Which part?"

His Adam's apple bobbed as he swallowed. "I have a meeting with the Magister tomorrow."

My mouth flopped open. "What? Why?"

"To talk to him about returning to the Order."

"Why would you do that?" I asked, stunned to hear that he was even considering returning to the Order, let alone that he actively sought it out after everything he'd said about them. "I thought you didn't want anything to do with them?"

"I don't. Not really," he said with hooded lids.

"Then what's going on? Why are you doing this?"

"Why do you think?" he answered gruffly as he tightened his hold on me. "After what happened with Engel? I need to protect you, Jemma. I thought I could do it without the Order, without all their politics and bullshit, but I need their resources."

"You don't have to do this. We can find another way." It was bad enough I was dragging him into this, but making him feel like he had to return to the Order after everything that happened with Linley was more than I was willing to put him through.

"It's not about that anymore." He tucked a wavy strand of my hair behind my ear and dropped his voice to a baritone whisper. "I have to do this for you, Jemma. Now more than ever. We need to find out what the Council knows and what they're planning."

"But you're playing right into them, Trace. This is exactly what they wanted to happen," I reminded him, but he didn't seem to care about that anymore.

"It's different this time," he assured me. "I'm going in with my eyes wide open. They're not going to control anything because I'm not doing it for them. I'm doing it for us."

He leaned in to kiss me again, to wash the bad away, but I put my hand against his chest and stopped him.

"Trace, I can't let you—"

"You're not changing my mind about this, Jemma," he said adamantly, making it clear I wasn't going to win this battle.

Trace was going to willingly throw himself down the same rabbit hole that I'd been free-falling through for the last few months, and there was nothing I could do to stop him.

There was no telling what kind of secrets and smokescreens he would encounter along the way or how many of them could potentially tear us apart...for good.

I shook my head, crestfallen. "If you're going to do this, I need you to promise me something."

His blue eyes met mine in the dark, piercing me with their willingness to give me anything I could ever ask for.

"Promise me that whatever you find out, no matter how bad or scary it is, you won't keep the truth from me. You won't keep me in the dark. Promise me we'll always fight them together."

He watched me for a moment, his jaw muscle pumping as he held me tightly in his arms and considered the weight of my request. "I promise," he finally said and then leaned in to me again, eager to seal the deal with lips that were clearly made to move against mine.

The world slipped away from me again, fast and hard, and even though it was only a temporary reprieve from the storm that was churning over my life, it was heaven like this with Trace and I never wanted to fall from its grace.

39. AN AFFAIR TO REMEMBER

Saturday came draped in an ethereal fog that spread over the town like a gathering of lost souls. There was something in the air, something sinister hissing in the wind, whispering as though it knew the town's secrets and sought to make them known to me.

I hugged my arms for warmth and pushed the uneasiness away. I couldn't let it sidetrack me. This was Taylor's special day and I was determined to make sure it was perfect in every way.

We pulled up to the Valentines' residence that sat on a sprawling acreage not far from Weston Academy, bordering the very same woodlands that our school grounds did. It was a beautiful, Queen Anne-style mansion fit for a real-life princess, right down to the matching turret that overlooked the yard.

Even though Taylor no longer remembered anything about me or our friendship, I was still beyond happy to be able to attend her party and welcome her back home with the rest of her friends and family. And, it didn't really even matter that it had to be from a distance as Trace's *unnamed* plus one.

A seven-piece orchestra was playing as we walked into the glitzy backyard. The Valentines had clearly spared no expense for their daughter's welcome home party. It was exactly the kind of bedazzled extravaganza Taylor went apeshit for.

Strings of twinkling lights crisscrossed above the dance floor like a blanket of stars suspended in the air. Lanterns and small spot lights lit up the gardens throughout the yard, making it look like a scene out of a modern day fairy tale. A fairy tale that Taylor deserved every moment of. There was even a full wait staff on hand, dressed in white tuxedo jackets and black pants, and carrying trays filled with tiny appetizers and fancy Hors d'oeuvres I couldn't pronounce.

Looping my arm through Trace's, I scanned the yard in search of familiar faces and the guest of honor. I found the latter planted at the crown of the dance floor, surrounded by a group of attentive admirers, most of which were of the male variety. She looked like an angel in her flowing white dress and loose locks of blond hair. I wanted so bad to run up to her and throw my arms around her, to tell her how happy I was to have her home and how much I missed having her around, but I knew I couldn't do that. I had to keep my distance and stay out of her *normal*, human life.

More importantly, I had to keep her out of my abnormal one.

"You look amazing," said Trace, taking in the black, mermaid dress that clung to my body like a second skin. He ran his hand down the length of my back, sending waves of electricity shooting every which way. "That dress is...something else on you."

I smiled up at him. "It's not too much?"

I had less than fifteen minutes to shop after my shift at All Saints earlier today and ended up grabbing the first black, formal-looking dress I could find on the rack at some small boutique on Main Street.

I'd never been to parties like this before and was always

doubting my fashion sense when it came to my wardrobe, especially since I didn't have Taylor to set me straight anymore.

"Too much?" He circled his arms around my waist and pressed me into his thick, muscular frame. "Maybe."

"You're supposed to lie and say I look fine!" I said indignantly.

"Fine doesn't even begin to describe how you look, Jemma." He craned his head towards my ear and breathed me in. "You're dangerous in that dress."

I arched a brow at him as I sprouted a smile. "Dangerous, huh?"

"It's taking everything I have not to rip that dress off of you right now," he whispered huskily, brushing his lips below my ear. "The only thing stopping me is the thought of anyone else getting to see what's under there."

My eyes widened at his confession. "Trace!"

"I guess I can always just lie and say you look *fine*," he continued nonchalantly, "pretend I'm not dying to finish what we started the other night."

Steamy flashes of our last bedroom session took over my subconscious, heating my cheeks and body simultaneously.

"We *really* should fix that," I agreed.

"I plan on it," he said, pulling back. His eyes were filled with love and lust and smoldering fire.

It was impossible not to get swept up in the inferno. "When?" I whispered, anticipation swirling deep in my belly.

"Tonight. After Taylor's party."

This was news to me. *Good* news, obviously. I suddenly had the urge to cut the night short and head home.

"Don't tempt me," he warned, pushing my hair over my shoulder and then dropping a kiss at the base of my neck, near my exposed collarbone.

I shivered from the contact as a feverish heat skirted over my skin. Hot and cold; I wasn't even sure how that was possible, but I wasn't surprised with Trace. He had a way of inducing feelings in me that I'd never felt before. Just the thought of giving myself to him fully made my entire body ignite.

"Thank you for tonight by the way," I said, running my hands along the lapel of his black tuxedo jacket. "For the Barrier and everything else you did so that I could be here."

After everything that happened yesterday, I'd realized that it would be too dangerous for me to attend Taylor's party. I could have unwittingly led the Dark Legion and a whole lot of other trouble right to her doorstep. When Trace had seen how heartbroken I was over not being able to go, he came up with the idea of asking Caleb to put up a magical fence around Taylor's entire property, ensuring that Taylor and her guests would be safe and that anything unclean, undead, or otherwise Dark Legion related, would be blocked out.

The fact that he didn't think twice about putting his beef with Caleb aside for the sake of making this possible for me only made my feelings for him stronger.

"Maybe Caleb can keep the Barrier up for a while," I suggested. "Make sure nothing can get to her."

"How long do you want him to keep it up?"

"I don't know, as long as possible."

"That can be arranged," he said and then looked at me as though trying to figure something out.

"I'm not always going to be around to look after her," I explained, glancing across the yard at her and then back at him. "Promise me you'll do it when I can't."

"Don't talk like that," he said, his eyes darkening at my words. "You're not going anywhere. I won't allow it—"

"Everything's secure on my end," interrupted Caleb, walking up to us with a champagne glass in his hand and a lopsided grin on his lips. "Nothing's getting through that firewall," he added cockily and then threw back a sip of his drink.

"Mostly thanks to me," said Nikki as she stepped out from behind Caleb and joined our private little party.

"Thanks, man." Trace put his fist out, and Caleb bumped it. And, just like that, they were friends again.

"What about me?" asked Nikki, her eyes plastered on Trace like a love-sick puppy begging for attention.

"Thank you too," he said, tipping his head to her.

"Anything for a friend. Taylor means so much to all of us," she said, sounding like the phony bitch that she was.

"Since when do you give a crap about Taylor?"

"Since always, Jemma." She shook her head at me and then clicked her tongue. "You'd know that if you actually took a minute to get to know me."

"I've already taken several minutes, Nikki, and I didn't like what I saw. But thanks."

"I'm sorry you feel that way."

"I'm sure you are," I scoffed and then turned to Trace. "You're not buying this, are you?" She was really pulling out all the stops tonight, undoubtedly for his benefit.

He frowned.

"There's nothing to buy. Everyone knows that there's nothing I wouldn't do for someone I cared about," she went on, her words stained with dark undertones that sounded a lot like a warning.

"I'll make sure to remember that."

"You really should, Jemma." There was a smile on her lips, but her eyes...her eyes glowered at me with venom.

"Hey, Pratt," said Caleb, nodding over to Ben, who was making his way up to us.

"What's up, gentlemen. Ladies," he greeted everyone jovially. He'd been in an infinitely better mood since the night we brought Taylor back home. Clearly, it wasn't a coincidence.

"Did you run the perimeter?" asked Trace.

"Yup. Everything's clear."

"Told you," said Caleb smugly. "Nothing's getting through that thing. That's some of my best work right there."

"I thought your dad was out of town?" said Ben to Trace suddenly, gesturing over to the sprawling white tent that housed dozens of white tables and matching bistro chairs.

We all turned at the same time.

I quickly spotted Peter Macarthur standing by the bar, having a drink with some other guy.

"Isn't that your uncle, Jem?" asked Ben, ticking his chin at the whispering duo.

I looked a little closer at the man standing beside Trace's dad and immediately noticed the patch of white hair along his ears. "I think so," I answered and then looked at Trace for confirmation.

He responded with a slight nod.

What the heck was my uncle even doing here? I mean, okay, so tons of other parents and Hollow residents were here tonight, celebrating Taylor's return, but still. Something wasn't sitting well about it. Plus, why didn't he mention it to me? Then again, I *had* (sort of) been evading him lately...but still!

Trace leaned in closer. "I'm sure it's nothing," he whispered reassuringly, making sure the others didn't overhear.

None of our friends knew anything about my bloodlines or the fact that the Dark Legion was hunting me down, and I wanted to keep it that way. The fewer people that knew about the secret that could potentially *end* my life, the better. Especially people like Nikki, who would undoubtedly hand-deliver me to the Dark Legion herself.

I pushed away all my ailing thoughts and smiled back up at Trace, fully intent on enjoying the rest of my night with him, and whatever else may follow. He wrapped his arm around my shoulder and dropped a kiss on the top of my head.

"Trace, can I talk to you for a minute?" asked Nikki, purposely interrupting our moment.

My eyes glazed over with hate—hatred for her and her conniving underhanded ways. Hatred for the way Trace's name sounded when it passed between her scowling lips.

"It's important," she quickly added.

I hated that she was even here with us, and that she was going to be here with him long after I was gone.

"Jemma?" Trace looked down at me to get my okay.

Mostly though, I hated that she was probably going to live the life I'd always dreamed of having with him—the life I was supposed to have with him. Chances were, Trace and I weren't ever going to get our happily ever after, and letting Nikki know that she was getting to me would only make her step up her efforts.

"Come find me when you're done," I told him and lifted onto my toes to pull a quick kiss from his lips.

Without looking back, I walked off towards the dance floor, taking in all the smiling faces as I listened to the haunting classical piece being played by the orchestra. Everyone was having a good time, it seemed, and none more so than Taylor. She had the most contagious, beautiful smile plastered across her pink-glossed lips, and it made my heart cheer knowing that I helped put it there.

My eyes continued to circle the grounds, noting all the guests and their chosen company, until they settled on my uncle and Trace's dad, who had now moved to a table near the back of the tent. Keeping my distance, I watched their interactions, looking for clues as to the subject of their hushed conversation. Stopping at the bar, I asked the bartender for a soda while continuing my recon as inconspicuously as possible.

Uncle Karl appeared to be heated. Leaning forward, his

eyebrows were rutted together and his forehead was creased. I noted his hands jerking back and forth as though he were angrily trying to get his point across. Whatever it was they were discussing, it didn't appear to be pleasant.

I picked up my drink and casually strolled in their direction, hoping I might get close enough to eavesdrop on them.

"Hi."

Shit. I turned slowly at the sound of Taylor's bubbly voice as I tried to prepare myself to face her. I was completely caught off guard and had no idea what to say to her. "Uh...Hi."

Wow, genius, Jemma.

"I know we haven't like, formally met at school or anything, but I just wanted to thank you for coming to my party." Her smile was big and warm, letting me know she was being nothing but genuine. "You and Trace are totally cute-sauce together."

"Thanks," I said, smiling back at her without even meaning to. "And thank you for, you know, having me."

"For sure." She tilted her head to the side and stared back at me with a strange look in her eyes.

"What?" I said, fighting off the urge to check my teeth on the back of the silverware. "Do I have something on my face?"

"No, no. You look great, it's just..." She continued staring. "You just seem really familiar. Have we met before? Like out of school or something?"

"Um, nope. I don't think so."

"Weird," she said, sort of to herself. "I feel like I...I don't know." She shook her head and laughed at herself. "I think I just had a little too much champagne tonight. That open bar just wouldn't stop calling me."

I couldn't help but laugh. *God, did I miss her.*

"So, yeah. I just wanted to say hi and all that...hopefully I didn't completely weird you out," she laughed again but there was definitely a nervous pitch to it this time. "I'm not usually this awkward. I swear it."

"Not awkward at all," I assured her. "It was really nice to talk to you, Tay. Ler," I quickly added, catching my mistake.

"Yeah, you too," she said, laughing—probably at the strange stutter she now thinks I have. "See you around, Jemma." She waved me off as she spun on her heels and headed back towards the dance floor and her waiting band of admirers.

I stood there for a few seconds too long, watching her go with my hand still hanging in the air like I was some kind of human stop sign. Snapping out of my daze, my eyes quickly darted back to the tent.

The table was empty.

"Shit."

"Language, Jemma." My uncle walked up beside me, holding a cigar between his index and middle finger. "It's a lovely night for people watching, is it not?"

I looked over at him as he stared into the tent. Was he referring to the fact that I was trying to spy on him earlier? Had they seen me? "Yeah, sure. I guess so."

"You'd be amazed at the things one can learn by watching."

I felt a strange chill run down my back, making the hairs on my arms tremble. "I'll have to try that sometime."

He looked down at me for a moment and then pulled in a puff of his cigar. A cloud of smoke billowed out of his mouth and floated up to greet the night's sky. "The Council would like to meet with you tomorrow. Perhaps you can stop by my office before work, and we can go together."

"Meet with me?" The hairs were now standing straight up. "About what?"

"About your future with the Order, of course."

"Right. My future." I glanced over my shoulder, looking for Trace. He was still with Nikki, talking privately. Damn that stupid heifer for monopolizing his time!

"Sure thing, Uncle Karl. Tomorrow sounds great. I'll just check my schedule and then, you know, get right back to you." My phone buzzed in my hand, causing me to nearly jump out of my skin.

"Goodness, Jemma. What's gotten into you?"

"I'm just stressed out about everything that's going on," I blurted out and then quickly tried to cover up my blunder. "You know, with school exams and everything. Will you excuse me, Uncle? I have to take this," I added, pointing to my still-vibrating phone.

"Of course." He took another drag of his cigar. "Enjoy the rest of your evening, Jemma. You never know when you'll get another chance like this."

My eyes rounded out as I backed away from him. What the heck did that mean? Had he just threatened me? Turning away, I hit the green button and put the phone to my ear.

"Hello, angel," greeted Dominic on the other end of the line.

"Something really weird is going on," I said in a panicked whisper. "I think my uncle just threatened me."

"I thought you were attending a social function."

"I am. He's here too, and so is Trace's dad." I glanced over my shoulder at where we'd just been standing, but the spot was already vacated. "I think they're up to something."

"Who?"

"My uncle and Trace's dad! And God only knows how many other Council members are here." I looked around nervously, trying to spot any familiar faces or suspicious persons-of-interest.

My eyes immediately fell on Nikki. She was alone now and walking clandestinely, like she was Nancy-freaking-Drew, looking over her shoulders as she skirted towards the wall of forest that kissed the edge of Taylor's backyard.

"What did he say to you?"

"I don't know, something about enjoying my night," I said

distractedly, following her.

"Oh, well, yes, that sounds highly suspicious," he said sarcastically. I could hear rustling in the background.

"It was," I insisted. "'Enjoy your night, you might not get another chance'," I repeated, trying to mimic his eerie tone. "Where are you anyway?"

"He actually said you might not get another chance?" he asked. "I'm close."

"Or that I never know when I'll get another chance?" I tried to recall his exact words but couldn't get my thoughts to run in a linear fashion. "Whatever. It was creepy and it sounded like he was trying to threaten me, or like, warn me about something."

"Speaking of which. We need to talk, love."

"About what?" I asked, watching curiously as Nikki reached the border of the forest and then flipped open her phone.

"About Engel."

"Can it wait? I'm kind of in the middle of something."

"Well, he's back in town, and that isn't even the bad news. You decide if it can wait."

My heart skidded to a full stop and then exploded into overdrive. I quickly scanned the sprawling yard for Trace and spotted him alone at the bar, ordering a drink.

"What's the bad news?" I asked, turning my attention back to Nikki.

"For starters, he isn't working with the Dark Legion. I'm not sure that he ever was. He appears to have his own plans."

"Which means he's still after the Amulet," I guessed.

"It's a little more involved than that."

"Meaning what?"

"Not on the phone, love. Can you slip away?"

"I think so. I just need to get Trace," I said distractedly, watching as Nikki took one last glance over her shoulder and then slipped into the woods through a thin, skeletal opening.

"What the hell is she up to now?"

"Who?"

"Nikki," I answered, rushing towards the spot she'd just disappeared into. "She just took off into the woods. She's up to something! I'm going to follow her." My heart thwacked hard against my ribcage at the thought of finally outing her.

"I strongly advise against it."

"And why is that?" I asked without bothering to slow down.

"You don't know nearly enough about her to attempt to take her on. How do you know you're not walking into a trap?"

"I don't," I answered simply. Stopping at the edge of the woods, I peeked over my shoulder to make sure no one was watching me. "She's up to something and I'm not about to let her get away with it. Besides, I have the Amulet, remember?"

"You're getting careless, love."

"I know what I'm doing, Dominic. I'll call you right back," I said and then hung up before he could say anything else.

I only had a few seconds to make a decision. There was no time to think twice about it or run back for reinforcements. Nikki was definitely up to something and this was my one chance to finally out her for the red-handed witch she really was.

I pushed through the pines and stepped into the woods.

40. SEASON OF THE WITCH

Skeletal branches scraped against my skin as I weaved through the dark forest, peering around looming pines and evergreens that seemed to reach all the way up to the pitch-black sky. The fog was dense, swimming along the forest floor like smoke, beckoning me forward into the land of the lost as I tried to gain some kind of visual on Nikki.

In the space behind me, I could still hear the muted sounds of the orchestra playing the echoes of a ghost song I couldn't name. Unknowing party-goers dancing contently among a slew of liars and cheaters who would gladly feed them to the enemy in the name of keeping their precious secrets.

A branch snapped up ahead of me, pulling my attention forward again. The tip of Nikki's blue dress caught my eye right before it disappeared around the bend of a narrow path that twisted and turned its way deeper into the woods.

Kicking off my shoes, I picked up my dress and started running after her, my feet crunching against the slush of earth and twigs and dead leaves I couldn't see under the thick skin of fog. My feet pounded hard against the ground, colliding with branches and rocks that sent sharp stabs of pain shooting up through my feet and legs. It was as though the forest were alive and well, and openly playing for Nikki's team.

I slowed down my pace as she came further into view. She was walking at a steady clip, weaving her way through the woodlands with an obvious motive and a clear destination. The further I walked into the woods, the louder my heart became, banging against my ribcage like gunshots sounding off inside my ears.

My eyes shifted from her to something further up ahead; a glimmering wall that fell from the sky like a translucent sheet made of soft blue lights and air.

The Magical Barrier.

What the heck was she doing near the Barrier?

I knew she was involved in casting the spell with Caleb and could have easily been checking on it to make sure everything was alright, but this was *Nikki* after all, and something was telling me her intentions were far less noble and pure than that.

She came to a full stop in front of the ghostly wall and waited, fidgeting with the phone in her hands as she gazed through the sheer Barrier.

It looked like she was waiting for someone. But *who*?

Hungry for more clues, for answers, I shuffled forward towards a thick, moss-covered oak tree, rooted in its yesteryears just a few feet away from her. I already had a good enough view, but I *needed* to get closer still. I needed to get close enough to testify against her in the court of Trace's eyes.

A branch snapped beneath my foot, freezing me mid-step.

Nikki spun on her heels at the sound of my fumble. Her narrowed, aquamarine eyes immediately fell on me as a sliver of a smile appeared on her deceitful mouth. "Well, isn't this rich," she said, casually strolling towards me.

I brought my strangling foot to the ground and silently cursed the branches that decorated it. "What the hell are you doing out here, Nikki?"

"I was going to ask you the same thing," she sneered as she crossed her thin arms across her chest. "Do you stalk all your boyfriend's exes, or am I just the special one?"

"If by special you mean a rocket-sized hemorrhoid in my ass, then yes, you're extremely special, Nikki."

"Is that what I am?" She put her hand to her chest and feigned surprise. "Gosh, Jemma, I didn't know I was affecting you so very much. It's nice to know my efforts are paying off."

"What are you doing out here?" I demanded again, choosing to ignore her obvious bait. "Who are you meeting?"

"None of your damn business."

She tried to turn away from me but I quickly grabbed her shoulder and pulled her back.

"You're standing in the middle of the woods right next to the barrier that happens to be keeping everyone I care about safe right now, and you think it's none of my business?"

"Get your damn hands off me!" she said, slapping my arm away.

"I know you're up to something, Nikki, and I'm not about to let you get away with it, so you might as well just call it off."

"What makes you so sure I'm up to something?" she challenged. "Are you a Seer now too?"

"Yeah, I'm a seer. I see a wicked bitch in front of me that gets off on messing with people's lives."

"I bet your boyfriend would disagree."

"Actually, I happen to know for a fact that he wouldn't," I retorted, each word slow and measured to ensure she got the point. Trace was on my side of the line. Not hers.

Her eyes darkened with fury. "Well, I guess we can't all be as special as you, *Daughter of Hades*."

My stomach bottomed out.

"Didn't think I knew about that, did you?" The corner of her lip pushed up into her rosy cheek. "It's actually quite poetic if you think about it. I mean, I already knew you were a boyfriend-stealing skank, but who knew you were actually the she-devil herself?" Her biting laughter reached out through the air like a whip and slashed at my skin.

"Screw you, Nikki. You're just mad because Trace doesn't want you anymore. He wants me now."

"Yeah, and how long do you think that will last?" She laughed again, little bursts of mockery peppering the delicate space inside my ears. "It's only a matter of time before he wakes up and realizes what you really are, and when he does, he's going to leave your sorry ass and come crawling back to me."

"You're so delusional," I said, refusing to let her know that she was even remotely affecting me. "Trace doesn't want you anymore, Nikki. He doesn't want anything to do with you. We laugh about how pathetic you are all the time," I added, wanting to cut her the way she was cutting me.

"You're lying," she seethed, though her voice was shaking when she said it, and I could tell I was getting to her. "Trace would never do that to me."

"Well, maybe not to your face," I shrugged innocently. "He just doesn't have the heart to tell you himself."

"You're such a bitch." Her gaze shifted over my shoulder at the sound of my name being called in the distance. We both immediately recognized the voice as Trace's.

"See. He calls my name now, not yours."

"Well, let's see how long he calls it when he's standing over your casket, you stupid bitch." Her lips curled into an evil grin that sent chills running scared all throughout my body.

"Are you threatening me?" I asked, instinctively taking a step away from her. She was a Caster after all, and God only knew what she was capable of.

"More like promising you." She uncrossed her arms and

tilted her head to the side. "I think I'm really going to enjoy this."

"Enjoy what?" I asked, taking another backwards step.

"Watching them all fight over who gets to put you in the ground first. Right where you've always belonged." Her eyes flared like two warning signs.

I didn't have a chance to say anything back.

Arms came out from behind me, plucking me off the ground like a poison that needed to be eradicated.

"Get the hell off—" My command was quickly killed by a hand clamping down around my neck, pressing down and squeezing as if to encase my throat in a tomb. I tried to scream out for help, for reprieve from the sudden onslaught, but I couldn't pull in enough air to accomplish the feat.

Panicked, my eyes darted back to Nikki, pleading with her for help, for allegiance, but she just stood there motionless, watching my attack like a horror movie she was dying to see.

This is what she wanted all along, what she'd been working towards since day one. And now here she was, watching contently from her front row seat.

Fingers ripped through my hair, grabbing at the roots and using them as an anchor to yank my head back. My gaze snapped from Nikki to the pitch-black sky peeking out through the thick canvas of trees and overgrowth, and then to the silver blade that appeared in my peripheral. It glinted murderously, blurring out the rest of the world as it caught the light from the moon and reflected its deathly message back to me.

Realization hit me like a train.

He wasn't some random Revenant that wanted a taste of my blood, and he wasn't here on behalf of an ex-cheerleader with a sour score to settle. He was here to make sure I didn't make it out of the forest alive.

A startling burst of adrenaline shot through my veins,

screaming at me to fight for my life. I bucked wildly against his back, my feet swinging relentlessly as I tried to kick out his legs from under him, to break his hold on me. He tightened his grip, dragging us further back into the brushwood, his breathing coming out fast and heavy in my ear as he struggled to keep me contained—to keep me in position.

Jerking my head back once again, he lifted the blade in front of my eyes as if to taunt me with it, as if to warn me of what was coming, before lowering it beneath my chin.

I felt the cold steel press against my neck and gasped as he pushed down and then slid the blade across my neck, from one side to the other, as easy as slicing through warm butter.

And then he released me.

My hands shot up to my neck, covering myself as I spun around to look my attacker in the eye, but the coward was already gone, darting back through the woods from which he'd come, back towards the flock of unsuspecting party-goers.

Hot, wet liquid seeped through my fingers and down my neck. My gaze fell to the strange, wet sensation coating my body like a blanket.

Blood.

My blood.

Everywhere.

I tightened my hold around my neck, trying to stop the wound from pouring out, but the harder I pressed, the more blood came pulsing out of me. I turned back to Nikki, my eyes wide and petrified as I fell to my knees at her mercy.

"Hheee..." I tried to speak but the sound was being distorted by a strange gurgling, choking noise. It took me a few moments to realize the sound was coming from the back of my own throat.

Nikki just stared down at me in silence, not saying a word and not moving a single muscle to help me. I was literally going to bleed to death at her feet, and that was if I didn't drown in pool of my own blood first, and all she could do was stand there with that stupid look on her face and watch.

"What is this?" boomed a voice from behind her—from the other side of the Barrier.

I knew that voice. I *feared* that voice.

Nikki turned to Engel, her shoulders raised as if she were going to shrug the whole thing off.

"She...someone...I—"

"Speak, foolish girl!" snapped Engel as a wall of vampires moved up behind him.

"Someone jumped her from behind! I don't know what happened!" she shouted, backing away from the Barrier and the army of Revenants.

"Bring her to me," he ordered, his voice rattling through the forest like thunder. "Bring her to me now!"

Nikki hesitated, her eyes bouncing between Engel and me and then back again.

Gripping my bloody neck with both hands, I shook my head at her—begging her, pleading with her not do this. I was dying, there was no doubt about that, but I still had the Amulet. There was still hope. Handing me over to Engel would end any chance I had. He would surely finish the job and probably so much worst.

"I will not tell you again, child."

All expression disappeared from Nikki's face as she straightened her back and stepped towards me. The vacant look in her eyes confirmed that not only was she going to hand me over to my sworn enemy, to a murderous, centuries-old vampire, but she wasn't even going to think twice about it.

I tried to retreat from her, to run away from her and save myself, but my legs quickly gave out, causing me to tumble back onto the ground. The blood was pouring out of my neck at unsurvivable speeds, weakening my body and slowing down my breathing. My heart wanted so bad to get up and run, to fight to the death, to go out with my fists blazing, but I couldn't even find the strength to keep an even pressure on my neck.

My eyes blinked tiredly as Nikki closed the gap between us. Blackness seeped in through the corners of my eyes, darkening my world until only specks of my former life remained.

The sickening sound of dry leaves crunching under Nikki's feet barely registered as she calmly bent down beside me. There was no remorse in her eyes, no love lost at all. I may have even noticed a smile.

And then, there was nothing.

41. AS I LAY ME DOWN

My lids fluttered weakly, struggling to stay open as though the weight of the world were resting on them. I fought hard to push away the darkness, to stave off the sleepy confusion that had seeped into my fragile mind, but I could only hold onto my consciousness for tiny gaps of time.

I knew I was still in the forest; I could smell the pine, taste the dense fog in the air, see the twisted limbs of trees...

But I wasn't alone.

I was being carried off against my will; carted away from the warmth of the protective barrier and the raging party just beyond it. Away from my heart's keeper, and everything else that was good in my life. I was being hauled off to my death, forced into my final resting place.

An ember of fire still glimmered in my heart, urging me to do something, to stop them, to kill them where they stood. But it wasn't enough. I didn't have the strength to fight anymore. I didn't have the ability to run. And even if I did, where would I go? Back to the party? Back to my faceless attacker who was masquerading as a friend amongst an endless sea of my enemies?

There was nowhere left to go, and no hope for rescue. So I

didn't. Instead, I did what I had to do to survive the moment. I let it go. All of it. Hope. My life. My dreams...

Him.

I let it all fall away through space and time—back into the past, back into the twisted maze of secrets and lies that left me breathless time and time again, broken up only by the small moments of peace when I was with *him*; the only boy I'd ever loved. My own version of a true heaven on earth.

But all of that was gone now. Only darkness remained; a darkness as thick and suffocating as the destiny that was written in my blood long before I was ever born.

My enemy had won the battle. He'd collected his prize and strung it over his shoulder like the carcass of an animal that never had a chance in hell of making it out of the forest alive. He was free to do with me as he pleased, free to hand me over to the Dark Legion, to let them have their way with my blood— with my soul, to obliterate any remaining light I had left in my heart. He was free to keep me for himself, to torture me until I handed over the Amulet and begged for my own death. The possibilities were endless, and time was infinite, for no one would even know to come looking for me.

Death was racking its nails against my door, begging for me to let it in, but it was all just a formality. It wasn't asking my permission. It was taunting me with its presence. Tormenting me as I tried to figure out the grand finale.

I didn't know when or how, and I couldn't understand why. There was only one thing I knew for sure.

The end was coming.

Bonus Material

Visit the author's website for information on new releases, deleted scenes from Invidious, and exclusive teasers from book three of The Marked series:

www.biancascardoni.com

GLOSSARY

ANAKIM
A race of people born with the spirit of man and the blood of angels; Descendants of Nephilim

CASTER
A Descendant of Magi Angels; ability to cast magic, control elements, and manipulate energy

CINDERDUST
Magical powder created by High Casters that sends a Revenant to Sanguinarium

DARK LEGION
Descendants that have turned against the Order; pledged to the dark side/ Lucifer

DAUGHTER OF HADES
Descendant of Lucifer, prophesied to raise Lucifer and bring on the end of days

INVOCATION
An ancient ritual used by the Order to invoke Anakim abilities

LUCIFER
The first angel to be created and the first to fall; imprisoned in a tomb in Hell

REAPER
A Descendant of Transport Angels; capable of teleporting, time travel, and mind reading through touch

SANGUINARIUM
Realm of perdition for Revenants that have been vanquished

SEER
A Descendant of Messenger Angels; ability to communicate with the Spirit Realm and predict the future

SHIFTER
A Descendant of Guardian Angels; capable of shifting into animal form, and telepathy

SLAYER
A Descendant of Warrior Angels; possess super strength and ability to sense demons, siren-like blood

THE ORDER OF THE ROSE
A secret organization that oversees all Anakim affairs

ANAKIM INDEX

SLAYERS *(Warrior Angel Descendants)*
Jemma
Tessa
Gabriel+
Karl
Thomas*
Jaqueline*

REAPERS *(Transport Angel Descendants)*
Trace
Peter
Linley*

CASTERS *(Magi Angel Descendants)*
Nikki
Caleb
Carly

SHIFTERS *(Guardian Angel Descendants)*
Dominic+
Ben
Julian

SEERS *(Messenger Angel Descendants)*
Morgan

* Character is deceased
+ Character is a Revenant

ACKNOWLEDGEMENTS

A huge thank you to Keri Karandrakis, for proofreading my second-born on the absolute shortest notice possible, and for doing an amazing job at that. Thank you to Andrei, for designing a stunning cover that beautifully captured my vision and tone for this book (and for putting up with my endless notes and revisions). A special thank you to Derek, whose design expertise and generosity of his time saved me from a whole lot of heartache and grief.

Thank you to my awesome parents for continuing to love and support my dream, whether it be by cheering me on, talking me off ledges, or babysitting my little one so that I could write into the wee hours of the night. I'm truly blessed to be surrounded by such a loving and supportive family. My cup seriously runneth over.

Thank you to my other half, Jeffrey, without whom, this book would probably not even exist yet. Thank you for taking such good care of me and our son, and for making it possible for me to live out my dream. You've listened to me rant and rave about my characters for months on end; consoled me, encouraged me, filled me up when I had nothing left to give, and supported me wholeheartedly every step of the way...even on my *horribly* bad days. For that, and too many other reasons to name, I love you (still s'match).

Thank you to my little sunshine, Jaxon, for making my days shine brighter than I ever imagined they could. You may not have had a hand in writing this book, but you are the very reason I'm sitting here writing this. You inspire me to do better and be more, to work hard and live out my dreams so that one day, you too, will live out yours. You are proof that magic exists in this world, and that insta-love is real. That's right, I said it. Mama loves you, baby.

And, finally, my absolute biggest thank you goes to you, the reader. The fact that I even have the honor of saying that still boggles my mind. This past year has been one of the best years of my life, and I owe that to *you* for allowing me to live out the dream I *almost* didn't allow myself to dream. Thank you from the bottom of my heart for choosing to read my books, for loving Jemma's story as much as I do, and for encouraging me to keep writing. You've given me all the feels and I seriously can't thank you enough for it. Seriously. *Thank you.*

ABOUT THE AUTHOR

BIANCA SCARDONI is a paranormal fiction writer who resides on the East Coast of Canada with her family. She graduated from college with a degree in web design and went on to build an online writing community in 2004. When she isn't writing, she spends her time reading, watching vampire shows, eating junk food, and staying up too late.

For upcoming book releases, bonus material, and additional information on the author, please visit her website: www.biancascardoni.com

93489027R00194

Made in the USA
Middletown, DE
14 October 2018